29/1

CW01621937

Mrs. Keiller's Marmalade

S M Boland

ISBN 978-0-9934071-5-4

Published by Warblebox

www.warblebox.com

What could be more divine than the soothing embrace of a morsel of marmalade upon the tongue? What could be more invigorating than the devilish delight as that most sublime of conserves journeys from mouth to soul? An intimate, personal passage from the golden jar which rests upon a table illuminating a subtle turn or a fleck of bejewelled peel, betraying this glorious preservative's regal heritage from the scorched plains of the Sierra Nevada . A creation which at once inspires and arouses, confounds, envelopes and cajoles; a sumptuous gift to every country kitchen, its opulent hue announcing to the world that this is a marmalade which has fire in its belly!

Contents

Step 1: Select the sturdiest Seville oranges for your marmalade

Religion had once held a precious place in Maggie Keiller's heart. Her father was a fervent Catholic and early morning Mass was a ritual in his daily routine and twice during Lent. As a young girl Maggie was encouraged to worship likewise and often she did, although primarily with the aim of impressing her intimidating father, rather than the Holier version thereof. It was 1925 and Maggie was sixteen years old when fate visited upon her.

He lingered uncomfortably outside the Church doors one dark Dundee morning, cigarette in hand, waiting for friends and transgressors to appear. He caught her eye as she ascended the grey, parochial steps of the church, and was instantly converted. He smiled. Her heart raced. After that first revelation, it became a ritual to seek him out, hoping each time that he would re-appear behind the besotted statue of the Virgin Mary. Always a pace behind her father, she could steal but an ephemeral glance in his direction, looking beyond the plasterwork of a cross. This striking boy, with dark hair and fine clothes had captured her imagination like no altar boy or saint ever could. That he came from the other side - the Protestant side – simply roused her fascination. His dancing eyes held her heart and it beat faster each time she found him, and sunk a little lower when he was not there.

For his part, where once he had waited impatiently for contrite friends, he now found himself craving the illicit vision of a Catholic girl. As the weeks progressed and his fervour grew, he found courage to deftly pass a note into her threadbare pocket. She felt his sleight hand close to her skin and sat in the pews throughout the service feeling the note burn through her winter coat and many layers. She thought not about the hymns she sung, or the actions she followed, only about the note and what wonderful words it might say. The automation of Mass seemed penitence that day, knowing that she could not reach into her pocket while her father studied his daughter's lips. If he found it, he would destroy it and she would never know the thoughts of her wonderful stranger.

When they eventually returned home, Maggie raced up the rickety wooden stairs to her secret place between the alcoves. With no one at her back and full view of the doorway should anyone approach, she slowly placed her hand in her pocket and felt the folds of paper warm inside. His hand had touched its rough edges and smoothed it at the crease. Removing the note, she felt the sudden realness of their secret bond. What if he wanted to take her off to Gretna? Would she go? Would she leave her home, her mother, for the promises of a stranger? She looked at the piece of paper, seeing the dark shadows of many letters contained within, feeling on the cusp of intimacy.

'My luve's like a red, red rose,

That's newly sprung in June.

O, my Luve's like the melody,

That's sweetly played in tune.

As fair art thou, my bonnie lass,

So deep in luve am I,

And I will luve thee still, my dear,

Till all the seas run dry.

And beneath it the greatest word of all - 'Billy'. His name was Billy. Throughout the warming months of summer his boldness produced other notes - Byron, Wordsworth and Shelley. She loved their words, but more than that, she loved his. As his confidence grew, he wrote more of his own and less of qualified verse. The circumstance of religion inadvertently became the foundation of their match, the Church the amphitheatre of their union.

Billy was a Keiller and that meant much in name and fortune but it was a destiny which consigned them to a difficult life. Maggie may have had much to qualify herself in terms of morality, but those qualities held little value when enveloped in a working class mould. All attempts towards a more pleasing etiquette counted not a jot in the monochrome life of Dundee's high society and the moneyed Keillers. It was quickly announced that she was not of good blood, and despite character and kindness, John Keiller would not be swayed towards his son's choice of wife. He was not known for his soft heart, nor his predilection for reason, a character which had served him well in the support of the Keiller marmalade business. His opinion once formed, forever rang true and his reputation tended to obstinate cruelty. Rumour told how he had held a grudge against a glass jar manufacturer who had made the mistake of sending him one bad specimen in a batch of five thousand. Outraged at this omission, Keiller had taken this lapse as a personal attack on his business. He severed all ties with the poor manufacturer, slandering the name of this unfortunate throughout Dundee's merchant community, effectively putting an end to the man's operation. The poor fellow hung himself after his wife and five children had taken to the poorhouse. All for the sake of single bad jar. John Keiller of course, took no responsibility for the man's demise, and scored his untimely death down to bad business. Such was the nature of the man whom Billy and Maggie had hoped to turn in their favour.

So Billy gave it all up for Maggie, alongside the comfort of an easy life. She felt sorry for his sacrifice, that she was never worth the trouble, but he had courted her with a spirit which would not be denied and despite the outrage of his Protestant father and the disappointment of her own Catholic clan, they were married nine months later. It was an intimate affair with an audience of two. She found him pacing the granite steps of Dundee's Caird Hall, tugging at buttons which were too tight about his collar and shoes with no grip or give. He oozed discomfort in such formal surrounds, but relief saturated his eyes when he saw Maggie approach. For Maggie, the gloriousness of a fine Scottish day seemed like a blessing from the heavens, that theirs was a union which despite its difficult beginnings, would endure.

They arrived at their marital home in the summer of 1929, brimming with blissful newlywed infatuation and the beginnings of a deeper, truer love. Gone the grand house and docile servants of a sheltered upper class Keiller life, gone the luxury of a sure footing and a sound future - replaced by Rose Cottage on Auchobane's jagged cliffs. But their isolation in both the physical and emotional sense, seemed only to increase the idyll of their precious world. There were none to interfere, none to please and bend for. There was only the two of them - soon to be three. Patting the round of her stomach, Maggie gazed lovingly upon her husband and his fortitude, and thought herself the most fortunate woman in all of Scotland.

The village of Auchobane was a small enclave which nature had the audacity to perch on an exposed cliff top along the unforgiving coastline of the Kingdom of Fife. Facing eastward, the huddled houses which formed the village seemed to eye suspiciously the North Sea, its neighbour, enemy and friend. Fifty meters directly below the village's position on the cusp of oblivion, sat its tiny harbour where boats bobbed enthusiastically like children's bath time toys. Auchobane consisted of no more than two hundred townsfolk, all fortressed in identical red sandstone dwellings excavated from Scotland's plentiful mines.

Rose Cottage, like its occupants, sat upon the fringes of Auchobane - not close enough to be considered kin, not remote enough for anonymity. Unlike the dusky houses of Auchobane, Rose Cottage was constructed from the white granite of Ailsa Craig which gave the cottage a rustic feel, a charm further augmented by the picture-perfect garden which wrapped around the building like a reassuring, colourful blanket. The name 'Rose Cottage' came, unsurprisingly, from the wild roses which clambered curiously by the door and seemed year on year to defy the strong winds which blustered in from the sea. The cottage was reached via an overgrown pathway from Auchobane, a path which grew organically from the village and wound its way for about a mile along the cliff edge until it reached the security of the cottage's old, red gate. It was an inconvenient distance to travel on foot without purpose or inclination.

There was however, one of Auchobane's residents who felt such physical exertion was morally essential. Mrs. McLintock, purveyor of condiments, aficionado of gossip and covetous by habit, was a vindictive and vociferous woman. Being the wife of Auchobane's Church of Scotland minister, and descended from a devout lineage of the same, she felt blessed with an ample pulpit from which to spread the Good Word and launch hellfire against the heathenism of non-believers. A lady of principal and unassailable pride, Mrs. McLintock felt it was her duty to convert the unconverted, to guide the unguided and to break the unbreakable. As the new inhabitants of Rose Cottage enjoyed their halcyon days, Mrs. McLintock demanded that her pastor husband visit their new unconverted neighbours, for fear that some misfortune would chance upon them and they would be cast for all eternity into the depths of hell. It was his religious duty after all, and her duty to remind him of it, and to accompany him one Sunday afternoon on the path to Rose Cottage. Being a meek man, and much maligned by his belligerent wife, he trudged the mile to Rose Cottage with her sparrow fingers prodding at his ribcage throughout their journey along the cliffs.

"Good morning'", he began, hat in hand, his eyes cast downward with timidity and marital burden. "My name is McLintock, Reverend McLintock. I'm the minister fae Auchobane."

Maggie stood before him, surveying the sight of such a broken man with the frame of his overbearing wife looming large behind him.

"We dinnae care fer religion in this house", replied Maggie.

As she went to close the door, a thin foot slid between it and the old wooden frame.

"We're a God fearing folk here in Auchobane", added the shrill voice of Mrs. McLintock, fuming at this easy slight to all she held dear. "Dinnae be quick tae shut your door."

“I’ve nowt against you and your kin”, Maggie replied. “I’m sure as far as God fearing folk go, you’re as repentant as the next, but I willnae have religion in this house. It’s brought nowt but pain tae me and mine. Have a good journey home.”

Maggie closed the door more forcibly, extricating Mrs. McLintock’s pins from beneath her lintel, much to the fury of its owner; and then she thought no more about the McLintock’s religious zealousness and pontificating. But for Mrs. McLintock this brief interlocution set the tone for a lifelong battle.

“Oh, she’s an immoral woman”, Mrs. McLintock raged as she briskly walked back along the cliff top path, easily outpacing her belittled husband. “Nae cross upon her neck, nae stockings on her legs. The Lord doesnae care for bare flesh. He will see her punished. I’ll see tae it. Aye, our Lord is a just God.”

With that she increased the speed of her step, her husband skipping awkwardly on uncomfortable stone just to keep up.

“The sermon this Sunday”, she stopped as they entered the Rectory, glaring through him. “Immorality. And make it a long one.”

What Mrs. McLintock would never care to admit, lest of all to herself, was that this newly awakened loathing for a stranger revealed more about her own character than perhaps she intended. She had become accustomed to inflicting her will upon others with increasing success. Her husband was possessed with a complete absence of courage, and after a decade of being berated, his flock was similarly compliant. To discover quite unexpectedly that there existed those on this earth with the audacity to challenge her righteous resolve and by extension, that of the Lord Almighty was shocking. That they should live not a mile from Auchobane and present such an immediate menace, was more contemptible. Maggie Keiller had to be overcome. She must be shown that religion would improve her life, inhibiting as it did, an otherwise self-indulgent existence. It would give meaning where it was lacking, and more, much more; it would make a life useful. For what was life without rules, but a lackadaisical one, a dangerous one? By the time Mrs. McLintock had returned to the cobbled streets of Auchobane she had determined that Maggie Keiller would be persuaded to turn to God, and if she could not be persuaded then she would be defeated.

Maggie Keiller foresaw the great storm of 1929 long before it devastated the Dundee coastline she called home. She dreamt of its impatience, as it churned death within its swollen bowels, wreaking havoc in the dark, dark ocean of its fearful belly. The waves swirled with a violence no storm had ever done before, dread and trepidation its only object. She felt its hostility in her bones, its revenge in every dissected current; it was a rage which demanded to be unleashed upon a land which had for centuries been its impediment. The closer it moved, the more anxious she became, sensing her own grief in its form. Her dreams became increasingly vivid and disturbed as it whispered its desire for death and she awoke that warm September morning dripping with a dread she could not shake. Confused, she rushed from her bed and sought reassurance at the window turned towards the sea. What she saw was no catastrophe of her dreams, but the familiar calmness of a landscape which soothed her troubled soul. Her love stood as he always did, his worn shirt discarded as a token hindrance to the swings and blows which he unleashed upon an unaccommodating earth. She watched the rhythmic oscillations of his arms, a machine but one with heart; her heart. She had lost it on those Church steps, somewhere amongst his pleasant features and sound character.

“Aye, aye wifie”, he smiled, feeling her look and returning it with affectionate eyes. He stopped and wiped his brow. “These tatties‘ll come good before the first winter frost, you mark my words.”

He looked down upon the mess of green stalk and potato which scattered the field and made it appear more dishevelled than it was. It was a blanket of honest food which would see them through the harsh winter months. A few extra haddock in the fishing run, smoked and tailed, and a clutch of rabbits from Auchobane’s hills, and he would feel more comfortable in this new practical skin. His regrets were numerous and he wrestled with his responsibility to provide for his burgeoning family. He hoped fervently that their hardships were transient and that the imminent arrival of a new Keiller would soften his father’s heart but for now, he occupied himself with earthly rewards, the only ones he could offer until his family saw past their prejudices and welcomed them back to the fold.

“There’s a storm coming’”, replied Maggie, her troubled dreams still fresh upon her mind. Her mother called it a gift, but she doubted it was so.

“Storm? What storm?” cried Billy, examining the perfect blue horizon. His thick black hair stirred in the sea breeze, like the tugging of autumn’s foliage from reluctant trees.

“It’s brewing’”, she continued, determined that the duplicity of Mother Nature should not overcome him. “I’ve seen it.”

It was true that the quiet of the ocean betrayed little of the storm she had seen in her dreams. Still as glass, it unnerved her. It was almost too calm, a lulling siren to those in search of just one more catch. The sea's history was strewn with the watery bodies of fishermen who had ventured farther than their luck, for one haul too many, compromising reverence for greed or necessity.

"Tarry close tae the shoreline this mid-summer."

The days were rapidly growing shorter, and soon the little cottage upon the cliff would be enveloped in the darkness of winter when nothing could be done or gained. Billy Keiller was acutely aware that his small harvest of potatoes was unlikely to satisfy them. A good basket of salted fish was required should any of their home-grown supplies be found wanting.

"Tell me again about a storm when I've brought ye a basket full of white fer salting."

"What use is a basket without a husband tae carry it? You'll find nowt but death on those waves this night."

Maggie's dread was increasing, her heartbeat rising with her growing anxiousness.

"I'll no stand by and watch ye be taken from me, and from this bairn", and she put a warm hand to her blossoming stomach. If he could not be persuaded for her sake, then perhaps he could be turned for their unborn child.

He looked at her with large, soft eyes and walked gently towards her. As he reached the window where she stood, he whispered.

"Hush now hen."

He cupped her flushed cheek with his palm. "It was nowt but a dream."

"But I saw it clear as I see you now."

"I know ye did."

"Did my mother not say I had the gift?"

"She did."

"Don't go", she whispered, the whites of her eyes glistening with the onset of tears.

"Isn't it possible", he began. "That this dream held more truth about yer own fear than any passing of mine? Is it not that ye saw what ye were afraid of seeing, rather than the truth of it?"

He rubbed her cheek gently with the coarse skin of his thumb.

"I've strength enough for any storm. Have faith in yer husband."

"I do, but…"

"In this dream of yers, did ye see me taken?"

Maggie hesitated for a moment.

"I didnae. But…"

"If ye didnae see me taken, then there's nowt to be fearful of, is there?" his voice was soothing, reassuring, a voice Maggie longed to trust.

"You'll do nowt but fret yourself and the bairn with such talk. I'll make ye a bargain - I'll return to the quay afore night falls. I'll no stay out with the big boats this time. The catch'll be smaller, but it's a fair price to pay to keep that pretty head of yours safe."

He took himself inside the cottage, the wooden floorboards creaking beneath the weight of the man and his muddied boots. He quickly deposited them on the step, revealing thick woollen socks patched through more times than they ought.

"Now, this fisherman's in need of extra sustenance if he's tae fight this great storm", and he pulled out a chair from beneath the table, its legs scraping the floor. He sat himself down and looked up at Maggie, his talk and manner encouraging her to action. He knew that the quickest way to ease his wife's concern was to keep her busy, and why not at something in which she excelled.

Billy took as naturally to his refreshment as he did to the spade, and Maggie watched him intently as if it were his last meal. When he had left, she turned towards the ocean, and watched as he disappeared across the horizon, towards the little harbour of Auchobane where another Maggie, his old fishing boat, bobbed enthusiastically waiting for her master. Maggie watched the light fade across rumbling waves and felt the wind grow stronger, toying with the wooden gate of Rose cottage. At first it was a playful kind of game, but soon it escalated in strength and menace. She saw dark clouds rush with speed across a dusky sky, succeeding in their haste to escape what ferociousness followed behind, feeling the shadows envelop the small kitchen as a heady draft extinguished her only flame. Then there came only nothingness.

Billy Keiller had long lost the cliffs of Auchobane, with its sheltered harbour and buttressed walls, by the time the swell turned and the winds increased their volume. His little boat, 'The Maggie', stood little chance when confronted by cyclonic currents and a plunging ocean. It struggled against a gale he could never defeat and lowered the sail which had hampered his purpose, the ropes shredding his hands as he gave them their freedom. He fell a thousand times upon the dampness of the deck, losing his footing with frustration. The boat spun wildly as each wave bred only the next, grasping hard upon the stern for fear of flying overboard, but the salted wood proved little comfort. His hands fell away as the spray washed them clean of any grip. The rolling waves came stronger, roused by an agitated wind and in the distance grew the largest wave of them all, near fifty feet high, ominous and fateful. His eyes betrayed the fear which rose inside him as this wall of death approached. He thought of Maggie, his family, his life and wished with all his heart that he was seated next to her by the fire. Tears welled as he realised that he would never see her again and he would never know his child. He was not ready to go, not so soon and not so alone.

The boat was calm and deathly quiet as it travelled up the breach of the giant wave. Once the boat had been set upon its course, Billy felt the helpless serenity of one who knew that his journey ended only at the pearly gates of heaven. So the boat progressed, advancing near vertical as it approached the crest, and he struggled to remain with his vessel. But he was determined that at the end, if he could not be with his love, then he would be with her namesake. And as the summit of the great wave was reached, both boat and occupant omitted one last desperate groan, collapsed and disappeared into the bowels of the sea.

Maggie awoke with a start in the early hours and knew instantly that he was gone. A pitiful hope drove her along the slippery pathway which led down the steep path to the village and its harbour. She found herself face to face with a multitude of fishing boats strewn in various shades of disassembly, ravaged and discarded by the unforgiving storm. Many were abandoned high upon the harbour wall, some bearing the marks of angry confrontation with their snapped masts, damaged hulls and disintegrating wooden oars. A throng of locals had gathered on the stone swept quay and were staring downwards at the water's edge, murmuring in hushed undertones. When they saw the woman of Rose Cottage come amongst them, they parted compliantly, eyes brimming with inquisition and mouths repressing knowing sneers. Maggie passed through them and their caustic gazes.

He lay upon the gangway where local men had removed him from his dance upon the lapping waves. He had lain there for hours, sloshing by the quayside for all to judge, a pearly white, ghostly figure. His features were swollen by the excess of water which had passed through him - the cool, crisp air which his lungs required having been replaced by a suffocation of salty liquid. His arms were spread wide, as though ready for a cross against which to be affixed, pleading for a retraction of his fate. He would have hated such a religious analogy, and she bent down to gently place them by his side. Worst of all were his eyes, which stared blankly upwards with pained despair at this unwanted death.

The body was placed on two salvaged pieces of watery wood. Maggie recognised them from the hull of their little fishing boat, the blue boards ruptured and splintered in similar devastation to its master. He was hoisted high by fellow fishermen, with the respect reserved for one of their own. As she passed through the prying throng, one of the women whom she recognised as the Rector's wife could no longer hold her tongue.

"'Tis the Lord's revenge," she snapped, pressing her lips into a tight spot in the middle of her face. It gave her the appearance of a sparrow, with her thin claws and sharp outlook. "He wasnae a God fearing man."

The men continued on their steep incline from the harbour, Billy raised high above the rocks and earth. It was as close to heavenly transportation as she could hope to give him. In the village, the body was rested in the back of a cart and two men buried their heads low and began the journey up to Rose Cottage, pulling the cadaver behind them. It was Maggie alone who followed the procession on its final winding coastal path; in the brightness of a full moon, a million stars her only companions. She felt all the heavens watch their journey, an honest audience to her grief. Each star seemed to radiate comfort, their brightness guiding hers, shoring a strength that should not fail on these last few steps. She felt him too. The shell of his human self lay lifeless on the rickety cart she followed, but he was not there. He walked beside her all the way, and she knew he would not leave her throughout.

At Rose Cottage, the men stopped and moved the body into the house. They laid him out on the floor and with token sentiment, bowed their hats and blessed their own fortune. They left this newly born young widow with much relief.

With a slow, methodical hand, Maggie undressed and washed him. In the whites of his fingers, despite a rigorous cleansing from the salt water which had seduced him, she still found traces of the earth around Rose Cottage, ingrained deep beneath his fingernails where they had dug eagerly at the soil.

“Am I doing it right?” she asked him once.

Standing in the corner comforting his widow’s first and hardest chore, he nodded gently his approval. She would come to imagine him there in troubling times.

She wrapped him tight in their wedding linen - white, cotton sheets which had celebrated the consummation of their love. When she had finished, she looked at the cocoon which lay in front of her on the wooden floor. The contours thrown by shadows from the single candle which illuminated the room, gave no indication of any human form beneath its curves.

She rose and rested at the kitchen table, one dram for him, one for her, both untouched. Then she sat with him throughout the short time which remained of the night and they talked through the practicalities of preparation for the hard Winter months.

When the sun gave intention of rising next morning, Maggie made her way to the lazy hills behind Rose Cottage, and spent some time pacing; a well-worn shovel by her side. She stopped and gazed out upon the vastness of an ocean, its vista an eternity which had used to calm her, but now stirred nothing but distrust It was not her resting place she sought but one which would please Billy. One from which he would always be close and see the seeds he had sown grow to their fruition, one from which he could admire the sunrise on Spring days, and set in warm Autumnal haze. She found a suitable spot not thirty feet from the gate of Rose Cottage. As she began to dig, she thought of him cold upon the hillside, she thought of the snow which would fall on his chest, and the rain which would make him wet, seeping through the linen and moulding his swathe.

By the time she had finished digging to what she felt was an appropriate depth, the sun had passed through its common trajectory and had now disappeared behind her and the Auchobane hills. She gazed down at her work, wondering what kind of beasties lingered down there, and if they knew the distinguished feast which was about to be placed upon their table. The earth was sticky, clumping around large stones which made the sides of this grave seem uneven and untidy. It was not a funeral fit for a Keiller, a broken woman digging a bad hole on a hillside, but it was all she could do and she hoped he would not mind greatly.

He said as much.

She rested the shovel in the excavated dirt and returned to the cottage, finding herself suddenly surprised to see his body resting by the door. She knew that in the days, perhaps weeks which followed, she would see it there a thousand more times like a missing piece of furniture expected out of habit.

With a great deal of difficulty and inelegance, due in part to the weight of the man, and the inconvenience of her pregnancy, Maggie lifted the body from the floor to Hamish, the new barrow Billy had spent five shillings on and never regretted. Through the gate of the cottage they stumbled and then to the grave.

She rolled him down into his new resting place, feeling each bump and knock as his body fell against the uneven earth. Through the deep darkness she felt a compulsion to remain by his side, for no reason other than to just 'be'. The sun had disappeared completely now, and she was in company with only the moon and drifting galaxies. As her eyes adjusted to the shadows, she began to make out the white flecks of linen still visible through clumps of earth as his body settled into its new home. She could not bring herself to cover him entirely with the freshly dug earth which lined his grave. So she sat upon the disturbed soil and wept.

Perhaps it was the finality of it all. Perhaps it was the exhaustion of the day. But the tears came freely and easily, too easily she reprimanded herself, for one who should know better. Their history had been intensely intertwined. Now amongst the quietude of stars, she was forced to consider a future in isolation from him. She saw herself alone, running though the monotony of day after day without words, without companionship. It was a bleak picture she painted, one without laughter or love. Exhausting years outstretched, with nothing of hope in them. Her mind ran to misery, as she finally found resolve to pick up the shovel and complete her final morbid task of filling in his grave.

In the days which followed Billy's death, she kept to bed, neither eating nor sleeping, but instead waiting for the hours to pass and with them the streams of tears to subside. She would weep until sick at his absence and the thought that he would never again cross the threshold of Rose Cottage, that she would never again be held tight when the wind rallied up through the cracks between the stones. Exhausted from sobbing, she would rest and be calm for a time, numbed by the physical exhuming of her feelings. Then as she recovered, she would remember once again the reality of her loss, and plunge back into the depths of mourning until fatigued and anesthetized in turn. And so the cycle continued for what seemed an eternity, but could not have been more than weeks.

In the month which followed Billy's death time seemed to adopt an ethereal tone. Although Maggie moved physically about the cottage, she knew not where or why. She felt an extremity of emptiness, as though she were but a hollow shell, and breathed in stagnated air. It seemed that this new indeterminate state would last forever, that this was the new Maggie, vacant and lost, and would be for all the years to be endured until her own end.

She had buried a husband. Soon, she would also bury a son.

The pain was excruciating, unrelenting, and terrifying, bearing into the very core of her, buckling her legs so that she could no longer stand, and she writhed in agony on the kitchen floor, not far from where Billy's body had once also lain. She looked towards that vacant spot longing for a vision of him, if only to give her support, if only to tell her that she was not alone. But she was alone, and the empty floorboards were a stark reminder of it. The snow fell thick and fast outside the cottage window as she thrashed and fought to appease the pain, and arrest the execution taking place in her womb. She saw the stains of blood, their mark clearly visible on the hard wooden floor and felt its inevitability. She knew there could be none, but she clung on to hope until the heartbreaking end.

For minutes, likely hours, she lay there as a sharp, thick pain grappled within her stomach with a ferocity she had never before experienced. She tried to remain perfectly still to allow it to wash through her, but as the agony became more insistent, she knew in her heart that it would not leave her without taking with it her most precious thing. She had ruminated over the child's sex, whispered to it and gently stroked the bump of a head where she thought it might lay. The baby was part of her and with Billy's death it had acquired greater significance as it was an extension of him. She had wondered if she would see his face again when the boy - she was sure in herself that it would be a boy – was born. Not only would Billy be with her in spirit then, but also in something more tangible, and she had willed the months to pass with speed so that she would no longer be entirely alone. It was the last star in a dark, dark sky.

She wretched again in agony, shutting her legs tight and willing the baby to remain, closing a cervix which might release that which she was determine to keep. But her legs grew tired after many minutes in fierce contortion, and the blood oozed more terribly from her than it had done before. It seeped through the microscopic splinters which formed each floorboard, staining them forever.

She felt the baby leave her, just as she had felt Billy's death only weeks before but this time it was a very physical desertion. She felt the small, perfecting formed being pass through her and she named him Angus. It took just a moment and it was, ironically, the most peaceful of them all. The pain subsided with his stillborn death, her body in relief at his release. There was no sound. Secretly Maggie had still hoped to hear a cry, but miracles were not her joy. She lay back upon the wooden floor, distraught. The sweat rallied in beads upon her forehead and her clothes wrung with the wetness of her physical pain. She shivered from the sudden cold of a draught from beneath the door and yet she dared not move, should a leg brush against the dead baby at her thighs, should she catch a glimpse of his lifeless eyes, tiny toes and fingernails. Would it look like Billy, with darkened hair and soulful eyes? She rolled onto her side clutching her empty stomach and found herself gazing upon a discarded pillowcase, the same linen used to dress Billy for his grave. It was fitting that his child should be similarly laid.

She tried to cry, but the tears would not come. Her face folded in the direction of ghost tears and she felt the convulsions associated with them. She wondered how more grief could be heaped upon her and wished for death so that she might complete their family in the grave and grew angry that she should be denied her own swift relief.

In her rage against God, Nature and Fate, she inadvertently sat upright and found herself quite unexpectedly facing the white cosseted baby which had been wrenched from her. Encased in a white, transparent jelly, tinged with blood and womb, he was curled peacefully in a foetal position, his hands clasped together and his eyes closed. His face, though not fully developed, clearly had Billy's mark. He would have been a beautiful boy, strong and tall. She dared not touch him lest she disturb his tranquil sleep; instead she counted his ten toes and fingers, and noted the beginnings of black hair upon his head.

He was buried next to his father, with a view of that which would have been his home. She found what little comfort she could in the thought that they lay together and would guide each other through whatever semblance of a life existed beyond this one.

Step 2: Scrub the fruit to release their natural goodness

It was soon after that Morag came to Rose Cottage. Billy's sister, she was nearest to him in age and character and was the only Keiller who had dared to side with the newlyweds against the wishes of her imposing father. She wrote constantly to her brother during his days at Rose Cottage, always encouraging and observing that she saw a softening in their father's heart for them, and that she was sure they would soon return to the warm embrace of Dundee's social circle. That embrace was fated never to happen, and now she arrived in mourning trudging through the great swathes of snow which marked the devastating Winter of 1930. She roused Maggie from her sorrow with a forceful knocking on the cottage door. Maggie opened it without question and found her modest sister-in-law dressed in a black hat and cloak, standing on a doorstep coated in ten inches of whiteness. Morag's hair was neatly pulled back against the solemnity of her face but the red curls which framed it were still irrepressible despite all attempts to subdue them. They softened the grieving clothes, and in the brightness of her eyes there remained a warm comfort, in contrast to the blanketed hills behind Auchobane.

"Snow?" asked Maggie quietly.

"Aye Maggie, these four weeks straight altogether now", replied Morag, empathizing with the emptiness in Maggie's eyes. Maggie avoided her gaze, fearing that her face might reveal the true extent of her disintegration. She was afraid too that Morag's easy charm would send her spiralling back into those initial days of loss. Morag had Billy's look, and Maggie knew that to see it again without courage was more than she could bear.

“I’m so sorry Maggie.”

Morag took her sister-in-law in her arms and embraced her with all the fondness of their first meeting. She had excused herself from the grief being exercised by the family in Dundee, and travelled the small roads and sharp bends treacherous with fresh snow, to make her way to Rose Cottage. The two women held each other close, conjoining thoughts and memories of the man who had shaped their lives. Maggie’s body shook as she fought back the tears which flowed too compliantly.

Morag gripped her even tighter.

“I’ve come tae lend a shoulder and a hand”, continued Morag, once both had strength again to stand apart.

Maggie opened the door wide for her unexpected guest. Morag could see she was a broken woman and if she was shocked by the disarray which greeted her inside the cottage, with rotten food and unkempt surfaces, she did not show it. Despite her own discomfort she removed her cloak and hat and began to put all she saw back in order. Maggie sat in the darkest corner of the room and watched her friend set to work on the restoration of her home.

“Forty days o’ snow now”, Morag continued, talking for its own sake. “They say it’s God’s own punishment, but I think we all just forgot ourselves with these past easy winters.”

“I miss him Morag”, said Maggie, taking opportunity to voice her thoughts and feelings out loud for the first time.

Morag took a seat realizing her legs would not take the weight of such conversation.

“I know ye do Maggie”, she replied. “He was a great man.”

“I cannae live without him.”

“Dinnae talk like that Maggie. It’ll take time but you’ll be right again.”

“I’ll never be right again”, whispered Maggie.

Morag hung her head. She struggled to comfort with words when she knew that none would soothe.

“He had a happy life”, Morag continued. “Draw consolation fae that. He was with the woman he loved and there’s no many can say as much.”

She drew a deep breath.

“Some of us will never have such a marriage as yours. Some walk this life without a soul mate. Is it no better tae have loved and lost him than never tae have known him at all?”

Maggie sighed and sunk into the weight of the chair beneath her. She felt as though she would never rise from it again.

Morag stayed through the thawing of the snow and the lengthening of days, through the first seeds of Spring and the overrunning of the sleeping garden with a multitude of colours. Rose Cottage had never shone so bright and although it made no sense to her, this new vibrant home, with its budding roses on the kitchen table, gave Maggie hope.

It was on one of these brilliant mornings that Morag sat, near enough to three months after her arrival, perfectly still, waiting for Maggie to rise. When her sister-in-law presented herself through the bedroom door, she beckoned Maggie to sit next to her by the table.

“Is it time?” Maggie sighed, foreseeing a return to solitude.

“Aye”, replied Morag. “But before I go I have a wee something which I hope will help in the times ahead.”

She slid a simple paper book across the table.

Maggie peeled back the cover. It was an old scrap book, with the words ‘Mrs Keiller’s Recipes for Marmalade’ carefully inscribed on the inside cover.

“All the Keiller marmalades that‘s ever been”, continued Morag.

“But I wasnae born a Keiller”, said Maggie, delicately peeling back the pages of this ancient recipe book.

“Your more a Keiller than any of us”, replied Morag touching her sister-in-law’s hand gently. “You have the same spirit as these women and our Billy knew it.”

Maggie flushed at the mention of his name.

“But I’ve never made marmalade in all my life.”

She surveyed the many pages of recipes, of advice and instruction from women who were strangers to her.

“Our mother used tae say that the most important ingredient in marmalade was heart. You have that in spades. The rest is just fruit and sweetness.”

“I cannae take it Morag. ‘Tis your history, no mine.”

She slid the heirloom back across the table to Morag.

“Take the book”, replied Morag, pushing it back towards her sister-in-law. “’Tis what Billy would have wanted. It’ll see ye through the dark days and quiet mornings.”

Morag’s words struck Maggie deeply. She had begun to sense the wall of solitariness which was outstretched before her. Billy knew how to distract her mind, how to occupy and constrain those sinister thoughts which lurked in the shadows of her heart. In an instant he could ease her anguish - could the occupation of marmalade do the same?

She picked up the fragile recipe book once again and this time gave greater consideration to the steps outlined in each of the handwritten pages. Full of passion and pain in equal measure, she saw through the process and method of the marmalades to the women who had suffered for them. Their hurt and grief was just like hers, poured out into the recipes, as much an ingredient in the marmalade as the fruit.

Morag rose from the table and took her things in anticipation of catching the Dundee bus from Auchobane.

“There’s one last thing.”

She handed Maggie an envelope.

“All that was due him is yours.”

Maggie peered inside. It was more money than she had ever seen in her life. She handed it back forcibly.

“I dinnae want your father’s charity.”

“Is no charity Maggie. He’s a broken man. He’s lost his only son and on bad terms. He wants tae make amends.”

“It’s too late for that.”

“I know it. And so does he. But let him do what he needs tae, fer he’ll not be much longer of this world. He’s not a well man Maggie. Billy’s passing’s taken all the life from him. From all of us. Let him pass tae the next world with one good deed in his soul.”

Maggie’s stomach churned at the thought of appeasing the hateful old man who had disowned them for nothing more than a social convention. Why should she soothe his heart when he had tried to break hers? She held nothing but hatred for the Keiller patriarch but similarly she could not refuse any request which came from the heart of her beloved sister-in-law. Her kindness and actions brought back memories of her husband, and to refuse her would be to defy him.

She knew Billy would have wanted her to take it, to give her comfort where he could not. But what did she care for comfort without him, without someone to share the ‘come see this‘, or ‘isn’t that grand‘? It was nothing without him.

She thought about the happy times such money might have brought them if he had been alive. Would they have moved to town? No, she thought, he would have rejoiced in his new found calling on the land. A farm then, with a pretty farmhouse, painted windows and great oak fireplaces, upon which would hang the reward of successful hunts. She saw a little boy, maybe three years old, with the same wild, dark hair and brilliant blue eyes as his father, rushing about with smiles and excitement. It was a vision too far - the smile faded from her face, and the tears returned to stain the kitchen table.

Morag returned to the high society into which she was born and the busy life of a merchant's daughter. She promised to write, which she duly did every week thereafter. Maggie's days passed slowly at first then assumed a flitting regularity. The routine of her day, seemed to increase their speed, as one day was identical to the next, and the one which followed, to such an extent that she could not single them out as individual hours. Just as the sun rose each morning, so did she, and as it set behind the Cottage, so she retired too.

In winter, when the cold became so suffocating it pained the tips of her toes and the bones of her face, she wondered if this were her time, if the march towards death were over and its frozen hand would take her now. But the warmth returned and she remained. With every rattling storm which unleashed its strength on Rose Cottage, she imagined herself blown away by one of the deafening gusts which beat down powerfully on the flimsy roof and fragile windows. But the storm passed, and to her disappointment, both she and Rose Cottage stood firm. The Keiller recipe book which Morag had given her took pride of place on the kitchen table. She would delve into its pages when she sought strength, devouring it on difficult days and grasping it tightly, on the very worst of them.

One morning, months into her solitude, Maggie watched as a strange man moved amongst the graves of her husband and son on the hill behind Rose Cottage. She watched him idly walk back and forth, leaning down to inspect the engravings then out to sea to admire their view. He seemed at home amongst the dead, without that overly reverential unease so common with the living.

After a time spent bowed downwards, his face then turned towards the Cottage, and removing his hat, Maggie watched him quietly approach. The wisps of his hair extended in the breeze and his large green coat flapped with every gust. Although she tracked his footsteps upon the path, Maggie still jumped with surprise at the thumping of his fist upon the door, as though she had watched his arrival outside herself, in a kind of dream of habit.

It had been too long since she last received a visitor. Throughout months and years, she had not uttered a word, all conversations taking place only in her mind. To express any sentiment seemed irrelevant - there was no one to reply. A momentary fear of unfamiliar conversation with an outside world took hold but the dutiful woman of Maggie's youth soon suppressed any indulgent whims, fancy or fears, and at the second rattling of the door, she opened it to this stranger.

Outside, swathed in the dullness of an overcast day, stood a gentleman, quintessential in thought and appearance but for a gaudy polyester vest draped across his torso. The man's face twinkled with anticipation, and he removed his Glengarry so that the rain dripping from the porch ran unrestrained over his prematurely hair-free head.

"Apologies Mrs. Keiller fer the uninvited nature of my call like", he began, his lilt marking him out instantly as more Northern than their local lot. Maggie was all the more intrigued for it.

"I have taken upon myself the position of grocer down in the village", he continued nervously. "And would care to know if ye would be interested at all, in a regular delivery?"

His words increased in speed with his embarrassment. He was not a natural salesman, but a simple man who sought to support his modest living.

"I'd happily deliver tae Rose Cottage come hail or snow… ye can count on that. Maybe just one or two things tae start with, an' see how we go? If yer happy with the service of an old soldier, we can talk again."

He stopped for breath.

It was a simple request, and a surprising one. Maggie had adopted an entirely self-sufficient life and the slightness of her emaciated frame would attest to this being not an entirely successful existence. She had God's own rainwater, vegetables for stew and more potatoes than she could possibly want to eat through seasons which passed her by. There was only one thing which she had coveted quietly.

"Have ye got any oranges?" replied Maggie.

"Oranges?"

“Aye, oranges. From Spain”, continued Maggie. “From Seville.”

Dougie scratched his thinning hairline.

“Seville eh?”, replied Dougie, “I didnae know there was such a thing, but ye have my word Mrs. Keiller - I’ll no set foot on this step again without a Seville orange, or my name‘s no Douglas Stuart MacGregor, of the second battalion of the Argyll and Sutherlands.”

He was true to his word, and days into the month of March, there came another unannounced knocking on the door of Rose Cottage.

Dougie stood there with a crate of radiating Seville oranges, rolling and knocking against each other from the melee of their unusual journey. Maggie took the fruit in hand, examining each one, the rough texture of their skin, the vibrancy of the colour; it was unlike anything she had seen before. They lifted her spirits like the roses by the door or the blue of the sky over Fife. She placed them on the table, next to the Keiller marmalade book.

After the oranges came the jars a month later, then the labels and lids shortly after. Maggie’s hours became consumed by marmalade production. The mundane was replaced with hours of peeling, chopping, imbibing and creating a very own personal conserve, one which overflowed with the heartbreak of her life. She delved deep into the hearts of the oranges, tearing their skin, releasing the tart, citric smell which enlivened a mournful Rose Cottage. Everything was alive again, she was alive again. Maggie embraced the occupancy of the process, enjoyed the physicality it demanded, delighted in the distraction it afforded, releasing her from months of introspection. Her hands ached with their new use, but she was reborn. With the birth of her first batch of marmalade, Maggie found herself with purpose and a friend, and Dougie for his part found enough excuse to present himself at the door of Rose Cottage even when there was no reason to warrant his trip.

The following year, Dougie opened his order book one day in early spring and found, written in pencil, the words 'Mrs. Keiller's Seville Oranges' at the top of the page. He smiled as he recalled the sensation of the marmalade, the sweetness on his tongue and the warmth in his heart. It was with this memory as fresh upon his mind as if it had been yesterday, that he placed another order for a consignment of oranges for the marmalade woman of Rose Cottage and a new routine was born. Two weeks later and the exotic fruit was delivered, ready for the final mile of its journey, up the coastal path to its new home and its ultimate destiny within the gloriously decadent surrounds of a beautiful clear jar. His precious cargo was placed carefully inside a wooden crate fastened to the fading black handlebars of Constance, his trusted delivery bicycle. He shut the door to his little shop with as much kindness as he afforded the lost souls of his fallen comrades who rested in old photographs and newspaper cuttings adorning the walls of his humble flat. He carefully wheeled Constance over the cobbled stones of Auchobane, which threatened to usurp her delicate mission, and turned towards the coastal path and their ultimate destination, Rose Cottage.

His quiet journey through the village was tracked by two discriminating eyes from the Rectory. A certain Mrs. McLintock took a keen interest in his progress as she sat by the window of the breakfast room. It was a small room set off from the entrance hall, comfortably furnished, but its most important feature and the reason Mrs. McLintock preferred it above and beyond all others in the Rectory, was its perfect outlook onto the street outside. It provided an exquisite vantage point from which she could monitor the comings and goings of Auchobane's residents and ensure that the strong moral fibre of the village remained intact. She knew each and every inhabitant - their history and their secrets, and believed that it fell heavily upon her devout shoulders to speak up where she saw standards beginning to wane. And she had no qualms about speaking up, pontificating from the window, much to the consternation of the unfortunate villager in question. She would deftly un-latch the handle, and raise her voice to Mr. Emslie about the excessive number of visits he was making to the public house, or Ms McEwen about her expensive new shoes when the church donation box remained undernourished, or young Sandy Stott, whose pocket money was being frittered away on frivolity when it could be more frugally employed in improving the lives of the poor. Her eyes were judicious and her words were as sharp as her admonishment of any villager whom she felt was descending into immorality. The movements of Auchobane's new grocer, a stranger amongst the kin of the village, were therefore of great interest to Mrs. McLintock. Distrustful of those in whose habits she was less than secure, she had taken particular interest in his provision round. The brightness of Dougie's consignment of oranges on this particular day was as conspicuous to Mrs. McLintock as a red flag beneath the heaving nostrils of a bull. Her hand flew at the Rectory window latch, unleashed with speed and purpose, the shrillness of her voice piercing the sea air.

"Mr. MacGregor", she shouted from her pulpit. "Mr. MacGregor, what is it ye have there?"

Dougie froze, fixed as though he had been spotted by a sniper in No Man's Land.

“I can see you Mr. MacGregor”, Mrs McLintock’s bitter tone came again. “What are those provisions?”

“Oranges”, he replied with a heavy heart.

“Speak up Mr. MacGregor. I cannae hear you.”

“They’re oranges, Mrs. McLintock. Just oranges.”

“Oranges is it?”, she replied.

“Aye”, said Dougie.

“That’s a very fanciful produce Mr. MacGregor. Tell me, who has ordered such fruit?”

Dougie winced. His mind flickered in brief consideration of a mistruth, but Douglas Stuart MacGregor was a brave man with an honest heart and the notion of lying to ease his way grated with his conscience.

“Mrs. Keiller”, he replied.

“Who was that Mr. MacGregor?” Mrs. McLintock wanted to ensure she was in full possession of the facts before unleashing her divine tongue on the unsuspecting grocer.

“Mrs. Keiller, of Rose Cottage. They’re fer her marmalade. I’m hoping tae persuade her tae enter the competition at Caird Hall this year.”

He waved a leaflet in Mrs. McLintock’s general direction.

“I see”, she replied. “Could I take a wee look at that piece of paper?”

Dougie slowly moved across to the window and duly handed her the leaflet.

Mrs. McLintock read it through twice. She had initially hoped that the loss of a husband might have turned Mrs. Keiller back towards a Godly light, but it appeared that stubbornness had prevailed. Mrs. McLintock, also recently widowed, was left with no option but to persuade Margaret Keiller of her oversight. With the leaflet, a delicious revenge suddenly presented itself. Such public humiliation as might be obtained through a marmalade competition could provide greater clarity of religious direction than merely removing her provisions. The irony that marmalade could bring about the downfall of a Keiller was not lost on Mrs. McLintock and she determined that this was a direct message from God. She folded up the leaflet neatly, pressing down the edges to make a clear, clean crease and handed it back to the grocer.

"On yer way then Mr. MacGregor", Mrs. McLintock nodded as she shut gently the clearly polished window. "We cannae keep a Keiller waiting."

Dougie stood for a moment at the retracted window, relieved but a little surprised at being allowed to pass unscathed. He turned and continued on his journey to Rose Cottage, leaving Mrs. McLintock to muse on the details of her revenge.

"Have ye ever thought tae move down tae the village?" began Dougie as he sat next to Maggie and the small fire kindling in Rose Cottage not an hour later.

Maggie shook her head.

"Is no for me", replied Maggie.

Maggie looked out of the window towards the hillside and the two weathered headstones which stood against the rushing grass.

“I’ll never leave. I’m here as long as they.”

She thought of her husband and son, dressed in their white linen, their bodies preserved in eternal youth. She saw their faces, pale but beautiful, surrounded by blackness, and wished with all her heart that this would be the day she joined them. It was the same wish she held out every day - it was her waking dream. Her eyes assumed their sad solitary complexion as she remembered the years already lost in waiting.

“If you’ll pardon me for saying, there’s plenty of living yet tae be done. There’ll be many a winter’s passed before you’ll be ready for the grave.”

“I hope not Mr. MacGregor, I hope not.”

“I came across something that might interest ye”, continued Dougie, and he took from his large coat pocked a piece of paper, neatly folded and kept.

Maggie read the notice advertising the Silver Spoon marmalade competition. It was the location of the event - Caird Hall – which touched her heartstrings. The same place from which she had set out on her life journey, arm in arm with her love and their hopes and dreams. She wondered what ghosts she would find there now, amongst the soaring columns and grey façade of the building and felt a sudden desire to see again a place where she had been at her happiest. So she took the pristine paper from Dougie and placed it on the table next to her new consignment of joyful fruit.

Down in the village of Auchobane, Mrs. McLintock, stirred by more than her usual religious fervour, set about creating her marmalade, secure in the believe that God would put his hand upon the jar, and bless the transparency and consistency of its contents. Just to be sure, she added a cupful of holy water to the mixture. The marmalade competition, she had determined, was a suitable platform, not only for conserves but for creed. Mrs. McLintock was acutely aware of the Keiller name, she was also aware of the claims that clan had made on the history of Dundee marmalade. Such heresy fuelled the fires of her intent to humiliate their descendant. Her plan was to defeat Maggie's irreverent marmalade which sullied the hallowed name of Dundee and its proud produce, with her own morally superior version and to press upon Margaret Keiller the role the Lord had played in its creation. It was Mrs. McLintock's duty, as the personification of all that was honourable and decent, and morally preached by her Protestant forefathers, to crush the Keiller woman and her marmalade, publicly and completely.

"Margaret Keiller lords the Keiller name over us all", Mrs. McLintock pontificated the following Sunday at Church. "'Tis a name steeped in ancestral lies. Invented marmalade? The good Lord invented marmalade, not the Keillers. Well pride comes afore a fall and there's a mighty big fall coming to that woman, you mind my words."

Maggie set about the conception of her own entry into the Dundee Silver Spoon Competition with little drama or direction, oblivious to the furious activity underway in Auchobane's Rectory. In contrast to the exorcisms being executed in Mrs. McLintock's kitchen, Maggie's marmalade necessitated heavenly intervention of a different kind - the ingredients were unblessed and unwashed, torn from orange trees on the banks of the Guadalquivir, the sunshine of the Sierra Nevada being the only God in which she trusted. Marmalade was more than blood, it was kin.

The Keiller matriarchs had bequeathed a passion, passed down through generations. It was this inheritance which Maggie potted in a shiny new jar and took with her on the short bus ride along the rugged coastline to Dundee and placed upon the judges' table on a rainy morning in 1932.

Caird Hall stood apart from the other grand buildings which lined the main square in Dundee. Its elegance was a mark of a glorious revolution now passed, its iconic pillars supporting this status, peering with expectation through grey granite, in search of a return to their momentous ascension. On this particular day however, the event was far more humbling - nothing more than a local competition and the guests who passed through its fine oak doors, inconsequential dignitaries. It was a suitably noble setting for a battle of marmalade proportions, but the notice outside the hall simply read 'Marmalade Festival - entrants enquire within'.

Inside the main vestibule, cornices and panelling abounded in grand interiors foreign to the rural visitors. A stern lady who greeted all with a homemade clipboard and an efficient pen, instructed both women to place their respective marmalade submissions on a colourful judging table, which overflowed with shiny glass jars. Mrs. McLintock placed her sanctified offering in a prominent position upon the table as was fitting for such a divine marmalade. Maggie Keiller's blasphemous jar by contrast, was almost hidden amongst the motley company which had filled the back of table by the time judging commenced at three o'clock precisely, or as precisely as Lord Tavistock could be persuaded to traverse the hall following a hearty lunch of roast beef and puddings, washed down with a supply of port wine.

Lord Tavistock was a popular and accommodating local landowner, not dissimilar in appearance to that of a walrus. A rotund man, his amiable girth ensured he could always be counted upon as an enthusiastic judge in competitions involving perishables. His preference was for home baking, being much persuaded by macaroons, a Dundee cake and a shortbread or three. These were closely followed, hopefully in time as well as proximity by ale and whisky competitions. In fact, if a month passed where he had not been invited to attend any such events, he would lobby the local luminaries until such an invite was forthcoming. It was not unheard of for a new competition to be created simply to satisfy the intimidating whiskers of the House of Lord's member. On this particular Sunday afternoon, much buoyed by his port and an enthusiasm for food in general, Lord Tavistock, accompanied on either side by sober and submissive fellow judges began their studious examination of the marmalade produce, venturing enthusiastically along the judging table, picking up jars, holding them to the light, checking for consistency.

A jar must be clean, the liquid transparent, the peel ought to glisten and twinkle like a starry night on the Trossachs. Many were dismissed, but with the conclusion of their scrutiny both Mrs. McLintock and Maggie Keiller's offerings held firm, successfully passing the judges' critical assessments.

The second round of the competition demanded more intensive inspection, the jars being opened, and tasting commenced. Spoons were dipped delicately, plummeted profusely and ladled languishingly. Jocularity rang out as Lord Tavistock tickled the humoristic taste buds of his like-minded judges and relished the syrupy sugar which caressed the back of his throat and then the lining of his ample stomach - the perfect digestion aid to a satisfactorily indulgent lunch.

After much deliberation, especially upon the not inconsiderable whisky marmalade section, only four finalists remained. As the names were announced around the voluptuous hall, Mrs. McLintock was perturbed to learn that her agnostic neighbour's unreformed entry was amongst those still being considered for the great prize. This was a Godly trial of monumental proportions, but her faith prevailed, rallied by the assurance that her loyalty would be as triumphant as the second coming. Maggie, unaware of her neighbour's keen interest in her modest jar of marmalade, was simply contented that the Keiller name should stand once again amongst such exalted company. As the judges huddled conspiratorially around the final four jars, the two women stood only meters apart, nervously anticipating a final decision.

Finally, Lord Tavistock raised his spectacles.

"After due consummation and much consideration", he boomed. Mrs. McLintock's heart pounded as she pressed her rosary beads furtively against the bone of her pious fingers. Maggie closed her eyes and thought of her little home.

"The Dundee Marmalade Silver Spoon of 1932 is awarded to…" Lord Tavistock paused for effect, ever the showman, "Mrs. Margaret Keiller of Rose Cottage. Congratulations Mrs. Keiller."

Applause erupted in the hall as Maggie stepped forward to accept her prize and the warm congratulations of those around her. The spoon was presented, photos taken, and Maggie was somewhat overwhelmed by the adulation for her simple jar of marmalade. But there was one whose congratulatory hand remained firmly within her practical coat pockets. To have accepted defeat with courtesy and grace would have been a truly Christian virtue, but unfortunately Mrs. McLintock's religious pride would not allow such benevolence. Nor could she simply allow the moment to pass without some condemnation, some cutting comment about her competitor's unworthiness. As Maggie stood receiving the honest congratulations of her fellow competitors, Mrs. McLintock felt a compulsion to say her piece and make her feelings known. She sidled up to her unsuspecting conqueror with intent, with many words to say, but only a few made it through the firmly clenched teeth she bared with fury.

"You may outwardly appear righteous unto men, Mrs. Keiller, but the Lord sees all hypocrisy and iniquity within", she snapped viciously. "He will have his vengeance."

With that, she swept ungraciously out of the hall upon her sanctimonious coattails, vowing never to face that woman again, and praying fervently that Mrs. Keiller would suffer irrevocably on judgement day.

Maggie watched Mrs. McLintock rush from the hall, baffled by her strong sentiment other than the obvious disappointment in the face of defeat. If Mrs. McLintock's intentions were to make known the greater good for which she fought, she had failed miserably to convey it to Maggie Keiller. Clutching the silver spoon in her left hand and a ceremonial bunch of forget-me-nots in the right, Maggie sat on the back seat of the old diesel bus which wound its way around the byways of coastal Fife, thinking about Mrs. McLintock. As she looked out upon the tempestuous wind beating down ferociously upon the wild sea, she saw again her vengeful eyes. On the walk up the grass track to Rose Cottage, she remembered the words of wrath hissed through clenched teeth; and as she placed the silver spoon in its final resting place in the drawer beneath the sink, she thought of the pointed finger which had been brandished with such acrimony by a woman she hardly knew. And then she thought of Mrs. McLintock no more, nor of the resentment which simmered within the Rectory for the unwavering woman of Rose Cottage.

Step 3: Immerse the Oranges in Water

Maggie sat in the darkness, listening. The small, thin window panes rattled like the drums she could hear when the parades passed through Auchobane. She sat upright on the hard wooden kitchen chair, staring into nothingness, expecting at some point that her eyes would acclimatise and she would start to make out the vague shapes of furniture and the room's situation. But the blackness was too complete and she found that she enjoyed the novelty of a different view. For years she had been confined to the vista of those same four walls, those same characters of wood and fabric, all unchanged since Billy's death. His face still came to her as vivid and real as the day he had set out upon an ocean and promised he would return. She hated this vision, but adored it too; for although she saw his death a thousand times over, she also saw quite clearly those beautiful eyes she missed with every heartbeat of every day. She could pretend in the darkness that he sat but a foot away from her, just beyond her touch.

It was only when the new sunbeams of an early dawn appeared that Maggie lost her smile. Her secrets died as the room and all its common shelves and chairs revealed itself with the light and she sat alone again. With the years, the young woman with thick blond hair and a youthful bloom, faded. Not that Maggie noticed her withering. What did she care for looks? What use were they to her now, to one who had lost her love? She had died the day he did, and all that came thereafter was but the slow and painful passing of time until their eventual reconciliation.

Year upon year, Maggie's day began with the sun's appearance upon the rolling Eastern horizon. She took her breakfast alone in silence; she looked out upon the same landscape framed only by the large white washed stone which hugged the kitchen windows of Rose Cottage. The only distraction became the now more frequent visits from Dougie and the growing list of provisions necessitated by her increasing age. He brought with him not only those essentials which Maggie could not provide for herself, but also a chance to step away from the moroseness of her thoughts and back into the lives of those who still enjoyed their living.

It was on one such morning, as she waited for Dougie to appear upon the pathway up from the village, that Maggie spotted a solitary magpie sitting upon the gatepost. Although the wind ruffled its dark feathers, it stood firm with determination to fulfil its portentous duty and when the animal was sure that Maggie had acknowledged its presence, it turned and flew off in the direction of the graves, stopping briefly on the mark of her husband, before returning to whence it came. Not an hour later and its omen, in the form of a letter, arrived at Rose Cottage.

The note came from Morag, which in itself was not unusual as Morag had kept her promise and written regularly for near on five years by this point. The constant of Morag's letters had become part of Maggie's routine and she would dedicate an afternoon to savour this sacred communication with the outside world. It was an intimate affair between the two women, and Maggie's scarce companionship meant that she relished this opportunity for connection with another. She would brew a pot of tea, arrange a few pieces of bread, and open a new jar of marmalade to welcome Morag's words into her home.

That Maggie never replied to any of Morag's letters may have seemed odd, but in truth Maggie could never find more than a sentence or two to mark a passing week. She had tried on several occasions to replay the course of her days, but it consisted more of a list of chores than of any notable narrative or insightful observation. So she had put her pen to one side and decided that if there were nowt worth living for, then there were nowt worth writing. But her inability to reply to Morag's letters in no way dampened her enthusiasm for their arrival and their significance continued throughout the difficult years at the small kitchen table in Rose Cottage.

Morag's life had been sprinkled with much excitement, since the two women had last crossed ways. She was married not a year after her brother passed - to a shipbuilder from Dundee's docks. Her father had again disapproved of his child's choice in matrimony, but having learnt some semblance of a lesson from his son's demise, had been less fierce about their match. John Keiller had lost his independence, followed by his memory and his dignity. It was a slow degradation and Morag had been with him at the end when he had lamented life's unfortunate turns, but nothing of his culpability in his son's death ever passed his lips. He left this world on a bitterly cold night, ten years to the day after his only son.

Morag gave birth to a daughter a year into her marriage. For Maggie, it was a difficult letter and she consumed it with a lump in her throat as she willed happiness for her sister-in-law but fought tears at the theft of her own motherhood. The girl grew like her mother, with a plethora of curls and freckles to match. A photograph was produced and enclosed in one of the letters, falling unexpected from the envelope as Maggie tore at it to release Morag's words. She placed the child's picture in a box filled with secret things which lay next to her quilted bed.

Such were the engaging correspondences which had scattered the welcome mat of Rose Cottage, and Maggie had no expectation that the letter heralded by the solitary magpie on that day in 1954, should be any different. It looked exactly like every other letter written by Morag's hand - the same steady, clear script, the same clean lines; it was only the contents which were markedly different.

This latest letter had a more serious inclination. Instead of a gentle introduction into her spirited world, she poured her heart out to Maggie. She pleaded for help in rescuing her daughter, shamefully pregnant and in need of support. She begged Maggie to take her in, hide her away from the world, until the baby arrived and arrangements could be made. Maggie's heart wrenched. Her heartache and her stillborn child would need to be forgotten. She remembered the photograph - the girl with the scattering of curls and wondered whether she was Morag's daughter in character as well as looks. Maggie determined to repay her sister-in-law the kindness she had shown to her, in those first months of suffocating grief.

Kirsty Keiller arrived at Rose Cottage a month after the letter which detailed her predicament. Furrowed clouds, briskly shifting across an expansive sky were audience to her journey up the coastal path from Auchobane, where the idling regional bus had deposited her. She carried within her the baby of a man whose blows controlled and dominated her to such an extent that she buckled beneath the fear of his physical presence. That morning, she had stolen from his bed while the sun slept soundly and her oppressor even deeper, with only the stars to witness to her secret journey, fear gripping her young heart and the foetus warm within her. As she reached the coastal pathway from Auchobane, alone and afraid, she knew that there was no going back. He would have risen by now and found her gone. He would have raged against the world momentarily but as an intelligent man, he would quickly have gathered his thoughts and begun the search for them at her mother's door. She felt terror even from a distance as she imagined his face and his clenched fists ploughing through any obstacle in his determination to fetch her home. She felt certain that he would eventually triumph and in her heart knew that this shelter at Rose Cottage would not be far enough to deliver safety.

Maggie watched her approach, the young girl trying desperately to hide her burgeoning figure as the wind whipped at her fulsome coat. Her eyes were like Morag's but with deeper inspection, Maggie found something colder in them and lacking the softness so prevalent in her mother's face.

"Ye have something of your mother's eyes", began Maggie, on opening the door to this unknown and yet familiar girl.

Kirsty Keiller felt overcome by her situation, both physically and emotionally and longed for the comforts of home. All she saw was the face of an old woman, one who had no notion of her own personal hell nor the sacrifices required to extricate herself from it.

"If you've but half her heart, you'll be just fine", Maggie continued.

The young girl burst into tears.

Maggie took her crying to be an outpouring of shame at the social stigma she had brought to her family and would now bear for the rest of her life. Fife was no place for an unmarried mother. She would forever be an outcast from her generation.

"'Tis no matter", continued Maggie. "You'll learn tae live quietly just as I have."

The girl sat stooped in a corner and Maggie brought out the book of Keiller marmalade recipes given to her in a time of desperation. It had been her constant companion through difficult days and might prove to be the salvation of another Keiller woman.

"Your mother gave this tae me when dark clouds rolled across this shore", Maggie began, handing Kirsty the old book. "It saved me from my own self, the worst demon of them all."

The young girl looked with disdain at the torn binding and discoloured cover.

"Wise words from your ancestors", continued Maggie. "They know you better than you know yourself."

"A recipe book?"

"Aye, the Keiller marmalade book", replied Maggie.

"Marmalade?"

"The best kind."

"What use have I for marmalade?" began Kirsty, holding the bump protruding from beneath her clothes. "Jelly's not going tae fix this."

"Less of the jelly lassie…."

"Mother said that you'd taken Billy's death a bad turn, but I'd no notion that ye were touched about the head."

"Occupy your mind when it wants tae flee and your heart when it wants tae wither", Maggie continued unperturbed. "It'll make the days pass quicker tae their end."

"I'm not ready for the grave", said Kirsty.

"But you've dug yourself one", replied Maggie unable to hold her tongue. "So as you give, so will you get? No laddie'll have ye now."

The young girl's tears came faster as she bit her tongue.

"No soul from dawn till dusk, nowt but sorrow at the door", said Maggie. "If ye willnae have the marmalade, ye may as well settle with the father of that bairn. Quiet can destroy a woman."

"A man can do that and all", replied the girl suddenly finding her voice and that it was fierce. "As mother tells it Billy was a good man, so what do you know of a bad one?"

Maggie was taken aback by the fury of her anger and the words cut by one so young. In her generation, the respect due to elders was unconditional. It was a sign that the world had turned without her to hear such insolence from her niece.

She sighed.

"Ye cannae put an old head on young shoulders".

So went the first fiery words between Maggie and Kirsty Keiller, aunt and niece. Kirsty stayed at Rose Cottage just one day. On the next Maggie rose to find the cottage door ajar and her young guest gone. She assumed that her niece had returned to the life fate had designed for her, burying deep a youthful impetuousness, but she was wrong. Kirsty had been stirred instead by the vision of a fallow future painted for her by Maggie. The shallow existence of her aunt had provoked her to choose an entirely different path. If Maggie had intended her wise words to soothe a rebellious soul, they inspired the opposite, driving Kirsty Keiller to greater ambition. If she was not ready for the grave, then she would mould a life on her own terms. She had escaped as far as Rose Cottage – why could she not go further? London would save her and her unborn child, but she left behind her innocence on the doorstep of Rose Cottage. She left it with kin, failed by a mother who could not protect her and an aunt who would not support her.

Hours after Kirsty left, a man arrived at Maggie's door.

"Is she here?" his broad chest extended with the direction of his threat and he glared through Maggie and beyond, his eyes scouring the dark interior of Rose Cottage for his intended.

"There's none here but my own self", growled Maggie.

"I was told she was here", he replied, as he muscled his way into Rose Cottage's kitchen.

Maggie understood at once the terrors of her niece's plight. Here was her perpetrator come searching for the easily intimidated.

"Ye were told wrong", said Maggie.

He began to uncover and set the room to disarray.

"Where is she?' He thumped the table in frustration.

"Away and boil yer head", replied Maggie, standing tall, all five foot of her. He glared at Maggie, and then rushed towards her with his fists raised.

"Will I ask ye again with these…?"

"You'll get the same answer."

Her words were short because her heart flew fast with fear. At well over six foot in height and not much less in width, he towered over her, using his bulk to terrorize.

“Biting and scratching is a Scots folk’s wooing”, he snarled. “I dinnae know what she’s told ye, but it’s between me and my lassie. This is nowt’s business but our own.”

Maggie tried to suppress the natural trembling of her limbs.

“She’s away”.

“Away where?”

“I dinnae know. She didnae say.”

He rushed towards her again, threatening violence.

“Yer off yer head!” Maggie screamed, closing her eyes and hoping that her resilience was a strong enough defence.

He stopped and whispered in her ear.

“I’ll find her… and I’ll give her an extra beating just fer you.”

He flew out of the door just as quickly as he’d entered it. Dougie told her later that he had stayed down in Auchobane for a time, perhaps hoping that Kirsty Keiller would return, perhaps looking for another victim. Then he disappeared one night and never returned. Kirsty, for her part, settled successfully into a London existence far from the destructive influences at work in Dundee and remained forever distant to mother and aunt for at least the latter’s remaining life.

With the loss of her daughter, Morag succumbed prematurely to old age and was swiftly removed to a care home. Maggie‘s correspondences ebbed as a result, before they stopped entirely a few months later. It was with a sense of inevitability that she learned of Morag's passing. Maggie felt as though her last connection with the past had been severed, and the loneliness which had enveloped her on Billy's death, crashed over her again like the great wave which had taken him from her. Morag had known Billy longer than she and loved him longer than she. With her death, Maggie became the last person on this earth who would remember him, who knew the man and his spirit. If she forgot, then it was as though he had never lived and so she began to resuscitate her memories of him daily to prevent them from failing.

It saddened her that Morag had died alone, in an unfamiliar place without friends or family as she moved from this world to the next. No kin readied her before she was placed in this earth. None sat by her in her new resting place, to ease the transition from light to dark. She would never have a view. Maggie could not help but place some culpability upon her niece.

Step 4: Disassemble the Fruit

In a townhouse in London, two very different creatures sat, beating out their individual rhythms. A mother and a daughter and between them a gulf of age and understanding. As one sat writing a carefully constructed note to her Keiller relative, the other stared vacantly out the window, loathing her insipid life and longing to assume that of someone else's.

Kirsty Keiller scribed her ‘t’s with a flourish. It was not an expression of creativity, but rather a painstakingly slow concentric turn of the wrist, forced to its unnatural duty over many years. The paper on which she wrote was carefully chosen for its royal mark, the pen she used for its finest quality. The words were considered and reserved. She would not beg, she would not plead. The note became all the more vague for this reason, but it was a small price to pay to avoid elaboration. The necessity of the letter made Kirsty despise Maggie even more, which in turn placed greater pressure on that wrist which sought to maintain its artistry. What Kirsty Keiller sought was not just the convenience of Maggie’s exiled location, but the promise of financial gain which lay beneath her rural walls; the promise of a Keiller fortune which Kirsty believed had been handed to Maggie by her mother many years ago, and which she felt was rightfully hers.

The dwindling fortune of a once great empire had been a bitter disappointment. Keiller marmalade had travelled the world, and brought riches to her ancestors yet, on her mother’s deathbed, the hidden inheritance which she had hoped would materialize had evaporated like the breath from Morag’s body. The great wealth, she learned, had been meted out to John Keiller’s son and daughter decades before. Her mother had squandered her portion through bad investment, ill health and general excess; but Maggie she concluded, must still have in her possession the bulk of her capital. With mounting demands on her own limited funds, Kirsty Keiller decided to stake a claim on this potential source of income. Before this inheritance died with her aunt or worse still, ended up with some undeserving charity, Kirsty Keiller knew she had to act. She found a solution in the guise of her teenage daughter, Isla.

Experience had taught her that Maggie was not so naïve as to welcome with open arms the return of a prodigal niece. She was no fool, and would see through any sudden re-emergence for its true design. But a child might prove to be a more subtle tool. There was no history there, no animosity to prejudice her charm. She fashioned a plan to send her daughter to Maggie under the pretence of her own selfishness. As Kirsty saw it, she could simultaneously rid herself of a child who jarred with her social circle while securing the funding to support it. It was, she felt, the most satisfying of solutions.

The daughter in question sat studying her mother's face. Isla found it to be a curious image that particular morning, so serenely calm, with none of the histrionics of other days. Her mother had summoned the strength on this, their last morning together, to hiss faux concern for her daughter through pearly white-capped teeth, the handiwork of a prominent Knightsbridge dentist. The girl saw her mother's eyes strain under the pretence of it all, unable to hide the crow's feet which resurfaced from beneath her painted lashes however much she sought to bury them.

"Could you pass the milk dear?" her mother oozed with disdain.

Isla Keiller moped beneath the perfumed roses which adorned the breakfast room. Surrounded by the contrived beauty of her mother's pristine house, she teetered on a knifepoint between desolation and despair. On that particular morning she had a preference for the melancholy.

"Drink your orange juice dear", her mother's voice was condescending, yearning to replace the dour exterior of her teenage daughter for the blanket obedience of a seven year old. For Isla's part, she long mourned the passing of a loving mother - so vague a notion now, that she questioned whether it had ever really existed.

She had begun to embrace an adult world, driven by secret obsession for a stranger. She watched him, day after day, a tousle-haired boy with his dangerous eyes. From the security of her bedroom she followed him, as he viewed her and the world with equal apathy. It was a lifeless gaze, one which she instantly identified. It was their deepest connection. Every fibre of this boy's being screamed rebellion - from the dirty, torn clothes he wore, faded through neglect rather than fashion, to the unkempt dark hair which framed his lost eyes and jagged cheekbones.

They had met briefly in an alleyway, but long enough to form an intimacy. No words were required, only their lost souls connected. In the moment that defined their physical union, she grew a lifetime; it was a Monday when she became a woman. He said nothing as he removed those last constraints of her virginity, breaching the layers of self-defence built up through years of anticipation. Breathing heavily into the base of her neck, she felt the warmth of his violent panting turn to moisture and trickle down her back as his heart flew faster and his body reeled, struggling to maintain a rhythmic oscillation. The entanglement continued for a few fleeting moments, his breathing labouring, his body lurching. Her thighs grew tired in their unfamiliar stance and he placed his hand underneath them to support their failing strength. He penetrated deeper, with more vigour and determination than before and she felt his life within her. For those few minutes she overtook his history, his childhood, his hopes and fears, abandoning her own for those of another. The relief was exhilarating, heady.

She longed to remain in that transitory state forever, but they were seconds of escape destined to fade. In an instant it was over, their connection and her childhood, gone.

In seconds she had achieved freedom, and also the beginnings of a newborn life. The days which followed were marked by youthful confusion, mourning the loss of innocence, desperate to regain the acceptance and escape she had so briefly experienced. Like the most addictive of drugs, she craved and desired it. She thought of him night and day, became withdrawn, could neither eat nor sleep. Her mother knew nothing of Isla's transformation. But it was not her mother's attention she sought. She cared even less as the weeks progressed, and her body changed.

"You didn't think I liked you..."

The young girl shuddered as she recalled his last words. She was the desperate, clingy, embarrassed child while he revealed in the glory of another insignificant conquest. The despair, the sadness, the dull ache which welled inside her, rolling and swelling with every dismissive sound.

Sitting in the clinical surrounds of her mother's house that morning, she obediently drank her orange juice, its bitterness made worse by the little blue sleeping pills which swam inside it.

Maggie examined the unexpected envelope, noting the expensive, heavy weight and the convoluted hand which had carefully written the address. The postmark was stamped 'London' and it was only when Maggie recalled again the little girl with Morag's eyes and curls, that its sender became clear. She remembered Morag's letters lamenting how her daughter had removed to the lights of the large city and rarely had time to call. She was doing well for herself, Morag had explained. Not so well as to remember her mother, Maggie had thought.

Dougie looked over her shoulder at the pristine white envelope with its excessively ornate hand.

"Not bad news I hope?" he asked, gauging the hesitation in Maggie's movement.

Maggie opened the letter with less trepidation now that she knew its source. Morag's daughter was nothing to her, so her words held little fear for Maggie. The letter was brief. Her niece feigned pleasantries, trying unsuccessfully to ingratiate herself with Maggie. Her intentions were transparent, her words stilted and it was obvious that such niceties did not sit naturally with the writer. The letter went on to explain that she wished to leave something with Maggie and that it would be no trouble. What this item was, she failed to elaborate on, simply to say that she couldn't have it in London, it being increasingly troublesome to her.

Maggie read the note a number of times, but the letter revealed no more truths than her first interpretation. There was no return address, no expectation of a reply. Had it done, Maggie would not have obliged its owner with a response. Its ambiguity did however intrigue her and occupied her mind, interrupting the tedium.

The strained world of a city collided with the untamed landscape of Fife three days later when the mystery of the letter was exposed. It was revealed under the guise of night and a sky brightened by a thousand stars, as if they sensed some great, portentous event. The drone of an unfamiliar car engine trumpeted the procession's arrival at the door of Rose Cottage.

"Hello Maggie."

In the doorway stood a middle-aged Kirsty Keiller, swathed in darkness and a Dior mink coat. Her skin bore an unconvincing sheen, unnatural and unbecoming. Her hair, a peroxide yellow tone, once arranged in perfection atop her arrogant head, had collapsed and disintegrated in the damp coastal air.

Despite their brief history and Kirsty Keiller's difficult beginnings, Maggie found herself unable to warm to a woman who had abandoned her own mother to a lonely death in a care home. She knew of Kirsty's hardships but was unable to bring herself to like her. It was not the physical distance between Rose Cottage and the fashionable streets of fifties London which supported their mutual isolation - if they had lived side by side, the same brutal silence would have raged. But if Maggie's thoughts raced unbridled at this resurgence of her past, her face maintained its mask of dignity, and her voice a stony silence in deference to the contentious relationship she had with her remote niece.

"Did you get my letter?" asked Kirsty, gruff as was her habit.

Maggie pursed her lips forcibly together. She had much to say, but here, faced with opportunity, she enforced her own self-regulation.

"Let me inside", continued Kirsty, preoccupied with the biting wind which dried her skin and caused her to shake beneath her thick coat, "I don't want to catch my death in this God forsaken place."

Maggie winced. What did Kirsty Keiller know of death? What did she know of its arrival in a dreary retirement home where no daughter came to visit or cared enough to call?

Despite Morag's unyielding support for a daughter who returned none, Maggie's eyes were never blinded by the light of maternal love, and she saw plainly that Kirsty was in some part responsible for her mother's death.

"Ye willnae step inside my home", replied Maggie. "You'll tarry with the devil at the door."

Kirsty looked with contempt upon this small, old Scottish woman whose eyes were lined and face was discoloured from a basic diet and lack of any feminine attention. Maggie stood firm but unsteady in her position in the doorway, the limbs and bones of her age failing her now and then as she shuffled from side to side to try and spread the load. Kirsty refused to bow to the sympathy of age, her own heart had become as cold as the frozen earth of Fife which her inflexible heels navigated with care.

She had fled the claustrophobic landscape of her birth, fearful that it would suffocate her with its tedium. Her life in Dundee had promised only insular intolerance. Everyone knew everyone's business, and to try and achieve anything of note was met with blind derision. To accept ones place and order in nature, to aim for nothing and meet it with great success, to avoid all hope and ambition - that was the merit of all who lived amongst her. They were an infantry of mindless workers, in the factories and fisheries, without opinions, without hope, revelling in their down-trodden lives, finding comfort in their commonness with a camaraderie that they suffered together. This solidarity prevented them from striving for the stars. This destructiveness perpetuated, from mother to daughter, from father to son, in the steel mills and laundries, where youth died and hope drowned. She fought hard against the current. She fought so long that when the fighting was eventually done and she escaped the burning air of Dundee's chimneys, the struggle had become part of her. She had succeeded in outrunning the limiting life in Dundee's laundries, but rebounded into the embrace of an ambitious London. In this new life, she sacrificed that which she ought not to have in order to ingratiate herself with affluent society, one which could finally bestow those rewards she always knew were her due.

She lit a cigarette. The wind was starting to permeate her painfully fashionable coat, and her impatience increased in proportion. Maggie reminded her too much of a history she was determined to forget.

She had not for a second during those intermittent years regretted severing ties with the bleak Dundee hills, and although its isolation suited her now, she despised them for the sense of guilt she felt at her desertion. No one dared question her life in London, why the Dundee hills should feel authority to do so now, grated with her. As she stood beneath their shadow, they were all too close for comfort, those judicious hills.

"Fine", Kirsty hissed finally through expensive dentistry. "It's warmer out here anyhow."

She turned her back on Maggie, and surveyed the dim surrounds. She had expected nothing less than ambivalence from her aged relative. Nothing had changed in fifteen years. Theirs was a mutual stubbornness and Kirsty Keiller's had no inclination to seek the good opinion of an aunt who had rejected her. If Maggie had been a great socialite, or intellectual, she might have bent to some degree, but being neither in Kirsty's eyes, had led to an inevitable stalemate until the prospect of a great inheritance proved too much of an incentive to suffocate beneath pride.

“What is it yer wanting of me Kirsty Keiller?” snapped Maggie, searching for the truth behind her niece’s aberrant reappearance. She hoped it had been driven by contrition but in her heart she knew that this sudden visit was simply the pursuit of personal gain. This secretive convoy, its unconventional arrival under covers, plunging into the wilds of Scotland behind the blackened windows of an expensive car - it was all intricately planned.

“Did you get my letter?” asked Kirsty again.

Maggie gazed upon this middle-aged stranger, curt and cold. So unlike the child Morag had loved unconditionally a lifetime ago. What would she make of her daughter now? Maggie could see that the pretty young girl so deserving of a mother’s pride was gone for good; and even the memory of her childhood faded amongst the few still alive to remember. It had died, as real as any death thereafter. The adult who supplanted her, who stood before her now, was a stranger, and not one she cared to know.

“The…letter”, Kirsty repeated, louder and with an unmistakable note of irritation perforating every syllable. “Did you read it?”

Maggie had read it a thousand times over.

“Aye.”

“And? Are you going to do it?”

“Do what exactly?”

“I thought I made it clear.”

"You didnae."

Maggie awaited a truer response.

"I see."

Kirsty squirmed with discomfort. Her vagueness had been as intentional as her words. To reveal her plan too soon was, she felt, unnecessary and counterproductive. Better to take Maggie by surprise and force her hand. She was convinced that, beyond that dull, weathered exterior, lay the heart of a gullible and lonely old woman, who would not refuse to comfort a child given a second opportunity to do so.

"What is it exactly I'm to be helping ye with?" asked Maggie again.

Kirsty stood to one side, revealing for the first time, the unmistakeable shadow of a young girl asleep in the arms of a man by the gate.

"That."

The moonlight shone bright, illuminating a young girl's face, dazed by her nocturnal excursions and the depths of her mother's duplicity. She shivered occasionally in the unforgiving Northern air, unaccustomed to its temperature and intensity.

Maggie was stunned by the reappearance of the child who had been the impetus of Kirsty's escape to London. Here she was at Rose Cottage, being discharged back into a world Kirsty herself had rushed so readily from, and to the care of a relation so obviously despised.

"Why are ye sending me the bairn?" asked Maggie, doubtful of an honest answer.

"To keep you company dear aunt", was the response, laudable in its audacity and far from the truth.

"Rot", replied Maggie.

"Excuse me?"

"You heard."

Kirsty's face was slowly abandoning its mask of cordiality as transparently as she was abandoning her child. She had expected resistance and spirit from her uncompromising aunt, but was less prepared for the directness of her questioning. She considered briefly the pain of effort she was expending and whether the inheritance which she sought would be in proportion to it.

"Is she become a bother?" Maggie continued, resolute in her search for the truth, in the vain hope it might prove a revelation if not for her, then for her niece.

But Kirsty inhaled her cigarette and resumed her reserve, refusing to be swayed. The old woman was testing her patience, trying to rouse some kind of emotion from her - but she would not be goaded. It did not exist within her, she told herself, this notion of compassion and she refused to be shaken by an old woman without accomplishment or education, responsibility or influence. There was nothing to respect there but old age. Kirsty Keiller's good opinion had to be earned, and Maggie had done nothing of consequence in her long life to warrant it. No-one would remember the old woman of Rose Cottage. There would be no mark in history, no obituary, no plaque or indication that she had ever existed. What was the point of it all?

She sneered as she told herself such truths, unable and unwilling to repress that natural temper which longed to be unleashed on the undeserving. So what if Maggie was to know the truth? Her opinion was neither sought nor required and the truth, or the truth as she would reflect it, as Maggie so desired to hear it, could be hers. To Kirsty it cost nothing.

"It turns out I'm not the maternal kind", she slithered through pained relief, "It's not my style. People expect great things from me. Perhaps if she were glamorous, or beautiful, or even talented, something could be done. But as it is, she is just so painfully... dull. She hardly says a word, just stares out the bloody window, day after day after day."

Kirsty swirled her hand in an overly flamboyant gesture, disturbing her cigarette and sending ash floating like tiny fireworks into the night sky.

"She's an embarrassment and what's more she's ruining my reputation and everything I've worked for. How can someone so sophisticated, produce an offspring like... that."

Maggie looked with pity on her niece.

"My life is too important to ruin with a child. So here, she's yours. Do what you like with her. Up here, nobody cares. Make her useful. Set her to work or something."

Kirsty paused, realizing that she had said more than she had intended through Maggie's silence. She became suddenly anxious that her words and this extended quietness from her irritating aunt might have a less than positive ending.

“You are going to take her aren’t you?” she launched. “Because if not, you’ve got some nerve bringing me all the way up here, or was that your little plan? Be the big woman? Well, here I am Maggie Keiller! Do you feel like a Queen?”

Kirsty laughed with visible unease, the hinge which fixed her to her false reality, swinging as wildly as the gate to Rose Cottage did during the Great Storm. The skin across her cheekbones tightened as her pretence cracked, and lines appeared in the sham smoothness of its texture, contorting her face to a vision of abhorrence for this cold house and its owner.

Maggie waited as her niece’s emotions slowly subsided to their familiar control. She stood firm, fixed against the chameleon at her door, while audience to this intriguing battle, were two pitiful figures of the girl and hired help. They waited patiently by the gate of the Cottage for the two women to wrestle their insults, to see which victor would emerge.

“So this is the cause of yer trouble?” began Maggie, peering into the darkness and the shadows barely visible.

Kirsty nodded in response, exhausted from her efforts and the struggle against her inconsolable demons.

“Yer man best hoik her indoors then”, Maggie replied, conciliatory to a point and standing to one side.

With immeasurable relief, Kirsty motioned to the hired help to bring forward the various items of personal luggage, of which her offspring formed part.

"The hardship will sit well with her", Kirsty quipped as her daughter sloped past. "She's growing positively fat."

The slovenly demeanour of her daughter cloaked in dull, shapeless attire compared to her own colourfully tailored appearance, seemed to support Kirsty's decision to discard this unattractive version of herself. Her daughter was a painful reminder that she had not always been the confident, social dilettante.

"She won't be any trouble", continued Kirsty, sneering. "I often forget she's even there."

The small frame of the girl was moved dutifully forward, delivered by a tall unapologetic man in a chauffeur's hat, his mind occupied entirely with the thoughts of his own rampant children and loving wife miles away from this cold, inhospitable place. As they brushed past and into this practical, inelegant home, Maggie caught her first glimpse of the child's face - a girl of maybe fifteen or sixteen, on the cusp of adulthood. An awkward bundle amongst an array of infinitely more stylish bags, she was not like her mother, and it was a delightful smile which Maggie reflected inward. It may have been a lonely life, but Maggie knew that her loneliness was but a shadow of that her niece would suffer in the years to come. Life would have its revenge. Some called it God, there were many names for it, but in the end it would be the only victor.

So it was a willing Maggie who embraced her niece's castaway, watching as Kirsty sped back to her manicured world and the emptiness of a modern life which rested there. Inside the black leather interior of her quiet car, Kirsty Keiller sneered, grateful for the lack of cordiality which had greeted her at Rose Cottage, as though it reaffirmed her superiority over this old Scottish woman. She looked forward to the day when Maggie would finally join her long lost ancestors. It was overdue, and as she settled back into luxurious comfort, she hoped to return in more sombre, grieving circumstances. Moments later and her car disappeared entirely over the horizon – far from the judgment of Dundee's hills and her former self.

Maggie hoped she would never return, but guarded that expectation with practical thoughts as she looked upon her new guest who had settled into the comfort of a nearby chair and the warmth of an embroidered throw. The girl lay, amassed in layers of clothing, curled within the chair's embrace, clinging to it for warmth. She suddenly appeared many years younger and more vulnerable than before, instantly relinquishing herself to sleep.

She kept deathly still upon the chair, weighed down by the sleeping pills administered by her mother to make the journey more tolerable and did not stir, not for the many hours Maggie stood guard in the darkness of night, not through the chorus of songbirds which foresaw the dawn, not for the hours of drifting on the current of sleep and starting at the crashing of its' wave; not for the moments of deafening silence when the world stopped to regenerate itself in preparation for another exhausting day.

With the unforgiving early light of dawn, the mess of strawberry curls which framed the young clean whiteness of the girl's face became more vibrant, though the delicate frame which supported it remained unmoving. Maggie sensed now and then a struggle, as the young girl suffered through her heavy watery sleep. Maggie could do nothing but acknowledge the passing hours, in equal solitude and anticipation of a new and very different day.

Step 5: Separate the Pulp from the heart of the Orange

The cold was insatiable, as demanding as any newborn child. It pressed against Isla's exposed flesh; stabbing at the corners of her eyes, freezing the extremities of her colourless lips and causing their functionality to wane. The tip of her nose tingled with alarm as her body temperature continued upon its steady decline. Clothes which had seemed adequate amongst a city's shelter were rendered futile against this invading Scottish clime. Isla shook uncontrollably, every exhaled breath clearly visible, telling its own tale and lamenting its laborious existence. She pushed against her frozen flesh, in the vain hope of resuscitation, but every momentary respite faded. She peered with tired eyes around this intimidating, strange land - as foreign as any distant moon, far from her comfortable home in London. Isla shuddered with the recollection of its warmth, now but a memory amongst this dark, impenetrable cave.

Through the varying shades of blackness, Isla made out the figure of an old lady sitting at a table. This stranger hummed a soothing tune and seemed to drift superficially in and out of her own sleep. Isla could make out the deep lines of a worn face which told tales of harsh winters and difficult days. The only remnants of a once defining beauty were protruding cheekbones, exacerbated through an abstinent life. The old woman's hair was loosely encouraged into a haphazard bun planted at the base of her neck, and it bore a suitable shade of grey for her age. This submission to nature was a revelation to Isla, marking such a contrast to the fantastical circle of her mother's friends for whom the crusade against maturing years absorbed every coiffed hour.

Weary and pinned down with the weight of her young life, Isla felt the tiredness of her journey. Her limbs ached and seemed to seep from her, leisurely dripping onto the worn wooden floor. The past hours, days and weeks seemed fused together to form an incomprehensive pool of confusion. Her mother's abandonment, the uprooting of her life, the heartache of an absent lover - the intoxication of feelings rushed upon her and she became overwhelmed, feeling the pressure of a thousand hands press hard upon her chest, and she would not, could not, breathe.

It was not stupidity which had led Isla to this new, cold life, but inexperience. It was also the irrepressible desire to be loved. To be held close; to feel the protective warmth of tender affection; to be missed, to be wanted, to be loved. Was it love? Isla had thought so. An unspoken connection had drawn her to the tousle-haired boy she had left behind in London, but like so much which had been revealed to her in these past few months, she had been wrong. She could see that now. It was a distraction from the rejection advertised at home which made her abandon that ship before it inevitably sunk. And it would have sunk, how could it have survived the hurricane of her mother's ambitions? Isla had never understood her mother's slavery to a society she could neither touch nor feel. Unlike a daughter whom she chose to neither touch nor feel. Through her actions Isla had succeeded in controlling a future which had never felt her own, by destroying the sham image of the one her mother had created for her, for that obedient seven year old so easily manipulated. Here was her punishment - excommunication from a comfortable life.

Isla had always been acutely aware that she was supplemental to the mother's plans - that she was neither wanted nor desired. She had ruined an ambitious woman's figure, along with her hopes and dreams. She had quickly grown from a child who bowed to instruction to a teenager who rebuked it. She may have been bewildered by her new surrounds in Rose Cottage, but not the capacity of a mother who had thrown her there. High upon her social pedestal, she had divorced her daughter from her idyllic life, into the depths of an ocean strewn with little blue sleeping pills where she would tread its water until their effects dissolved. And yet Isla felt the hurt of her abandonment was tinged with hope. Hope that a life of colour might now reveal itself from monotone waters, producing an island of self-sufficiency and independence. She embraced her new found freedom, without the weight of expected failure which had been her constant companion.

Isla's tired eyes now began to feel the shadows less fearful than before. Sensation returned to her cold fingers, the tips of which tingled with a revived vivacity. It was the same foreign feeling of her tousle-haired boy first brushing her shoulder or leg. His abandonment had proved that desertion was not the privilege of her mother; it had escaped the pristine townhouses of affluent suburbs and permeated the heart and soul of a stranger. Isla's toes wriggled - a reminder that life remained there yet, that the pain of living was not yet done.

This was the same vessel which had already suffered through weeks of secret transformation. It was not just a child which grew within her, but a loneliness which had followed her out of one isolated home and into this new one. She saw that she had changed, not just physically and that however far she travelled in distance and maturity, she would always sit alone in a strange, cold place devoid of warmth.

As the minutes progressed, Isla's legs began their slow recovery, with a deepening desire to disentangle themselves from the shackles of prolonged sleep. She pulled her pregnant frame upwards, out of the confinement of a comforting chair, and once again felt her way tentatively, as if she were retaking cautious first steps.

"Where am I?"

Isla's voice sounded alien, as it reverberated around the closed crevices of this new, strange cave. Maggie remained fixed in her chair by the table.

"Auchobane", came her reply.

Maggie's words were no more enlightening than the whitewashed four walls which encapsulated Isla. The room in which Isla found herself, appeared to be an amalgamation of hall, lounge, dining and kitchen, all compressed into the size of one of her mother's hideously fashioned wardrobes. A low beam lay horizontal midway along the ceiling, the only indication of an attempt to segregate space. Isla stood directly beneath it, the thought that it might crash abruptly upon her was fleetingly entertained. It was one of many portentous thoughts which habitually skulked in her mind, involuntarily changing a mood. The other articles of furniture in this modest home were indigenous and neat, and consisted almost entirely of a bookcase, a large wooden chest and a small table, which provided inadequate real estate for the ambitious four chairs which hugged each face. Although light outside, the room struggled to shrug off its duskiness, hampered in its attempts by stacks of chaotically arranged jars covering every available shelf and space. Isla felt as though she were the only living thing in an oppressive vacuum.

“Where‘s Auchobane?”, she rang out again, perforating a claustrophobic silence.

“In Fife dearie”, came yet another uninformative reply.

Isla picked up a nearby jar from its resting place perched upon the edge of oblivion. The dark liquid inside sloshed with approval at her attention, rolling around the glass with delight. Within the dark brown substance flashed flecks of light, glistening like stars through the cloak of a night sky. On the top of the jar, in neat, almost child-like writing was etched the date ‘Spring 1939’. Isla returned the produce to its innocuous home and sought out further eccentricities. As she examined this efficient room’s secrets, the smell of its contents became abruptly apparent. It was a suffocating odour and the lack of air in this tiny space struck her violently. With some force Isla released the lifelessness threatening to overcome her through a nearby window and welcomed in the tart air of the outside world. Blissfully it raced around the room as though it had waited an eternity to enter that sacred space. The acute perfume of the sea betrayed their hidden cave’s location. Peering through a diminutive window, Isla saw before her a natural landscape to rival that of any picture postcard. In front of her and outstretching far into the distance, further than her eyes could comprehend, stood row upon row of the most dramatic, inspiring cliffs. They roared against a menacing sea which rampaged far below them, giants in all they surveyed. Their greatness was frightening in their scale to a girl so unused to perspective, so consumed by a concrete greyness and the sterility of city. This was no manicured world - this was a fire of vivacity, thrilling and menacing. Its danger energised Isla, rushing through her staid, closeted body. Smiling for the first time in many months, her thoughts were not of abandoning mothers and lovers, of lonely days and complications. Instead she relished the first taste of freedom from their repressive hold, and their tired conventions.

“Where?” the only word Isla could vocalize confronted by such beauty.

“Scotland dearie”, replied Maggie, now standing at her shoulder.

The old woman’s musical lilt provided a suitable soundtrack to the expansive land in which Isla found herself. Gazing in silent inspiration at the momentous horizon, the roughened sea stretched far into the distance, its crest tipped waves unfolding, peeling back layers hidden underneath until Isla imagined it ranged forever. She felt insignificant and with it relief at her triviality compared to this majestic perspective. Somewhere, deep within her heart, she also felt a tiny tinge of joy.

Step 6: Finely dissect the Segments of Peel

"She's had her heart broke."

Maggie stood beside her youthful kin in awe of the familiar landscape and the magnitude of change which had swept through their lives.

"But fae hurt comes great beauty", Maggie continued. "A land such as that cannae be fashioned fae anything but a history filled with pain."

Isla examined the cliffs which seemed to abandon themselves to the ferocity which skirted at their toes. She saw nothing of this fearlessness in her own life.

"Yer mother said ye wasnae one for conversation", continued Maggie. "Well that's no bad thing. This here's a house accustomed tae quiet."

Isla was a faithful companion to silence. She could not remember the exact moment of their first introduction. A quiet day without a word became a week and longer, until she found that speaking had become the most uncommon thing. She would sit in her room for days, the only interruption an insidious comment from her mother or at school the echo of derisive peers, but she never joined their hum, emitting not a word. With time, she had grown worryingly comfortable with nothing but her own thoughts. A habit which overtook her with ease, lost forever in a dream, and one which would over time affect her soul.

Maggie read the girl's silence as clearly as any verbal introduction. She knew her name, but nothing more, but with every passing word unspoken, she understood a little further.

“I’m Maggie, if ye care tae know it.”

It was an introduction of sorts, however tenuous, marking a conclusion of painful pleasantries.

“How far along are ye now?” asked Maggie.

Isla was surprised by the question. She placed a hand on her burgeoning stomach, forgetting her situation, the increasing roundness in her adolescent figure betraying a new impending reality. She looked down at where her toes ought to have been, their view obscured by this bump, this thing which she forgot grew inside her. She felt sadder for its recollection.

“I don’t know”, she whispered in an uncommon voice. She had not meant to say a thing, but surprised at the quickness of the old woman and her forthrightness in asking such a personal question of a stranger, she found her voice just where she had left it.

“Does she know?”

Isla looked at Maggie with a child‘s eye.

“Yer mother?” asked Maggie again.

Isla shook her head. Any feelings of affection her mother may once have held for her only child had long expired replaced by a gulf of silence.

Maggie felt the loneliness within the figure standing beside her, and imagined the fears which must weigh heavy on her shoulders. Without the reassurance of a home and a parent, she had been thrust upon a stranger, in a seemingly inhospitable place, and all subjugated by the expectation of her own child.

Maggie could not help but contrast Isla's situation with her own happy days of pregnancy, surrounded by loving security, and although she was not fated to see her dream through to its conclusion, she felt a desire to redress even a portion of the damage inflicted on the girl by an indifferent mother. She felt a kind of responsibility for her Kirsty Keiller's failings, but could not explain why. Had she been more conciliatory, more understanding of her predicament when she arrived at Rose Cottage all those years ago, would that have change the course of all their histories? Would Kirsty have nurtured a warmer heart? Would her daughter have borne the happy results? And would she herself have been more contented through all those quiet years? Kirsty Keiller had unquestionably made a success of her life in monetary and material terms, but standing before Maggie was the consequence of such. The personal price she had paid for a luxurious lifestyle and the quest for affirmation, when she might have been saved the trouble through the right words or action forty years earlier. It was this thought which would not be wholly suppressed, and which skulked at the back of Maggie's mind. It distracted her and caused her to feel a semblance of guilt in the presence of this unhappy young girl.

"'Tis no matter", continued Maggie, hesitating only now to consider the uncharitable childishness of her actions when Kirsty had reappeared at her door. Even at sixty years of age, she was prone to the same overwhelming insensibilities of a six year old. She should have asked Kirsty to tarry a while, for the sake of the child, to ease the transition from old to new. But she capitulated to the intensity of her feelings, and ushered her out of her precious home and quickly from sight.

Maggie turned away from the window and began to busy herself with the various pots and pans which hung upon hooks above the fire She had learned the effectiveness of distracted hands, and their positive influence on an overactive mind. It was something which had been intuitive to Billy and a regular ploy when her dreams overcame her and she slipped dangerously close to despondency. She could almost feel again the tap of his finger on her shoulder when such thoughts resurfaced, she felt him now guiding her around the kitchen, diverting her mind.

"A strange thing, kin", Maggie mused.

Family. Isla detested the word and all its meaning. Forever elusive, how she would have loved the endearment of a close family life, with its tenderness and comfort. It was a vague notion she recognised, as she stood on the periphery and wished for another's life. She blamed her mother for its absence. She blamed her for a magnitude of sins, some deserving, many convenient, but the failings she had experienced throughout her formative years she felt were due to her mother's vilification. How could it be otherwise? She was just a child after all. Perennially treated as such, she had learned to take the part and make it her own.

"I have no family", replied Isla, her eyes fixed on the distant landscape. There might have been emotion in those words a year or two ago, but now she said them with a cold apathy. Her mind wandered from the long familiar rush of frustration at her closeted existence, to the clouds which raced freely across a vast expanse of sky. She imagined its blueness ranging across endless mountains and anonymous towns, from this cold clime to the more generous south and the gentle hues which encompassed her mother; it enveloped them both, this azure blanket, and the bracing wind which accompanied it. In some ways Isla wished she had been thrown further and saved the shame of being idly forced upon a stranger's kitchen.

The strength of the young girl's sentiment against family seemed to stun even the jars of marmalade which hugged the windowsill, and just for a moment their dancing flecks appeared to freeze. But if they were taken aback, Maggie was less so. A life of isolation in a remote world had pared back her own polished politeness and being but a solitary party to the majority of conversations which took place in Rose Cottage, she had naturally developed a style all curtness and direct. She saw a lifetime of neglect written in the girl's clear features and blue eyes. If her niece had the capacity to treat Morag with such contempt, why should she not apply the same resolution towards her daughter? Maggie thought to tell the girl the truth of her history, to have it out and let her decide who was good and who was bad. But she held back and bit her tongue, even though the thoughts and recollections of a dark past simmered beneath her grey Scottish exterior. She offered instead a large mug of steaming liquid which Isla took with gratitude her head still diving in and out of the cloudy waters into which she'd been thrown by her mother's medication. The mug dwarfed her delicate hands, and the smell of the strong whisky Maggie had added to the tea swam around her eyes and nostrils like smelling salts arousing the senses sharply and effectively.

"Tea?" she asked, peering into the despondent drink.

“A special brew”, replied Maggie.

Isla hovered over the mug suspiciously.

“Sip it slowly”, Maggie advised sitting down at the small kitchen table, just big enough for two.

On the tired tabletop sat a large plate of warm bread which Maggie now pulled towards her as she eased herself into one of the wooden chairs which hugged each of the table’s four sides. From inside an old ceramic jug which had in a previous life fulfilled the duty of a flower vase, she produced a curious jar of liquid, one of many which sprouted organically from unexpected crannies around the room.

Isla followed Maggie’s hand as she opened the pot with an unapologetic pop, took a sturdy knife and delved it deep inside the chunky liquid. She swirled it round so that it absorbed as much of the dark, thick mass as possible, rousing the flecks of peel so they clung to the flashing steel of the implement. The knife was swiftly retrieved and with a flick of the wrist, the mixture smeared lavishly on a chunk of the warm bread with joyful relish and deep satisfaction. Once Maggie was sure that every smidgen of its crumbling surface was coated, she raised the morsel to her mouth and took a hearty bite, her eyes retreating with delight at the succulent combination. Isla watched, mesmerised.

Once the bite had been thoroughly consumed, Maggie opened her eyes and smiled; her face transposed and regenerated.

“’Tis a miraculous condiment”, and she slid the jar across to her new guest. Isla viewed the jar with distrust, doubtful of its powers.

"What is it?"

"What is it!" exclaimed Maggie, contorting Isla's question into the absurdity of statement. "'Tis marmalade of course!"

Isla's mind was no more illuminated.

"Jam?"

Maggie gasped with outrage, the sharp intake of breath travelling speedily down her oesophagus and shaking her very core.

She briskly replaced the lid on the murky jar, grasping it close to her chest, sheltering it as one would an innocent infant from the destruction of its childhood.

"Jelly indeed! We're fair affronted."

Maggie turned away, and Isla failed to notice the glint in her eye which betrayed mischief at work.

Isla shuffled her feet. She remembered the shameful assaults of her mother. Too quick to cut, her words seemed formulated long before their expression. Isla's own responses were less mature, released in a moment, arguments lost in less. She was never on the winning side, and learnt early on to avoid the battle entirely. Better to be silent than suffer her scorn. Now from a stranger, such assaults seemed unfair. Had she escaped one tyrant only to be faced with another? With the promise of tears welling deep within her tightening throat and the frustration of their enforced containment, she reverted back to a submissive silence.

“’Tis not the conserve itself that’s upsetting, ‘tis the sentiment. You’re a Keiller and ye dinnae know the name marmalade! Crivens! How is that even possible?”

Maggie spooled around the kitchen in consternation, stopping as abruptly as she started.

She positioned an orange squarely on the table and pulled out one of the unsteady kitchen chairs.

Isla obediently sat. She looked at the innocuous fruit.

“Do ye know what this is?”

Isla nodded.

‘Of course. It’s an orange.’

“Aye, but this is not just any orange, this here’s a Seville orange. Do ye know the difference?”

Isla shook her head.

“Take a piece”, continued Maggie, slicing the orange into quarters and presenting one to Isla, who placed it in her mouth. Not a second later and her eyes began to stream with the tart citric taste, which stabbed forcibly upon her taste buds. It was more than her mouth could bear.

“It’s horrible!” she exclaimed through pained eyes.

“Beedy”, corrected Maggie with a smile, “Here’s a knife. Start chopping.”

“We have people to do this at home”, Isla explained.

“Aye, we have folk like that here too. They’re called - ‘you’ and ‘me’. Now cut.”

Isla took the small chopping knife and began to slice unconvincingly through the rind of the orange.

“When’s the last time ye readied the fruit?” asked Maggie as she began to deftly remove the rind from her own precious produce.

“I’ve never done this before”, replied a doleful Isla.

A loud chime as Maggie’s knife rebounded off the kitchen floor with surprise.

“Yer a Keiller and you’ve never skinned an orange?” Maggie shook her head. “Never chopped an orange; never made marmalade…. Did ye even know the Keiller’s invented marmalade?’

“Did they?”

“Away! That’s what we’re known for round these parts. Did that mother of yours teach ye owt? Or is she ashamed of her history? Ashamed of yer great, great, great grandmother Janet Keiller who created the very first pot of Dundee Marmalade? Aye, no doubt she sides with that old gowpin, Mrs. McLintock, oh she’ll spin ye some yarn about Robertson’s or Coopers being the first, but we Keillers don’t pay any attention to a crabbit old beezum who adulterates her marmalade with ‘neeps while Keiller marmalade is as pure as Scottish snow.”

As if to illustrate her point Maggie thrust her jar of homemade preserve up through the thin beams of light which pierced the dull glass of Rose Cottage, seemingly cast from heaven itself. The flecks of peel in the jar danced, invigorated by the old woman's passion.

"You dinnae get those glimmering chips with owt but the best oranges", she exclaimed. "Now eat!"

And with that Maggie thumped the jar back down onto the kitchen table in triumph, demanding her young charge join with her in abandonment to the glorious marmalade. Isla, infected by this rampant enthusiasm, duly obliged, casting off all restraints for only the second time in her life. On that previous occasion it had been to an unbridled, burning, youthful passion, but this time it was to her ancestral calling. Isla picked up the spoon and thrust it enthusiastically into the jar of golden liquid, stopping only briefly to examine the texture of the marmalade before placing it freely into her mouth.

It was at once a very odd sensation. Isla expected the tartness of the marmalade to overwhelm her as the fruit itself had done moments before, and initially it was a bitter taste which engaged her, but then came a strangely sweet sensation, startling and indescribable. And the aftertaste, the slow, gradual enveloping of her mouth with the smooth, syrupy warmth, intermingled now and then with the roughness of the peel - it transported her to the Mediterranean climes of Southern Spain, where the sun soothed her face and the warm waters tickled her toes.

"Now yer a Keiller."

Maggie smiled proudly having acquired this new convert to her clan, reassured that her forefathers could sleep soundly in the knowledge that the younger generations were being indoctrinated.

“Now we‘re kin.”

Isla pretended to understand the difference, as Maggie continued her reverie.

“Each and every day a brand new wind blows across those Auchobane cliff-tops, carrying with it exotic tales of far off lands”, and she leaned forward as if whispering her darkest secrets into Isla’s ear. “It’s never seen those cliffs nor myself afore it, but I know it and it knows me. For it’s all in here.”

Maggie grabbed Isla’s hand and clasped it to her breastbone.

“In here is my life. My mother‘s life and my mother’s afore her. I’m centuries old, and so is the wind, and that is why we know each other.”

Isla looked at Maggie. Her eyes sparkled with a magical energy, glinting in the evening sun, as though she had just imparted the greatest promise of them all.

“Look at yer hands!” Maggie exclaimed suddenly. Isla looked down at her entirely presentable offerings.

“Ye cannae make marmalade with green fingers!” she continued enthusiastically.

“They have tae be orange.”

She thrust out her own lined hands next to Islas. The contrast was deep and profound. Isla could not but compare their roughness to the smooth, unblemished skin of her own.

Her hands betrayed a quiet life with little use and pain. Maggie's hands, by contrast, were deeply excavated and proliferated with a multitude of lines and cuts, some partially healed, others faint scars forever engraved. Dark spots lingered where the skin had lost all its natural pigmentation. Isla understood the eventuality of it all, that this would be her fate too. Maggie's long fingers once elegant, enlivened, full of hopes and dreams extended, their tips permanently stained a deep orange hue.

Maggie saw Isla's eyes examining her weathered hands. She forgot too frequently that she was old. The days had crept by, the years much quicker, until one day she realised that her own twilight had snuck upon her quite unexpectedly. She didn't feel old, save for the creaking of a hip on a frosty morning. She still followed her own path and set her own direction. She could still chop a batch of oranges in a day, and boil up a hundred jars of marmalade in a month. She could still trim the roses and fight the elements, so who did they belong to, those tired old hands? Embarrassed, she removed her inelegant talons from the table.

Maggie sat placidly once more, closely examining several of the ripened oranges which sat centre stage in their large, wooden bowl. Eventually she singled out her elected fruit and began to peel.

"Fools look to the 'morrow'", said Maggie after a time, her voice restored to its familiar tranquillity. "Wise men look tae tonight. Never be feared of living Isla, only be feared of standing still."

But the irony of youth is its stubbornness to listen when the wisdom of elders floats casually by. Isla heard Maggie's words but she instinctively smothered them in caveat.

She took them as the regrets of an old woman yearning for the return of a black and white childhood which existed only in her own wavering mind. Isla's childhood was anything but utopian and she longed to leave it behind and embrace an independent adulthood without restraints and imposition.

"It's been such a time since there was any kind of enchantment at Rose Cottage", continued Maggie, slowly removing the bright, bumpy rind from her favourite fruit. She knew she made little sense, but what was sense, but the crutch of practicality.

But Isla didn't see any enchantment. What she saw was a lonely old lady, an outsider who had retreated from the world. Isla recognised that reclusiveness as it was a familiar friend. She knew it instantly when she saw it permeating the fortified walls of Rose Cottage. This was indeed a fortress, but not against the harsh Scottish clime, nor against the advancing cliffs, but a fortress against life. It was not dissimilar to her own, which although not completed, was sufficient to repel a wounding mother, and a destructive lover.

Step 7: Extract the Pips of the Orange from its Whole

Mrs. McLintock was now seventy years of age. Her husband had long departed this earth, and so it had fallen upon her son to take up the weighty mantle of faith. The son would have rather been a fisherman or taken trade, but his mother had put such nonsensical ideas out of his head with twenty years of tongue lashing and a couple of lashings of a different kind. He had subsequently preached without conviction from the Auchobane church pulpit for many years, his liturgies driven entirely, and often literally, by his mother's hand.

Home was no relief; his mother being unsuited to life without a husband to dominate had announced on the day of his father's funeral, that her son would be relocating his family to their new, moral position in the Rectory. She would sacrifice her own comfort by removing herself to the spare room. The villagers required spiritual guidance, even in the face of such a personal loss. The Rectory was small, and Mrs. McLintock's personality large and the younger Mrs. McLintock was no match for her mother-in-law. She suffered for many years before eventually leaving the marital home on Christmas Eve, never to return. With time, her sons, James and Ewan became ripe for the picking, and long before her own son's retirement, Mrs. McLintock's eyes had begun to fall upon her grandsons to ensure continuation of the McLintock name in the Auchobane church annals.

The elder grandson, James, had been made aware of his grandmother's loathing for the lady of Rose Cottage from an early age. Ever since he could remember, his grandmother's thoughts and words were ruled by a desire to see the Keiller woman defeated. When younger, and knowing no better, he proved his family loyalty by aiming rocks at Maggie's unfortunate windows. Often successful, he would return home and recount his achievements to his grandmother, delivering a smug satisfaction to the old lady's face, although she could never outwardly condone such behaviour.

"You're a good laddie", she would begin. "You're a McLintock through and through. Not like yer father. He's a weak man. Bur you, you're the Lord's gift."

James McLintock was now a shy lad of eighteen. He bore his frustrations physically, manifesting them in an increasing waistline which hung on the wrong side of plumpness. Even his appreciable height could not hide the comfort which he sought to conceal. With his conformist appearance - his hair had been pasted flat to his indented skull by choice not mother nature - gave the suggestion of additional years to those he had actually spent in the shadow of Auchobane's Church Hall. His only redemption lay in piercing green eyes which conveyed the impression of innocence, although corruption was entirely possible. Altogether he had a pleasing, if uninspired appearance; one which under-whelmed the female population of Auchobane. Motherless from an early age, he gleaned the truths about her from those around him. Their opinions had perpetuated long enough to become fact, and James now fervently believed that he had been abandoned by his mother for no other reason than her own selfishness. However, the memory of her kind face was an image at odds with the stories told to him by his grandmother and made him shift uncomfortably from side to side whenever her name was mentioned.

James was in a reflective mood the morning his grandmother called him into the breakfast room. As a rule James avoided this room at all costs - it had a suffocating air and the thought of what lay inside, that cutting tongue of the McLintock matriarch and her hard exterior, made his stomach churn. But it was not his actions under scrutiny that day.

“A black car passed through the village in the wee hours of yesterday morning”, Mrs. McLintock began. “It’s windows were black an’ it didnae stop, no till it climbed the coastal path and reached the door of Rose Cottage”

She paused for breath.

“I want tae know who was in that car”, she concluded. “And what was its business with the Keiller woman. An’ you are going tae help me find that out.”

James looked a little surprised, but stood to attention as he did every Sunday in Church, awaiting his enlightenment.

“Douglas MacGregor”, she continued.

“The auld grocer with the big green coat?”

“Aye, the same. He takes provisions up tae the cottage on the first Tuesday of every month. He doesn’t past his way, fer he’s a sly man, bur Mrs. Sweeney on the high road tells me he passes by her with a bicycle full tae brimming.”

She sneered as she spoke of one of whom she had yet to acquire the measure.

“You’re going tae be his new lackie”, continued Mrs. McLintock. “You’re going tae help him deliver his provisions up tae Rose Cottage. And you’re going tae tell me all of what ye see.”

Her grandson nodded.

“Keep yer eyes wide and yer ears even wider”, she finished, as she prodded him with her walking stick so as to emphasis her words. “Keep hold of yer wits an’ all, for he’s not a God fearing man, and there’ll be much said tae try and turn a strong McLintock faith.”

James closed the door gently behind him as he left the Rectory and made his way across town. As he scuffed the soles of his shoes against the solid grey cobblestones of Auchobane’s winding roads, he reflected on whether the old grocer might hold some new truths about his mother, truths independent of his grandmother’s influence. He found no new revelations that day, just an empty shop and a note explaining the grocer’s absence, but he resolved to effectuate not just his grandmother‘s end through this new scheming, but also something for himself.

In Rose Cottage that morning, Isla had spent what seemed like an indeterminable amount of time peering through one of the diminutive cottage windows as a succession of gannets tracked their way across a perfectly still horizon. Maggie was aware of the young girl’s distraction as she went about her own business of the day, a succession of obscure household chores, their only goal the acceleration of time.

“There’s a storm coming”, offered Maggie, as she brushed past her idling houseguest, temporarily disrupting the young girl’s reverie.

Isla looked doubtfully at the sky. It was a flawless, wholesome azure blue and the air was so still, it was as though the earth had momentarily stopped its rotation to breathe.

Isla was lost today. She was lost yesterday and for the many weeks which had preceded it. When exactly she had misplaced herself, she could not tell, all she knew was that she no longer recognised the depths of her own being. Perhaps it was the indifference of her surroundings, or the child she bore which sapped from her any desire for self-preservation. She spent her time wandering aimlessly from room to room, an easy journey as Rose Cottage held only two; or sitting vacant in a chair as she found herself that morning, looking who knew where, thinking who knew what. The hours she could not recall, the days she had lost forever. But it didn't matter. Perhaps it would matter in time and she would mourn these precious last few months of independence, but for now she could not bring herself to care.

"The gannets", continued Maggie, fighting the invading silence. "They're fleeing tae the safety of the shore. Means there's a storm brewing."

Isla said nothing, but then she had spoken few words since arriving at Rose Cottage. She had certainly never mentioned her mother whose face was beginning to fade from her memory like an old, worn photograph. Her success in severing all ties with her daughter meant that for Isla, her disdainful influence was also beginning to wane. As summer approached, there was a freshness dancing upon the Arctic air which rolled in across the North Sea, and with it came hope - for a new beginning and a new outlook.

Maggie too felt the change. Although weary, she felt the energy of associated youthfulness, and inspiration to soar above the sparsely dotted rain clouds which often clung to the Fife sky. With each new shower, the tired frame which held together an old soul permitted an unexpected vitality to reign. Maggie questioned whether it was a kind of second youth or whether her new companion had somehow infiltrated the foundations of Rose Cottage. All she knew was that she felt different, and she welcomed the alteration.

True to Maggie's word, before midday the first raindrops had made their mark on the panes of Rose Cottage and by afternoon they were slicing horizontally across the sky. The village of Auchobane was completely enveloped in their misty haze and droplets rebounded so fiercely against the roof tiles that Isla feared they would abandon their function, sending marmalade jars scattering in all directions. That same sky, at dawn a quiet blue, darkened with a multitude of transitory rain clouds, creating the illusion of a portentous dusk. With the rain came shearing gales and by teatime, the storm which Maggie had forecast, was in full flight across the familiar cliff-tops.

"Great things happen in storms", enthused Maggie as she deftly removed the peel from an orange as one would skin from a potato. "Keiller history began with a storm."

Isla blank expression was read as curiosity in Maggie's ancestral tales.

"A storm carried the first Seville oranges tae Dundee's shores, so it did", she continued. "If it wasn't for a storm, Keiller family history would have been nowt but a couple of chanty wrasslers."

The windows reverberated at her words.

"Aye - the most tremendous things happen in storms."

And just as she finished her theory on the advantageousness of tempestuous weather, there came a sudden and violent thumping on the heavily fortified door of Rose Cottage.

At first, the knocking was indiscernible from the pounding which nature was effectuating outside but then it came again - far too rhythmical to be anything but man-made. Maggie seemed unaffected, and rose calmly to prise open the defensive door - easily compliant at the behest of a familiar friend.

"Fine storm Maggie", beamed Dougie, his arms carried the soggy remnants of a crate of oranges. "Something big is afoot, I can feel it in my old bone.".

"'Tis well for you Mr. MacGregor, as some of us know nowt in our bones but the pain of rheumatism", replied a cynical Maggie, happily inviting this stranger into her cave whatever his cause. "Well, don't tarry on the step getting drookit. Take yourself inside."

The old soldier invigorated by the power of the wind, beamed impishly like a man half his age as Maggie's down-to-earth welcome revealed the warmth of their long friendship. Douglas MacGregor stepped dutifully inside the cottage, and shutting out once again a rampaging nature, he thoughtfully and thoroughly wiped the remnants of the outside world from the underside of his boots. Delicately he took off the heavy, practical coat which bore the marks of infantry, carefully hanging his most precious garment by the door. More inelegantly he dispatched his garish vest to the floor, happy to be ignorant of his gainful employment for just an hour or two. Maggie for her own part, sought to quickly unburden her friend of the citrus contents he bore, keen to progress her commencement of that year's delicious marmalade conserve.

Dougie sat down at the table, easily dwarfing one end, seeking and receiving silent approval before removing the comfortable boots which hugged his feet. Isla watched this well worn couple dancing their exchange.

Dougie gazed upwards with warm eyes and noticed Isla for the first time, standing as she was partially engulfed by the dark crevices of the room. He stood up at once, chivalry being the gem of his generation.

"My sincerest apologies, I was ignorant of company."

He stood awkwardly for a moment before continuing. "Allow me to introduce myself - I am Douglas Stuart MacGregor, of the second battalion of the Argyll and Sutherland - at your service."

He extended a great paw in greeting towards Isla, who took it with some trepidation.

"This is our Isla", interjected Maggie, seeing the awkwardness simmering in her young guest. She saw how the intimidating presence of a large man such as Mr. MacGregor could seem ominous to one so unused to boldness.

"It is a pleasure to make your acquaintance, Isla the Great."

He shook her delicate hand vigorously with charm.

"Just Isla", Isla mustered meekly.

Usually she was just Isla, more often she was nothing at all. Her mother generally avoided introduction of a daughter who might incidentally reveal her age. It allowed her to remain aloof on the subject, hoping that her suitors would err on the right side of forty.

A daughter could destroy that illusion, and any burgeoning relationship would be smothered before it naturally extinguished beneath the murky waters of her superficiality.

“It’s not the name that makes the man, but the man who makes the name. I can see the greatness in those eyes of yours, so I will call you Isla the Great.”

Maggie nodded her approval.

“There are precisely fifty-nine Douglas Stuart MacGregors in this world and what sets me apart fae them are the lines upon my face, the life within my heart and the boots in which I walk.”

Dougie sat back down, contented.

“Not these particular boots mind”, he continued, picking up the rain laden, hole ridden boots just recently removed.

“Poor laddies have seen better days. But my Sunday best, now there’s a pair o’ boots.”

He placed his sorry footwear by the fire.

“Well, Isla, what brings ye to our exceptionally sodden kingdom?”

A torrent of words flooded Isla’s mind, but none made it from her mouth. Dougie was quick to note her hesitation.

“Hiding out from the enemy eh? Mum’s the word”, and he winked knowingly at Isla.

“Yer no wrong there”, said Maggie as she peeled another orange.

"Away", replied Dougie, his eyes widening with the revelation of an accidental discovery, "have I happened upon your secret?"

He bent forward, as though the walls themselves had ears.

"If 'tis true in here', Dougie thumped his chest with admirable commitment. "then there's nowt tae be feared of out there."

He pointed in the general direction of a dark horizon.

"I've seen things in war as would make a laddie weep, but there was nowt as much misery as that which we put upon ourselves."

He shook his head dislodging shadowy remembrances from their habitual place on the dusty shelves of his mind and leaned back in his chair, exposing the holes which dappled his socks and beneath them, well worn feet. Isla wondered if Maggie had ever offered to mend them, and whether he would have let her.

He continued in a kind of reverie, "I remember it as it were yesterday, the speckled skies of St Julien filled with a million black clouds fae the anti-aircraft guns. They didnae stop the shell which dropped out of the heavens with our battalion's name on it. 'Twas the loudest din I ever heard. My ears rung like the bells of Westminster for weeks after. I came to in a shell-hole the size of a football field. There was another laddie with me, a young fella of maybe sixteen years of age, with nowt but scratch on him, and he says tae me, 'we're not all here Dougie' so I hauled myself out of the hole and found more laddies a few yards further fae the centre of crater. They wasnae so lucky.'

Dougie shook his head despondently.

“One soldier had nowt but the tops of his legs left. The rest had been taken clean off by the force of the hit. A fella fae Fife he was, and says tae me, ‘Straighten me legs Dougie’.

Dougie’s voice lowered with the sadness of his words.

“What could I do? I touched the bone of his thigh and that seemed tae put his mind tae rest. Then he says tae me ‘Get me hen’s photograph out of me pocket’. So I did that fer him. He couldn’t lift a hand, no a finger, but he held that photograph on his chest by some means, and I watched him die. I didnae mind admitting it - I thanked the heavens fer sparing me that day, and every one of the days which followed. Someone must have been listening. Fer all the shells and bombs, I made it home with only a couple of bits of shrapnel dug into the backs of my legs.”

And he lifted up his trouser leg proud of the scars which still marked him half a century later.

“That‘s a bonnie tale that is, Mr. MacGregor!”, exclaimed Maggie.

“‘Tis a kind of fate that I sit here today”, he continued unhindered, “when many a brave soldier didnae return fae those poppy fields. God rest their souls.”

And he stopped for a moment as his mind ran through the youthful faces of friends and strangers that never grew old. The years of war had inflicted few imperfections on the old man’s body; save for those few erstwhile shards of shrapnel, but inside his heart, the damage was inconsolable. A day was never permitted to pass nor a still moment relinquished without a respectful nod to the young eyes and mischievous grins of men who deserved the chance to live, but never got their opportunity. The names and faces of each and every one of those remarkable soldiers were etched inside the great heart of the man, who promised that he would never forget. For almost half a century, he had faithfully kept his word.

“Is no fate nor anything like it. Is just so. No use dwelling on it, no use wishing fer owt else. Take what life deals ye with as much grace as ye can bear and that’s the sum of it”, said Maggie, not wishing to linger on a time that history had set in stone. Mulling over heartbreaking events could not bring back old soldiers, no more than it could resurrect her Billy. “History is brimming with a sadness nae one can change. Life is fer nowt but surviving.”

“There is reason behind it all, greater than you or me”, replied Dougie. “Man didnae fashion those Auchobane cliffs, nor did he send the Great Storm which passed this way. There is a force of nature at work which nae one understands – no you and no me.”

“That’s a tale we tell ourselves tae make the days less long”, said Maggie. “Must every life pass with purpose? Every day folks pass quietly unheard. Is that fer some great reason too? Or is fate only those who are taken too soon?“

Maggie rose from the table.

“A wise man once said to endure is greater than to dare. A life lived long of this earth can have even greater purpose and destiny than one taken in bloom.” replied Dougie. “Old or young, there must be reason, whether we know it or not”.

Maggie deposited some tea on the table. Isla hoped it would prove to be a distraction. She was mistaken.

"There's no mistaking it Maggie", he continued. "Your life has great meaning and purpose whether you care tae admit it or no."

Perhaps she understood his words; perhaps she had always known their truth, but Maggie chose not to heed Dougie's argument and refused to meet his gaze when he turned towards her. It was enough of a warning to the old soldier that she wished the subject to be changed, so he turned back to their new, unchartered guest.

"So Isla, what's your tale?"

Isla's face fell. Uncomfortable at admitting truths to herself, she baulked at revealing them to a stranger, albeit a cordial one. She was fearful that the world should know that she was abandoned by those whom nature had placed closest. It was a somehow an admission of her own failings, she must have driven them away, brought it all upon herself or deserved such measured neglect. She was not ready to acknowledge her disappointments in return for kind words wrapped in pity. The thought of such condescension did nothing to lift her spirits; if anything it transformed Isla the Great into Isla the Inconsequential.

Dougie had seen those sad eyes before in the face of a young girl in an old photograph shown to him by Maggie many years before.

"You've no got her eyes."

Isla looked at his kind, elderly face.

“Her eyes. They’re not the same as yours.”

“Who‘s eyes?”

“Your mother. Yer no her daughter.”

Isla looked at Maggie, her mind flooded with the thoughts of covert conversations between adults, to which she had not been privy. She formed words her mother might have said to Maggie behind her back, arguments she might have made, lies she might have told. She imagined the hurtful things which must have been conveyed in secret between them. Those things must have been accepted as truth by an old woman who knew no better, regurgitated amongst her friends, so that they too judged and pitied her.

Dougie took Isla’s hand, gently rubbing the balls of her fingers in a soothing lullaby.

“We look before and after”, he began, tracking her heart line with his roughed finger, “and pine for what is not. Our sincerest laughter with some pain is fraught; our sweetest songs are those that tell of saddest thought…”

Isla’s eyes prickled with tiredness and memories of tearful days. She looked forward to the time when her mother’s features would merge into a mess of blurred lines and dull glamour and be finally forgotten. But that day had not yet dawned and those empty maternal eyes still stared back at her, too clear for comfort. She felt their assault, as painful as if the blows were physical, as though she stood over her in that small kitchen, her emotional attacks seeming to last a lifetime.

She extricated her hand from Dougie‘s encompassing grip, simultaneously escaping his pitying gaze and his soothing lullaby. Dougie allowed her hand its freedom. He sat back, his mind wandering and his melancholy sitting as it always did, upon his shoulders, where it had settled on his return from those difficult French shores and from where he had been unable to shake it over the subsequent years. He drifted off as was his habit, idling a moment or two in reverent reflection of the praiseworthy. After a time he leaned back effortlessly in his hard chair and stretched his ample limbs, "And tell me Isla, what do ye make of Auchobane?"

"It's very… small", replied Isla.

"It's as small as ye want it tae be", was his response. "Germany was too small fer some folk. It's all a matter of perspective, eh Maggie?"

"Aye, it is", replied Maggie, dressing the small kitchen table with the accoutrements of a marmalade tea, as though three solitary mugs were insufficient to mark the occasion.

"A mightily small distance it is for example, between Rose Cottage and the old Rectory in the village", continued Dougie.

"Rot", was Maggie's curt reply.

Dougie smiled. He bent across to Isla, mischief his intention.

"Did she tell ye about the caves?"

"What caves?" replied a sheepish Isla.

"Auchobane's caves! Only the best smugglers caves this side of Hadrian's wall. It's told that Maggie stores some of her best marmalade down in those sandstone caverns. The way I sees it, she's hiding the whisky marmalade fae the advances of an old army soldier."

"Yer head's full of mince Mr. MacGregor", said Maggie. "As if I'd stow my best jars in some damp caves."

"Lets you and me find out what's really down there!" Dougie winked at Isla, his amicable countenance sparkling "we'll take a visit of our own and see fer ourselves what's hidden down there."

"You're as daft as ye are days auld", chastised Maggie. "An old man like you taking a young girl along the cliffs? That's inviting trouble."

"I've tarried longer at Ypres in no-man's land", replied Dougie, extending his girth in line with his momentary bravado. "If I can see home the Hun, I can tackle a few of yer rowdy rocks."

"I willnae have ye dragging an innocent wee girl tae her death", continued Maggie. "Not in her condition."

Condition. It was an odd word, steeped in intentional vagueness. Isla had succeeded in ignoring the practicality of her pregnancy, so effectively that it seemed as though this 'condition' as it was called, belonged entirely to someone else, and she sat outside herself watching the events unfold with a contented detachment.

"Is it far?" asked Isla, deflecting from an uncomfortable conversation. If there was one lesson she had learned throughout years spent in the company of her mother, it was how to pander to an ego. People, she had discovered, loved to talk about themselves.

They simply required differing degrees of encouragement to do so. Her mother for example, required almost none; these new Scottish people perhaps more, but why not fan that flame of self-interest if it served to avoid that which she wished to remain unsaid.

"'Tis but a few miles along the rocks fae the harbour", replied Dougie.

"Aye but it's a dangerous walk", continued Maggie, glaring at Dougie. "With the footway flooding at high tide."

"Except on the Autumn Equinox", whispered Dougie. "Which is why the new moon in September is the best time tae go."

"Talking of time tae go", said Maggie, "away and stop bumping yer gums in my kitchen, Mr. MacGregor. You've tallied so long I thought ye were planning tae stop the night."

It was getting late and the sun had now entirely disappeared over the hills behind the cottage, the portentous rain had eased and the restless winds had regained their calm. An altogether more placid scene marked Dougie's departure to the one which had heralded his arrival.

Dougie rose from his chair good-naturedly.

"I know when I'm not wanted."

"If you'd known that you'd have left half an hour ago", teased Maggie.

"Cannae blame an old soldier fer lingering longer to enjoy the fastidiousness of company", he replied, feigning airs and graces he knew were not his natural lot. "Friends are lost by calling too often, and calling too few."

He retrieved his bright polyester vest from its discarded position by the door, and Isla could hear him sigh as he repositioned it across his decorated chest. Then he reapplied his Glengarry and his trusted old coat.

"From one lonely cloud the moon rains out her beams, and heaven is overflowed", he nodded waywardly but enthusiastically to Maggie as he opened the door to Rose Cottage. He saluted his farewells and closed the door, his lilting voice floating through the air as he made his way to the gate. And with that he was gone; back to Auchobane and his small room adorned with black and white photographs and more colourful memories to keep him company until his next delivery day. Remembrances of a time when a tall, skinny sixteen year old sat quietly on a bus and was presented with a white feather by two pretty girls who took him for more than his age. Back to the drill sergeant desperate to support the depleting ranks of the Sutherlands, first to battle, last to the clearing station. Back to the desolation of wounded comrades, like family, and the feeling of closeness reserved for those who faced death together. And back to the needless loss, of dead men to the left and right as far as the eye could see, contorted where they had fallen, a field of gruesome carpeting.

"How long have you known Mr. MacGregor?" asked Isla once the old soldier's tuneful voice had drifted off over the horizon.

“I think we’ve had enough clishmaclaiver for one day”, replied Maggie as she rose from the table.

And she carefully placed a bowl of the new oranges in the centre of the table, along with her tenderly placed peeling knife.

“Cannae abide all this blethering”, Maggie continued. “Harking on things that cannae be changed. Does nobody any good.”

And she placed a second peeling knife on the table.

Isla, assuming that the second implement was for her, pushed it away. Maggie looked at her with surprise.

“You’d rather chop?” asked Maggie.

“No thank you”, said Isla.

“Ye cannae sell the cow and sup the milk” replied Maggie. Isla looked at Maggie blankly.

“If ye want to eat marmalade, ye have to make marmalade”, Maggie explained.

“Can’t we just buy some from Mr. MacGregor’s shop?” asked Isla.

Maggie looked at Isla, perplexed.

“Why would ye want tae do that?” she asked.

“To save us the bother of making it”, Isla replied.

"Bother? Is nae bother. It's its own reward. I can open any jar in this room and know I made it with my own hand. I remember every orange that went in tae these jars, big ones, small ones. If I knew them any better, they'd be kin. Round these parts lassie, we shake our own mats at our back door."

Isla felt that she had nothing in common with this old woman and her staid, cold home with strange notions of life, death and marmalade.

"Humour an old woman", continued Maggie, "try it, and well, if ye dinnae take to it… I'll stop putting a second peeler out on the table."

Maggie's eyes had opened wide, forcing back the many wrinkles and folds which normally held them down. They were a piercing blue, and Isla saw for the first time the beauty which must have once existed there. She reluctantly took her place at the table, closer to those eyes and their honest appeal.

Maggie picked up her peeling knife and began her familiar process. Isla watched her for a while, gently scraping at the outer shell of the fruit, gliding her peeler back and forth as though she were Michelangelo searching for her David. Maggie's face was all calm contentment as she worked, a quietude washed over it like a gentle friend. Isla picked up the worn knife and an unassuming orange from the large bowl sitting in the centre of the table. For a time both woman became absorbed in their own activities, neither diverting their focus from the fruit, each considering it easier to believe that for those few moments at least, they sat alone with their contemplations in a very empty world.

Isla stared intently at the rough peel of the bright citrus fruit, its minute bumps and enclaves like some foreign moon. She focused hard upon its surface, examining every minor indentation and ever so subtly altering inflection and shade.

“There’s nowt tae be feared of”, she said, picking up another piece of fruit, careful of avoiding eye contact with the tacit young girl.

Maggie spoke honestly, the only way she knew how - around a table, hands and minds distracted by practical application. Many a problem had been solved for generations in this way, worries and introversions divulged, troubles shared and halved over the quartering of an orange.

“I’m not afraid”. Isla’s reply was more adamant than she had intended.

“Oh everyone has the fear”, continued Maggie. “Even Mr MacGregor, fer this life is much like peeling an orange. Oh, ‘tis fair difficult work at first. The skin doesnae want to give but the more ye work at it the better ye become, until one day to yer great surprise and with the greatest of ease, the whole rind gets carried away in one great, big... swoop.”

As she spoke, she whipped away the skin of the orange she held in her hands with one perfect circular motion, and let it drop onto the table, a wonderful concentric citrus cone.

Isla picked up the rind admiringly - a simple beauty of geometry.

“Try breaking it”, said Maggie. “Go on.”

Isla tugged at the orange skin, in various directions, but the stubborn rind refused to tear.

“It may look as delicate as any wee flower”, continued Maggie, “but that skin is as tough as Mr. MacGregor’s old boots.”

Step 8: Place the Pips in a delicate Muslin Bag

Maggie had lived alone for forty years, with none but her own thoughts and weeks into her new life in this Scottish isolation, Isla had still only encountered one other living soul in Mr. MacGregor, who came only by invitation and convenience. She had begun to grasp the reality of Maggie's existence - days, years, decades, the only voice her own, the only thoughts her own. It was on one such day, no different to the rest, that Isla watched Maggie sway emotionless by the door to Rose Cottage, oblivious to the world, oblivious to her. Maggie's face was frozen, oddly paralysed, her eyes were vacant and behind them a mind departed on a distant journey. She was completely unconscious of all but her own company, her thoughts a fortress, forcing out all interruptions from an outside world.

Isla knocked against a kitchen chair, its wooden feet scraping against the floorboards. The grating penetrated the silence of the room, but still Maggie did not move. Isla wondered what could occupy a mind so profusely, so absolutely that nothing physical could disturb it?

As the morning progressed and Maggie's abstraction continued, Isla's concern grew to fear that there was something more deviant at work than simple contemplation. If Maggie was suffering from an illness of her age and mind, had her mother known? Was there a darker purpose to her own abandonment here? Deeply cunning as she was, Isla doubted that her mother's manipulation extended that far, for if she had suspected some mental degradation, she would have dispatched Maggie to the cheapest care home as she had done Isla's grandmother, and reclaimed Rose Cottage as an inheritance of her own. If, as was more likely the case, her mother was unaware of any change in Maggie's mental state, should she reveal it to her? Give up the old woman in reward for her own return home? In this dark, cold corner of the world Isla still yearned for the warmth of London, for her familiar comforts and old habits and the continued ignorance of this imminently terrifying motherhood.

Isla studied Maggie's far-off face again, its gaze fixed, her mind wandering the many paths of the sub-conscious. Who was she to judge those meanderings, those hidden passageways? She had a myriad of her own psychoses to battle, each and every exhausting day. While she waited for Maggie's re-emergence Isla embraced the quiet which filled the small room in Rose Cottage. Finding herself in the solitude of a rural aspect where she could stand alone without the millstone of small talk was liberating. Without intrusion - light or personal, she felt a sense of complete concealment from an invasive world, from all its judgments and its criticisms.

She began to examine her own history with the advantage of distance and detachment and came to the gradual realisation that the common factor in all her failings was her own character. It was a revelation like a kind of religious awakening and so unmistakable a conclusion that she berated herself for missing it from the first. It made perfect sense that there must be something within her which attracted the loathing of others. It was unnatural for a mother to so dislike her first born, her only daughter, her only child, unless that offspring herself inspired it. She must have an absolute need to be rejected and to reject all that surrounded her. This new discovery was intoxicating and she imagined that she knew herself for the first time in her short life, that she fully understood the reason for each and every thought and action which could not otherwise be explained. She would gaze upon her baby in the knowledge that it was not possible to adore it, as it would eventually reject her out of hand, just as her mother had.

Isla wondered if this was where she too would come to stand in many years, an old lady staring into the middle distance, searching an invisible horizon, standing for hours with no one to interrupt, no one to whisper words of consolation. Isla knew that darkness lurked in her own mind, brooding until its future liberation. One day it would charge to the fore and she would no longer know herself. Like Maggie, she would lose her reality and plunge unwittingly into involuntary suspension.

Maggie turned and faced Isla, blankly at first, then with colour and a realisation slowly awakening. She flushed, confused as to where she was, and where she'd been. Isla tried to ease her obvious discomfort.

"I've put some more oranges in the bowl", she said, picking up one of the vivid articles as if to emphasize her point.

A fleeting bewilderment in Maggie's eyes betrayed a lingering disquiet. She had a sense of having missed several minutes, maybe hours. She picked up one of the jars of marmalade which sat innocuously by the door. Like an intimate book, the jars told a story, a very personal account of the years which had passed since Billy's death. Half a lifetime had passed since he had left and yet he still played upon her memory as clear as any symphony from her prized record player, enlivening the dull air of Rose Cottage for a magical moment. She missed him still after all this time; his words, his smell, his laughter, his role as rock and soul mate. He had left her too early, too unexpectedly, not a year into marriage so that she did not have enough time to explore the depths of his being. Maggie had felt his emptiness deep within her, so much that she questioned whether after all these years, she yearned for the man himself, or rather a projection of him - sharper, better, clearer than reality could ever hope to emulate? Was it even possible for the clouded mind of a sixty year old to accurately remember all the details as they were? Was it not more likely that, like her declining frame, her mind had become inconsistent and unreliable? That her memories would fail her, like a bad hip or rheumatic hand or the involuntary twitching in her right eye, blurring at the edges? Could she trust her memory and the stories it told? She feared it had turned upon her, and she had not recognised the change.

She saw her love as an agile man, his touch firm and strong, but it was not so at the end. The lungs which failed him, the watery bile which formed languidly in his mouth, his eyes extended by the anguish which travelled the length and breadth of his once firm frame --- these images which Maggie knew to be true never formed part of the memories she had of him. Her mind had applied its own censorship upon the truth - no doubt some euphoric gift to an old woman too fragile for the violence of reality. That Maggie struggled to recall the essence of each memory, good and bad and instead relied on vague images was in some way, a comfort. Only the good won out and no doubt Billy would have wanted it that way. What departed soul would wish for the cold, hard truth in their obituary? So Maggie chose for herself, her fondest recollections of the man. They may have not been those he would have chosen for himself but they were those she had cherished, the divine right of the living to remember the dead as they will.

Maggie considered the jar she held within her hand. Its contents delighted in the warming rays which pierced through the open door but its existence today pricked at her heart, a reminder of the hurt that still lingered there after all these years. Each day began with a dull ache, which gathered pace as the hours progressed and absorbed all other emotions until the wave broke upon her heart and almost suffocated her. Then she was lost to despair and the thoughts of her beloved lying in a grave beyond the cottage gate, or what remained of him, if anything, after so many winters. The beasties had had their feast of his flesh, and organs, once home to the warm beating heart, the insatiable intellect and humorous wit, all consumed. He was now a mess of anonymous bones, a skeleton like any other sheltering upon the hillside. He was gone forever, just like his son. The longed for child of a father in a grave and a mother broken-hearted. She saw herself again, sprawled next to her dead son, on the cold, blood-soaked floorboards of a home, as if hours not decades had past. The mess of existence and foetus sprawled upon the kitchen floor like the heart she wished would follow. The elongated head, the tiny body, not yet fully formed, eyes unopened, flesh a pale white imitation of humanity.

She would have wrenched fingers, torn limbs, ripped lungs, done anything to have given her child a life. She longed to do it anyway, to make his loss significant, to give physicality to the pain which overcame her heart and put it on display for all to see, so that all would know that she was scarred, and would remain so for all of her life. Maggie never wanted to recover. She needed to remain in that hurtful place to give their lives the meaning they deserved. But she had failed there too, her body had healed, the only scars which lingered now, lay within. She remained, year on year as others fell. She stood against the tide, wishing and hoping that it would wash over her and sweep her out to sea, where she could dream and think no more, where her unborn child floated eternally and her husband drifted upon the sands.

Maggie dipped a spoon into the jar of marmalade languishing before her and held out the orange, sparkling conserve for her guest's approval. Isla stepped towards her, reneging out of courtesy for her host, unsure as to the state of a mind which offered this conciliatory gesture.

The warm, soothing liquid enveloped Isla's throat, the sweetness sang upon her lips and the joy within the jar transposed her soul. How its seemingly unremarkable contents could touch the core of a person was beyond Isla's understanding. All she felt was the sudden ebbing away of all doubt and self-examination. Her soul sang out, unleashed, invigorated by the conserve.

Maggie saw the change in Isla's face, the eyes brightening, the frown of life's heaviness, softening. The weight upon the girl's shoulders lifted temporarily and she stood tall for the first time in years. No cloud hung over those fragile bones to beat them down. She smiled.

"Aye, 'tis a magical condiment", whispered Maggie. She turned away and rummaging in a nearby drawer, which appeared to contain a lifetime's worth of memories, retrieved a notebook, scraped and battered through years of neglect. She placed it gently on the kitchen table, its simple cover betrayed none of the secrets contained within.

"This was yer grandmothers. I tried once tae pass it on to yer mother, but she was no for having it. It's yours now."

The book had lain unopened in the kitchen cupboards of Rose Cottage for the sixteen years since it had been offered to Kirsty Keiller. It had memories of Morag etched upon it which marked it out as priceless; but Maggie knew that it was not written to be hidden away in a dark damp place without light or life.

Isla looked at the unassuming article.

“Recipes”, interrupted Maggie. “Everything I know and everything told me and generations before. Fae thick cut to whisky soaked; every marmalade that’s ever been produced by a Keiller woman.”

Isla looked down at the inauspicious notebook, frayed at the edges, faded through years of use.

This was Maggie’s life - the jars, the recipes and Isla felt that she wanted no part of her family history, neither the social aggrandisement of her mother, nor the cacophony of curious jars which trellised the walls of Rose Cottage. To Isla they were an equally unwelcome inheritance. So just like her mother‘s ambitious pursuits, Maggie could keep her marmalade and her recipes.

“Take it dearie, it’s yours. I’ve no use fer it now. Marmalade’s no fer an old lady.”

Maggie eyes lowered, saddened by the thought of her once bright youth, wilted and run to its customary conclusion.

“I’ve travelled the world”, she began, her mind drifting from its course, “but never ventured farther than Dundee. I’ve visited foreign lands but never left the four walls of this very kitchen. All the wonders I’ve seen have come to me fae the spices and scents in those wee jars. The marmalade opened my eyes and gave me a life I'd never have found on my own."

She had hope once. But it was lost so gradually, so incrementally, that she simply woke one day to find it gone. Not that she would have given up her Billy for its return. In her mind's eye, she could see Billy again, clearer than the blue of dawn's sky, sitting quietly in the corner chair, a fond smile cast across his ever youthful face. His black hair was curled playfully as he tapped the torn cover of his 'Luck of Barry Lyndon'. He had the look of their early days - it was one of Maggie's favourite images of him.

Maggie's poignant eyes weathered by time and the great storms of life, dropped a tear upon the bound leather of the recipe book, marking it with the heartache of yet another Keiller woman.

"Take the book dearie", sighed Maggie. "Ye dinnae need to do owt with it. Just keep it safe till it's needed."

Step 9: Add the Juice, Pulp and Peel to a Large Pan

As per his grandmother's lucid instruction, James found himself dutifully standing outside the green door of the grocer's shop in Auchobane on a bright Tuesday afternoon. The store stood amongst a gluttony of residential houses, its worn green exterior and wide windows the only indication that an affair of commerce lay there. Few people came to the shop directly. Its greatest asset was in the delivery of provisions, hence the shop itself acted as a transient respite for a tired old delivery man rather than the hub of a local economy. Had Dougie been more forthcoming in his knowledge of the comings and goings of Auchobane's residents, or been of a more local persuasion in his personal history, the nature of his business might have been significantly different. As it was, his advantage lay more in his usefulness than his personality, and the emptiness of the grocer's shop lay testament to it.

This was the reason James had failed to find the old grocer at home on his first visit and indeed his second and third call to the desolate shop and the reason why he had not expected to find his new prospective employer in residence on this latest attempt. He had anticipated no reply to his feeble knocking on the flaking green paintwork of the door, but as he gazed down at his knuckles, coated in a light dusting of emerald, the door swung open and he found himself face to face with the old soldier, his great coat not a dissimilar colour to the old, worn, door.

“Can I help ye laddie?” Dougie began. “Are ye lost?”

“I am nae”, replied James quickly. His thick accent seeped through his demure exterior betraying the suffocating strictness of his Presbyterian upbringing.

“Have ye come to buy owt?” said Dougie quickly, remembering the nature of his business and the prospect of a potential customer. This was not a calling to which he was naturally born, but one he had acquired accidentally. He was a soldier through and through, but one who happened to find himself with a gainful employment which would never be his passion.

“I havenae”, replied James.

“I see.”

“I’ve come tae ask fer a job Mr. MacGregor”, continued James, attempting to compensate for his lack of charm with an overabundance of enthusiasm.

“Oh aye”, said Dougie raising an eyebrow. “And what is it in particular about the grocery trade which attracts a young lad such as yourself to the profession?”

James thought for a moment.

“I just need a job Mr MacGregor.”

“Yer a McLintock, are ye no?‘

“Aye”.

James hung his head as though admitting a personal shame. He ought to have stood proud with such a heritage in Auchobane, but he was intelligent enough to recognise the burden which his grandmother’s overbearing presence could weigh upon a villager’s shoulders.

"Have ye no work at the Church? As I understand it fae yer grandmother, there's always God's work tae be done", replied Dougie, intrigued by this young McLintock.

James shuffled in the softness of his practical shoes.

"I'd like tae set my own course."

Dougie thought for a moment.

"Well who am I tae dampen the independent spirit of a young laddie" he replied. "There's a job here fer you, if you've a strong back."

He passed a box of groceries into James's arms and shut the old green door behind him.

"It's James is it?"

"Aye it is."

"'Tis a pleasure tae make your acquaintance. You can call me Dougie."

Both men headed off in the direction of the bedraggled coastal path.

The sun was holding forth in an ephemeral sky as Isla stood in the doorway of Rose Cottage, examining the expansive horizon presented before her, enjoying anonymity and relishing the spring delights of her hidden setting. She could gaze upon the shearing cliffs from a position of safety and with equal apathy surmise a powerful North Sea which plunged with abandon, rose and pounded down again upon a submissive earth. Wave after wave came crashing, unconquered by a treacherous edge of rocks which ringed the coastline. She was lost to her thoughts to such a degree that she failed initially to notice the two figures dithering their way along the grass track up to Rose Cottage. They plodded a laborious route along the cliff path, entrenched against a steady headwind which stunted their pace. Isla recognised Dougie, his concave shoulders hunched, their shape silhouetted by the heaviness of his beloved army coat. A playful gust tugged at the polyester vest he was obliged to wear, threatening to remove it and send it riding upon the coasting currents. The other man she had never seen before. He was as tall as Dougie and more upright, his youth and strength an advantage against the challenges of a wilful wind.

This new stranger carried in his arms a large box of provisions which was requiring full commitment from both of his hands, rendering him unable to repel the gust which whipped off his cap and absconded with it just as the two journeymen reached the cottage gate. Immediately he abandoned his delivery and pursued his headwear. Isla watched Dougie berate his young charge who had taken off at speed back down the pathway in retrieval of his precious hat. Maggie appeared in the doorway, stirred by the unexpected melee.

"Better late than never do well", she said disappearing enthusiastically down the pathway to rescue her provisions deposited at the gate.

As Maggie embraced her new consignment, Isla studied the progress of the younger man as he danced with the wind and his hat on the grass filled cliffs of his stage. He lunged desperately against Mother Nature, his step slow and steady as he lurched from tuft to tuft, each gust toying mischievously with him, and with his hat. He appeared to take its joviality with some frustration, his energy no match to that of the ambitious wind.

His indulged waistline hampered his cause, and the wispy hair of which his head held few was easily manipulated with each and every flurry. He was nothing like the tousle-haired boy Isla had left behind in London in charge of her heart.

Maggie returned from the gate with the large wooden box, and began to unravel her precious package. Dougie followed her inside, cap in hand - experience having taught him not to make the same mistake as his young protégé regarding the unpredictability of the weather and the importance of keeping a firm hold of one's headwear.

"I see you've got yourself a lackie", said Maggie, steering the subject to something more remarkable than a few essential condiments.

"Aye", replied Dougie, looking out the window at his charge still larking about on the cliff tops. "Thought I'd hoik him up this way – he might provide some company for our Isla like."

Dougie nudged Isla playfully.

"He has all his back teeth, ye know", he winked with spirit.

His hat retrieved, the young man of Dougie's misplaced mischief now arrived in the shadow of the doorway. His eyes quickly surmised the room for any outward signs of the infamy of its owner.

"Hullo", he mumbled in a barely audible, monosyllabic tone.

Isla looked at this unimaginative man, so unremarkable compared to that of the dangerous young lover who had unburdened her of her virginity back in London. His unruly, unkempt hair challenged the very boundaries of an insipid life and his clothes were torn by necessity rather than choice. He was everything this quiet, neat man was not and she had no interest in hearing his associated suffocating pleasantries.

With no kind of acknowledgement of his presence, James McLintock tried again to impress himself upon his desired audience, this time gesticulating towards the table and injecting himself into conversation with a cruder outburst.

“Why all the oranges?” he nodded to the bowlful of fruit sitting in the middle of the old oak surface.

Maggie eyes turned towards this interesting stranger under her roof and launched one of the finer examples of her produce at the diffident delivery boy. He caught it admirably.

‘Ye want one.’

James, tired from his exertion in reaching the cottage, happily began to tear skin from fruit to gain the reward held within. He abandoned himself with a hefty bite into its juicy heart, the remnants of which dripped freely from his chin onto the newly swept floor. For a moment or two he merrily obliged Maggie and his enthusiastic stomach, but as his taste buds began to deploy, his cheery countenance changed. A brutal grimace resurrected through that once bright complexion, ageing it terribly as the lines around his eyes betrayed a maturity that would develop in later years. He let out a roar, shaking the house to its core.

“It’s rotten!” he cried and gazed at the fruit with suspicion, searching for tell-tale signs of decay, but finding none.

Both Maggie and Dougie smiled at the spectacle, at the expense of a smidgen or two of the young lad's pride.

"They're supposed tae be beedy", Maggie laughed. "They're fer the marmalade. Ye do like marmalade, no?"

James thought for a moment. He remembered the many years his grandmother had spent lambasting the conserve and its immoral consistency so he dared not admit his predilection for what his family called 'orange jelly'.

"Yer looking at the silver spoon champion of 1932", said Dougie righteously. "You'll no find a better marmalade this side of the Firth than any that sit on the shelves of Rose Cottage."

Maggie beamed proudly through the scarlet hew of her blushing cheeks.

"Pick a year", continued Dougie.

"What?" replied James.

"A year. Pick a year", said Dougie again.

"A year?"

"Aye laddie, a year."

"1950."

"Is that yer birth year?"

"It is", said James.

Maggie walked across the room to a bookcase, took out her favourite Thackeray, and laid it down to one side. Her hand disappeared into the gap left by the large novel. A moment later and it reappeared firmly attached to a large, shiny jar. Maggie handed it to James, who read the label.

"Spring 1950."

He opened the jar and examined its contents.

"1954", interrupted Isla.

This time Maggie made her way to the dresser cupboard by the bedroom door. Crockery clattered, cups rattled but two minutes later and Maggie had retrieved another hidden jar, this one with a handwritten label.

"Summer 1954".

"There's one fer every year", said Dougie, "and each is magnificent."

"That's the oranges, no me", replied Maggie. "Every year the weather brings its own story and those tales are written down by the fruit trees. All I do is chop and boil and spoon them into the jars."

"How far back do they go?" asked Isla.

Dougie winked at her. "Why not find out?"

Isla looked for a moment, surveying the room. She spotted a jar half hidden behind the home-made net curtains on the window and stepped across the room to retrieve it.

“Spring 1942.”

“Warm and moist”, said Maggie.

James delved into an ornate vase on a shelf by the doorway, and retrieved his prize.

“1935.”

“Tart, but tasty”, laughed Maggie.

Isla’s eyes searched the room again, investigating every nook and cranny in this wonderful grown-up treasure hunt. She rummaged behind a great atlas on the bookshelf and sure enough the explored worlds revealed a dusty jar. She looked at the date and exclaimed.

“1933.”

“One of my personal favourites”, said Dougie swiftly relieving Isla of the jar.

Spurred on by a determination not be usurped by this young girl, James opened the cupboard under the sink and fumbled with purpose amongst the bric-a-brac until a jar was produced.

“Summer 1932”, he beamed, “that’s the oldest one!”

“Rich”, said Maggie, “and complicated.”

But Isla’s stubbornness was of a fierce kind inherited from her mother, and she determined to repel the man and his attempts to win their game. She knew there existed older marmalades. She had seen such a jar. All that was required was to discover it in this house of hidden treasures. A chest sat hidden behind a chair, unceremoniously covered by a tattered lace cloth. She fell to her knees alongside the old trunk and removed the veil which guarded it. Opening its heavy lid, she found to her surprise an assortment of old clothes - men's clothes - musty jackets and moth-eaten trousers, evidently stored for many years in this inconspicuous place. At the very bottom of the chest lay a small jar, unassumingly petit and covered in the same dust which coated every item in this mysterious box. The label was half torn, the jar opened, but she could still make out the date scrawled in an unsteady hand.

"Spring 1931", she proclaimed, thrusting the jar victoriously into the air.

The room was quiet save for Dougie's feet shuffling uncomfortably on the wooden floorboards, sanding the rough edges with the underside of his boots. Maggie took the jar from Isla, her face distracted by deep thoughtfulness.

"You win lassie", she said, sorrow hanging on her voice, "that's the oldest one of them all."

Maggie gazed wistfully at the small, ordinary jar. For her this pot brimmed fuller than any other in the room.

"We'd best be away", said Dougie, reading the discomfort in Maggie's voice. He rapidly retrieved his vest and made towards the door.

James stood, arms folded defiantly, next to his employer. He was unhappy and sensed some kind of unfairness at work. The girl must have known all along where the oldest pot had lain.

“I'll send the lad back tae collect the marmalade”, continued Dougie before any more awkwardness could permeate the already strained air.

“She can keep her beedy jams”, muttered James.

“Hold yer tongue”, Dougie warned as he manhandled his young charge out the door with a reminder of the necessity of respect. Cap in hand, he bid farewell to the two Keiller women and followed his new charge down the pathway.

As he reached the gate, James having recovered from his brief tantrum, turned and tipped his cap to Maggie, then promptly lost it again to another disobedient gust. As he chased his wayward hat and tangoed with the wind down the worn grass track, the old soldier ambled slowly behind, lost at Neuve Chapelle in 1915.

“Ye didnae take to the young laddie?”, said Maggie as she watched the two figures disappear from view.

“He was fat”, snapped Isla.

“He was here”, replied Maggie, “and that's more than can be said for the father of that bairn.”

“He'll come”, said Isla.

“No lassie”, replied Maggie. “He willnae.”

“You don't know anything about him”, retorted Isla.

“I dinnae. All I know is that there are men as will walk the length of this earth for their love”, replied Maggie. “If he's no here now, then he's never going tae be.”

Isla looked at the old woman. Of course she was right; she knew her tousle-haired boy would never appear at the Cottage door as he had done in her dreams, to sweep her up and smothering her senses as he had done that first and only time. When the rain beat down on the roof of the cottage, and the wind howled through every inch of brickwork, she dreamt that he would take it all away, to some unknown place of impossible peace and happiness.

"You're wrong", she replied defiantly, defending the dream as it lay exposed and dying. "He will come. You'll see. He will come. He will."

Her argument was unsteady and she knew it. She had no grounds for assuming anything about a boy she had known only minutes.

Maggie looked with pity on the girl. She felt privileged to have experienced her own consuming love. She could have said many wise words to Isla. She could have taught the girl about life and the futility of pursuing that which was lost. She might have explained what it was to feel the joy of requited love. Maggie considered all these things, but said none.

As the firmness of the grass track from Rose Cottage to Auchobane developed from the unsteady tufts of grass worn through years of occasional treading, to the more intentional stonework of the entrance to a village, conversation between Dougie and James resumed.

"Who was the lassie?", asked James, anticipating the caustic questions which would inevitably come from his grandmother's thin mouth upon his return. "Is she a relation?"

“Aye, she’s the bairn of Maggie’s niece”, replied Dougie as the burnt sandstone houses of Auchobane came into view. “She’s a bonnie wee thing, no?”

“I dinnae think so”, replied James, scuffing his feet against the small stones which skimmed the surface of the path. “So she’s a Keiller?”

“Aye she is. De ye no think she’s bonnie?”

“I think she has an awfully big opinion of her own self”’, replied James.

“Takes after her mother in that regard”, continued Dougie.

“Will she be at Rose Cottage fer a long time?”

“Perhaps. As Maggie tells it, the mother abandoned her but that’s good riddance I say. Let the wee lassie find her own voice. She’ll flower and no mistake.”

James’s thoughts returned to the grey walls of the Rectory. “I’ve nae time fer strangers.”

“That’s your granny talking now”, replied Dougie.

James McLintock flashed a look of fierceness at the old soldier at the mention of his grandmother.

“Aye, there she is again”, continued Dougie.

Dougie saw a look of simmering animosity within his young charge.

“I’m nowt like her”, mumbled James almost inaudibly.

“Aye, ye are”, replied Dougie, fearless in the face of his companion. “More than ye care tae admit it. She’s quick tae judge and long tae turn. If ye take the same path and cannae see past the end of your nose then there's as much hope fer you as there is fer that poor lassie in Rose Cottage. If she cannae overcome the hardships cast upon her fae her mother, and you cannae grow taller than yer grandmother then a right pair of lonely old folk you'll be."

He paused for a moment.

"There's nae life without hope, and nae hope without forgiveness. Absolve your enemies and you'll forgive yourself."

With that the village houses of Auchobane embraced the two men in the final footsteps of their blustery journey home.

Step 10: Diffuse the Rose Petals with Water

Isla rose uncommonly early with no other objective than to be awake. In those early hours, dawn had yet to relinquish its grip on a cold earth and Isla's exposed toes which peeked from beneath an ineffectual blanket. The physical discomfort was strangely refreshing. It was the height of summer, but in the Northern reaches, that season afforded scant improvement in the temperatures of arctic currents rushing in across the North Sea having gorged itself on cool Scandinavian fjords.

She noticed in her half-slumber that the door to Rose Cottage was fully ajar, welcoming in the harsh morning elements to the kitchen and much more importantly, her unprotected feet. She stumbled to the door to stop this uninvited breeze, hopeful of return to the peaceful sleep from which she had been so impolitely awoken.

The glare of dawn upon the cliffs of Auchobane caught her by surprise as she stood in the doorway exposed to its full brilliance. But as her eyes gradually acclimatised to the harsh light, Isla noticed a strange vision by the gate.

A dishevelled Maggie stood at the cottage's boundary with the outside world, surveying the stirrings of a village below, and a sky above. Fog had breezed in from the North Atlantic, carrying with it the last breaths of the many souls lost in its arms. It engulfed the unprotected rural community, enveloping each and every one of the small auburn houses within its ghostly breast. Rose Cottage positioned on higher ground and further along the cliff tops escaped its sinister attentions and stood guardian to the ethereal scene below. To Maggie, the parallel with her own plight was unnerving. Watching her own demise played out amongst the meteorological powers, her memories were those houses and the fog of old age which engulfed them was devastating. Her cotton nightdress afforded her little protection against the advancing gusts which thrashed her threadbare legs. Her hair was unkempt from a night which brought only restless hours, and as the sweet pea which climbed the gatepost caressed her swollen shins, she stared sadly out to sea, the resting place of her dearly beloved.

That morning the jars had mocked of the old woman, laughing merrily at her incapacity. Some days they chatted endlessly about old times and the hours spent in contemplating a life rather than living it. But today the glistening liquid had danced with disdain as Maggie floated quietly past before the dawn. Their ridicule rang in Maggie's ears, reminding her of the incompetence which now marked her days. She had tried to close her ears to their babbling noise, pressing her lined, dry hands hard against their surface. But still she heard their derisive tones ringing clear, poking fun at the paranoia which had lately taken hold. Their voices chimed together in one loud clamour for attention - demanding, threatening, intimidating. Why had she forsaken them?

So she was forced out into the exposed elements of the garden, where she had found no comfort but the meteorological representation of her failing mind. The sea carried her away, as it had done her husband many years before and she was lost to the sound of Isla rising at the new cold air, lost to the unspoken concerns which riddled her mind, lost to the girl's retraction even further into the ever-hardening shell of her young exterior.

The only thing which could revert the silence of a deafening morning and rebuke the menacing chatter of those ringing jars in Maggie's mind was the gentle touch of Billy's strong hand. He placed it gently on her shoulder. A comfort and a fortress, she thanked him every day for its luxury. Her mind had not retreated so much as to stop these daydreams, and he stood beside her, encouraging a retreat to safer ground. She dared not move, lest the strain on a fragile mind should cause the image of him to fade too. Frozen, she closed her eyes and disappeared into the precious moment of his spiritual presence.

Isla tried to stir Maggie from her distraction, but her dreams were too intimate for infiltration. Standing beneath the lintel of the cottage door, she could but watch and wait for her to return.

It began as nothing more than a twinge, as Isla clutched at the breach beneath her growing belly for support and comfort. For three days now she had felt none of the reassuring movement of the baby inside her. On the first day she had felt some relief, as its somersaults were an inconvenient reminder of its presence; on the second she felt a growing disturbance but reassurance that here was just another phase of pregnancy, a perfectly natural lull before the storm and on the third, she wondered whether she should say something or seek out a doctor in the nearby village below. They were an unnerving three days, not simply of growing physical concern, but of the realisation that despite her best efforts, a bond had somehow developed between her and this unborn child.

Standing in the doorway with the discomfort escalating, she grasped again at the growing pain in her abdomen; her whole belly lurching and contracting as though it clamped tight against the world. Her anxiety was honest, and her attempt to detach herself from the baby, unsuccessful. She looked at a distant Maggie by the gate, thinking to shout her fears, but she had no notion of what to say or how to begin. She made a vain attempt at a cry for help, but if a vacant Maggie heard such a feeble sound, she did not show it. Fixed in some other worldly place retrieval was somehow impossible.

“Please stop”, Isla whispered to the child within her, as again her belly shuddered with a cramping pain which caused her knees to buckle and withdraw their support so that she fell to the floor. She writhed upon the doorstep, assuming the same foetal position as her unborn offspring, clutching her stomach with an overwhelming fear but inside she was frozen.

Isla strained towards the gate, in search of salvation, but it remained steadfast with Maggie, unmoving and unrequited. The only movement came from the joyful roses which bobbed with every fleeting breeze. Rays of treasured sunshine kissed the pathway, their warmth inviting to those who had suffered through the annual storms. But no living soul traversed its surface to save Isla from the pain now encompassing every fibre of her being.

Isla’s lip shook despite the pearly teeth which sought to hold it firm. She bit down hard upon it, embarrassed and distracted by her incapacity, yet powerless to bring about its end. She wondered if this was the premature gasp before motherhood, the beginnings of an agonizing labour and she closed her eyes and wished for death.

“Crivens Morag!”

A concerned Maggie stood over her in the doorway but any hope Isla may have had that she was returned to her old familiar self disintegrated in the coastal breeze. The cloud of vacant distraction washed over her weathered features like an impenetrable haze. Maggie seemed more distracted than she had done at a distance, her eyes reflecting the waywardness of her words.

"The bairn is on his way!", and she pushed past Isla, thrusting her back upon the wooden floor, in her eagerness to support the child which she felt at any moment, would appear.

Isla's agonies seemed irrelevant in the presence of this unbridled woman, who seemed submerged in another lifetime. She felt robbed of her own expectancy, dwarfed as it was by Maggie's exuberance.

"I need... a ... doctor", Isla stumbled through the waves of contractions breaking over her frame.

"Rot Morag!" dismissed a rambling Maggie. "Hot water. That's what we need. Lots of scalding hot water and a good old tug. 'Tis been that way fer generations."

Isla was bustled backwards once more as Maggie whirled eagerly around the room, searching for something she had lost or thought she had lost.

"Please stop Maggie..." begged Isla in fragile tones, between laboured breaths. Her words pleaded for the return of the old Maggie, the responsible, lucid occupant of Rose Cottage.

Maggie flashed a distrustful eye at her patient, then she let roar with an unnerving exclamation of laughter, which disturbed Isla more than any dismantling appearance ever could.

“Have strength Morag and I’ll have this bairn out of ye in no time.”

“Billy!” she shouted in a dream, her glance darting around the empty room.

“Ach he’s no returned fae the boat yet”, she continued, suddenly asserting herself. “But he’ll be here soon. Dinnae fret Morag, Billy will see you right.”

The confusion within Maggie ran deep and rampant.

“Who’s Billy?” asked Isla.

“Hush now Morag.”

Maggie was in no mood for questions, being as lost to this world as her Billy. She rushed back out the door, searching for a sight of him.

“He’ll be down in the harbour, so he will” she cried with fervour. “I’ll go and fetch him this minute.”

And she disappeared down the garden path.

Whether Maggie’s behaviour was enough distraction from the pain enveloping her uterus or whether it simply gave Isla focus by demanding it from her, the result was the same. Isla’s heart beat a little slower, her blood pressure dropped and the once terrifying contractions in her stomach subsided, at least sufficiently for Isla to hear Maggie’s words and understand their implication.

“Wait!” Isla cried with some returned strength, her voice so loud and alien with a conviction of feeling that it alarmed both her and the jars of marmalade which stood audience to the disturbing events.

Maggie stopped, surprised by this sudden outburst.

"Don't leave me Maggie", continued Isla, regaining some of the composure which nature had sought to drive from her.

Maggie turned around.

"Morag!" she chastised with the authority of an elder sister. "You've never raised your voice tae me in all the years we've known each other."

Isla looked down at the doorstop on which she sat, encumbered by Morag's chastisement as if it were her own.

"I'm not Morag, Maggie. My name is Isla".

She felt the weight of this adult illness, but could not abandon Maggie to the destructive elements and the exposed Auchobane cliffs.

"Billy's not in the harbour", said Isla, with palpable panic.

"Then I'll tarry by the quay till he comes in", replied Maggie.

"He's not coming Maggie."

Maggie walked slowly back to the young girl standing in the doorway, and took Isla's trembling hand gently in her own.

"He's coming", she began. "I have tae see him home."

She let Isla's hand drift slowly away from her rugged grasp and set out once again on her journey.

"Stop!" Isla cried out once again. "Take this."

Isla grabbed Maggie's old familiar cardigan from the back of the door and held it outstretched, a gift for Maggie's weathered shoulders.

"Ach Morag", laughed Maggie. "I'm not an old woman."

Isla stopped. She knew now how to shake Maggie from her reverie, but it would be a brutal, violent awakening.

Maggie gently removed the woollen wrap from the young girl and took the remaining steps down the path towards the red gate, towards the harbour and beyond. Soon she would stray too far for rehabilitation, and this hidden secret of her drifting mind would be revealed to the world, and to her mother.

It was a difficult decision, but Isla unhooked the stained, worn mirror from its place hanging hidden behind the door, leaving behind an unmistakable shadow on the whitewashed wood. She stood in front of Maggie surrounded by the colourful flowers of a summer in bloom, and held up the unsympathetic item by its plain, etched frame.

"But you are an old woman Maggie", said Isla, loud enough to assuage her conscience and a determined Maggie.

For the first time that morning, Maggie's thoughts and actions were interrupted by an outside force.

"You are an old woman", repeated Isla, longing to soften the obliterating blow as it smashed through any reassuring hopes and dreams which lingered with reason.

Isla dared not look directly into Maggie's weathered eyes. They stared perplexed into the flawed mirror at the reflection which she was incapable of recognising as her own. She touched the mirror and its surface, believing that the image was some kind of cruel, insidious deception.

"'Tis a kind of trickery" Maggie murmured, her eyes looking up at Isla for confirmation that the reality she saw was not her own.

"There's no trick", Isla replied, standing firm with the mirror.

Maggie's eyes bore deeper, harder than before.

"Who is that?" Maggie whispered, "Who is that woman?"

"It's you Maggie", replied Isla, wishing she could construct some other, gentler truth.

"Away!" chastised Maggie, still protecting that youthful twinkle in her eye. "That's not me. I'm not old."

Maggie's life was slowly drifting back to her as she looked for familiar detail amongst the lines on a face which could not console her. She traced each and every one of the extended wrinkles around her eyes, touching them, watching the old woman in the mirror touch them in turn. She tugged unceremoniously at the loose skin, once so plump and firm, and poked irreverently at the brown spots which marked her discoloured skin. Tears welled in those soft eyes as grief overwhelmed her once again. The memories returned with a vengeance. None spared, none tempered. She relived their pain with all the force of their original conception, beaten down by sorrow in all its form and guises.

Maggie was persuaded to return indoors and Isla's heart beat a little calmer for it. Perhaps it was the cold snapping at those worn, old bones or the sudden dissipation of her youth, but she stumbled by the doorway, grasping at the damaged wood, weathered just like she. Isla reached out to help, but Maggie shrugged off her pitying hand, and steadied herself.

Within the sanctuary of Rose Cottage, Maggie found her rectitude at the kitchen table, always a friend in desperate times. Her head rested upon her newly lined hands, forming a cushion against the hard table surface. The vulnerability of her old age was tangible. After a time spent grappling with her sudden aging, Maggie's head rose from its insulation against the comfort of her own skin.

"And who might you be?" she asked, her voice calm but distant with this new stranger standing in her home.

"I'm Isla."

"Sent tae mind a silly old woman who's lost her head", said Maggie. "A woman with more lines on her hands than sense."

Maggie's self loathing came in floods. She had lost not only her youthful years, but she had also lost herself. She had a husband once, she had the expectation of a child, and in her mind it was all very real. Just for a moment she had felt absolute happiness. That precious commodity had sat within the palm of her hand, a hand now riddled with lines. She held it for all its briefness, before it evaporated and broke her heart all over again, leaving the empty shell of a lonely old woman. Maggie felt anger at her own self-deception and stupidity for admitting such deceit.

She rose from the table, a luxury not deserving of the delusional, and although still physically unsettled by her meanderings, she felt her way around this newly aged Rose Cottage. She came to rest by the window, and gazed upon this new world, so utterly unaffected with the passing of the years.

“The sea’s the only thing that never changes”, she whispered to herself, to lost husbands and sisters.

Isla allowed each painful year to settle back upon Maggie’s broken heart. They passed through her, decades not in days but seconds.

“Promise me you’ll not let them take me away”, said Maggie in earnest, her curt fingernails digging into the kitchen surface. “It’d be the end of me, just like it was fer your grandmother. She was a good woman, but your mother doesnae care fer good, only fer money. If she knew I’d lost my mind, she’d have me locked away tae speed its deliverance. There’s nowt more I’ll ever ask of you Isla than tae promise me you’ll no let them take me. Nae one listens tae an old woman, but they‘ll listen tae you. Whatever they say, promise me you’ll fight my corner and you’ll make them listen.”

Maggie’s words were strong, her armour robust and her determination stoic.

“I promise”, replied Isla.

“I want tae… I have tae… die in this house.”

Morbid thoughts wrestled inside the old woman. She had accelerated towards the end with sudden speed and now she saw it closer than ever before. A black cloud lingered, biding its time, waiting for a great gust to blow it in Rose Cottage’s direction.

“You’re not going to die”, said Isla.

“We all die”, replied Maggie. “My time is overdue. But it has tae be here, with all my kin. Else how will they find me?”

She looked up at the young girl whose journey still enviably lengthy and undiscovered. She hoped with all her heart, or what was left of it, that her destiny would be different and that the agony of her own loss would never touch her.

Maggie put her hand once more to the faded silver handle attached to the drawer beneath the sink, and tugged at it until it gave way. From inside its enigmatic tomb, Maggie retrieved a wooden box and placed it on the table.

The perfect detail of this box contrasted starkly with the fatigued plainness of the everyday table on which it sat. Unlike the table which had endured the attention of those who had passed through the Cottage doors, the box had been protected from the curious fingers, its position meted out as being extraordinary from conception.

“Go on”, said Maggie, as she pushed the box towards her young companion, urging her to be adventurous.

“I don’t want to break it” Isla replied, balancing her chair on two legs and her reservations on the others.

Maggie laughed.

“This wee box has survived decades in this clime, it hasnae the fear of you” said Maggie. “Go on, introduce yourself.”

Isla picked up the beautiful box, placing her hands where she imagined Maggie had done so many times before. She inspected its exterior, running her fingers over the tenderly crafted ridges which had been carved into the gently compliant bark. She could see where the patient hand of its architect had excavated deeply in parts, while other areas had remained virtually unscathed from the creative path, allowed to linger as nature had intended. The pattern embellishing the façade was unsymmetrical by design. Its lack of symmetry enhanced the box's character and propagated its charm. The chisel had been indulged, allowed to embark freely on a journey of discovery over the face of the box, until an abruption was met. The result was enchanting captivation.

Isla eagerly tugged at the lid of the box. It defied her for a time - its age and longevity in this damp corner of Scotland had increased its resistance to invasion. The reward was fitting. As the lid came away, Isla's eyes danced with pleasure at the kaleidoscope of colour which unravelled before her. Partitions of varying width and depth formed the main body, carved with the same patient intricacies as the lid of this treasure chest. The interior of the box was lavishly lined with a myriad of soft silks of pagan purple and orange.

"Indian silk", interrupted Maggie, proud that she had both knowledge of and access to such exotic materials.

As Isla's eyes feasted upon the spectacle of the colourful materials, her senses awoke to the aroma of the contents of the box, which had begun to slowly and subtly perfuse the air. Continents of wealth permeated the immediate space around Isla, transporting her to climes she had never been, across oceans she had never traversed.

Maggie smiled at the young girl's speechlessness.

Delving deeper, Isla tasted rustic cinnamon upon her tongue, became enraptured with the concentrated scent of musk dancing at her nose and aroused by the sweet texture of sugar upon the air. It was a coalescence of scent, a crowning perfume. She breathed in every tantalising drop, dizzily intoxicated by the salubrious fragrances. Lost completely in its foreign world of colourful kings and queens, she floated upon the waves of florid spice, absorbing their history, their vibrant tales. Reality dissipated with the incestuous droplets, along with her doubts and insecurities. She anticipated and expected the fragrances to fade as the musty surrounds of Rose Cottage infiltrated their world, but to her enjoyment, they triumphed, and Isla, confident of their constancy, began to explore the source of these exquisite essences.

The first and largest of the partitions, of which the box held five, contained a small blue velvet bag hiding its wonderful secret. Untying the ribbon, and peering tentatively inside, Isla found crystals of the most delicate kind, constellations more constant than any diamond she had seen on her mother's manicured hands. Enthralled she explored another compartment, and discovered West Indian cinnamon wrapped in delicate muslin, in another saffron stored in a shiny snuff box of pristine pewter embossed with the letter 'K', the next held a graceful glass bottle of fine Indian rosewater, and in the final compartment sat a ceramic jar of Italian musk. It was an orchestra of fragile, sacred scents.

Maggie watched as Isla drunk in the exotic history of spices which now wafted around the cottage, exploring corners and crevices numb for many stagnant years, conjoining with the old Highland wood, harmonizing its rustic flavour with their own aroma. For Maggie, these smells and fragrances transported her back to a time of happiness and delight. Their perfume instinctively cultivated an inner joy and remembrance of enchanted days and fond memories. To her relief, she could see the first gleam of a similar interest in the young girl's eyes, her face enlightened by the colourful ingredients.

"My wee treasures", Maggie offered, with pleasure, taking the box from Isla's enlightened hands and gently patting it, as though it were the most loyal of friends.

"What are they for?" asked Isla.

"Fer? Crivens! They're fer the marmalade of course."

"But they're so ...exotic?"

"Just as they ought, to make a marmalade fit fer Kings and Queens", replied Maggie.

She picked up the delicate glass bottle which was lying peacefully in the smallest compartment.

"Rosewater fae the gardens of the Raj", continued Maggie, the glass sparkling in the early morning sunshine which now drenched Rose Cottage, as though the sunbeams themselves were curious at the wonders being revealed.

She opened the bottle and soaked in the rays as if standing in the midst of a mountain of roses where the exotic scents of the East fused with the sweetness of each flower, drowning in their glorious delight.

Isla watched as Maggie then retrieved the cinnamon sticks, carefully unravelling the muslin as she lingered lovingly on the intensity of their flavour.

“Cinnamon fae the ember fields of the Caribbean.”

She passed the cinnamon beneath her nose, teasing her senses with its fired humidity, the tropical air dancing upon the atmosphere then quickly diffusing with the tumultuous hurricanes which tore across the islands, stirring flavours to their very core.

“Ah, my own favourite, Italian musk!”

Maggie pinched at the cork topped ceramic jar with fondness, teasing her fingers with the promise of its cool, moist touch.

“Fae the romantic springs of the Florentine hills.”

She drew the musk up to her nose and inhaled deeply its gloriously perfumed scent.

“All this for marmalade?” interrupted Isla.

“Great marmalade is not just fer the belly, but fer the soul”, replied Maggie. “These ingredients can fashion the most magnificent of marmalades, one which lingers in the heart long after the first morsel has been devoured.”

“I didn’t know it was so complicated”, replied Isla.

“Is not complicated, ‘tis passion. There’s nowt so sad as an undernourished marmalade.”

“You say that like it’s a human”, said Isla.

"'Tis not far fae the truth of it'", replied Maggie. "Like any bairn, ye get fae it what ye put in."

Maggie placed the lid carefully back on her momentous box of scents.

"Of course there is one final ingredient", she continued, "but all in good time."

Maggie placed a tired hand upon the table.

"Which compartment is that in?" asked Isla.

"Oh no dearie, 'tis not in any box, and it did nae fall fae any tree", replied Maggie, rising from the table and leaning on the haphazardly scattered items of furniture strategically placed to guide her to bed. "Could ye put the box back in the drawer for me dearie? So you'll know where tae find it."

And with that she shuffled off to her bedroom door, leaving Isla behind with her secrets.

Isla listened for a while as the strains of Debussy floated from Maggie's old gramophone, out through her bedroom door and into the intoxicated air of Rose Cottage. It was a sad tune. Isla instinctively pressed a comforting hand to her stomach as the baby inside her jumped with each dancing crescendo. She found unexpected relief in the child's movement, so she pressed a little harder, and soothed a little gentler, and allowed herself to think for the first time of its fingers and toes.

Step 11: Introduce the Orange Pips into the Pan

1969 was a good year for Kirsty Keiller. The months had passed swiftly since her return from Rose Cottage. Her days were filled with numerous parties and social functions. Invitations glided effortlessly through the letterbox of her fashionable London home and she exuded a confidence which came from one whose family constraints had vanished and whose future held only endless freedom. With such assurance came popularity, which in turn created further narcissism and so the infinite circle of sycophancy churned throughout the spring and summer. There was only one thing which grated with Kirsty Keiller - and that was the emptiness of her kitchen table. Superficially, that unassuming article looked remarkably the same as it had always done. It sat where it always did; the coffee tasted the same from the Meakin cups which sat upon its surface. It was just somehow, different. The empty chair at one end served to remind her every morning that she may have erased the physical presence of her daughter but her mind would not be so easily compliant. It was a brief moment of weakness in early morning when she imagined her daughter sitting before her, where she would have directed some cutting comment but now she looked up to find only vacancy. When an involuntary word escaped, only silence heard its acerbic tone. So the table had to go. After that, she took her coffee in her bedroom, and all unpleasantness, with a new routine, disappeared.

She thought often of Maggie's inheritance, calculating how much would have been originally distributed amongst the siblings, adding accrued interest applied over the years and concluding with a satisfactory figure with which to plan her new ostentatious lifestyle. Duping the old lady who had provided her nothing but a thorny shoulder as a young girl, gave her almost as much pleasure as the money she expected to extract from her. She had never felt as forsaken as she had done the morning she left Rose Cottage and she decided that some considerable recompense was due to her for such anguish. It was ironic that the deliverance of what was rightfully hers should be at the hands of the unborn child Maggie had sought to return to the fists of a beast and certain death. Her daughter had survived only through Kirsty Keiller's sacrifice and determination and now she would be the catalyst for Maggie's repayment in kind. Kirsty had no doubt in the success of her scheme. Isla's innocence and obedient conscience ensured easy manipulation.

Kirsty's plan was to swoop on the Cottage as soon as she heard of Maggie's death and offer a swift return to Isla into the bosom of warm family life and all that was familiar to her. She had no doubt that her daughter would leap at such an opportunity after months of isolation in the inhospitable Northern clime. Theirs would be a joyous apportioning of the Keiller inheritance - sixty-forty; no - eighty-twenty - Isla had simple taste. Kirsty Keiller smiled. This new world of restored order and reward seemed to her as tangible as a new Pierre Balmain silk gown, her first planned indulgence when her inheritance materialised.

In Rose Cottage, a million miles away, the months had also passed with speed. Autumn made its advancement with only the faintest hint of adjustment upon the ait.. James had become a regular companion on Dougie's visits to the Cottage. Together they trod the worn walkway amongst the high grass and plentiful wildlife. Making for the green tufts which held the cliff tops firm against the onslaught of the sea, they expanded their horizons beyond the cobbled streets and uninspired houses of Auchobane. Along the pathway they would plod, towards the Leap - the point at which the coastal path met its oblivion, so called because no-one ever leapt, but many wished they had; a half-mile further and they reached their destination of Rose Cottage.

Two miles was sufficient to build a bond between the two men. What began as idle chatter soon turned to personal confidences. Dougie would recall stories from his days at Neuve Chapelle, St. Julien or the Somme. James would listen with interest to a man who had travelled further than he. Dougie's casual acts of bravery he necessarily compared to his own ineptitude and lack of courage. James wondered what kind of man he himself might have been, had he been bolder. It was not too late to be that audacious person, he told himself as he crossed the few grey streets between his employment and the Rectory.

James's misplaced desire to exercise some bravery manifested itself one Tuesday at Rose Cottage. When the opportunity presented itself, he swiftly appropriated one of Maggie's pots of marmalade, deftly removing it from the kitchen surface and into his pocket, in a rushed exit. It was not the first illustration of James's sleight of hand. His more regular pilfering occurred with collection plate at Sunday prayer - it served to supplement his mediocre pay packet. As his father used to mutter in trying times - God never shuts a door without opening a window. The weekly offering appeared to him a transparent solution to his financial shortcomings. As he bounded down the cliff path on the return journey from Rose Cottage that afternoon, invigorated and alive, he placed his hand inside his coat pockets, reassuring himself that the marmalade, along with his courage, was secure.

Once engulfed by the cobbled, claustrophobic streets of Auchobane, he took his shiny new prize by its lid and altered its position in his shallow pocket so that it could plainly be seen by anyone scrutinising his person, from the closeness of a Rectory window for example. As he approached his grandmother's vantage point, he began to amble purposefully, sauntering almost nonchalantly towards the front door, his pocket swinging merrily in full view. He clunked his keys against the glass jar as he feigned a struggle with the lock, and he brushed the lid of the marmalade clumsily against the bulk of the doorframe as he strode across its threshold. It was not by chance that his grandmother discovered Maggie's little pot of marmalade and it was no unfortunate accident that placed it in her hands on that particular day.

Mrs. McLintock had indeed noticed the pot of homemade marmalade peeking out from her grandson's indulgent coat pockets on his return from deliveries that Tuesday afternoon. The look of it was unmistakable from the one she had seen on display on a Caird Hall judging table many years before. Her mind whirred with thoughts of that Keiller woman but she held her tongue until her grandson crossed through the Rectory door.

"James McLintock!" she bellowed from her position of power.

James looked at his father, who had come to greet him by the door. The fear in the Minister's eyes was familiar. He was a broken man, and cowered at the very tone of his mother's behest.

"Best get in there", he replied, stepping away from his son.

James knew that his grandmother had seen the jar of marmalade in his pocket. She sat at the Rectory window day after day, hour after hour, assuming the self-appointed position as moral regulator of a village which neither wanted nor desired one. At school he had been ridiculed for it - as idle as the gossip was surrounding the old woman of Rose Cottage, his grandmother had grown to similar fame through her own erratic actions. Friends never came to play; girls never came to call, everyone stayed away for fear of incurring the wrath of the old woman at the Rectory window. James buried deep the taunts and sneers of his childhood, but he never forgot the damage wielded by her actions. Most of all he remembered the integral part she had played in the destruction of his family life. He was four years old when the young family relocated to the Rectory. He remembered his mother's reservations, and the reassurances of her weak husband, which withered away within days. The verbal barrage which emanated from her daily may not have been of a physical kind, but their effect was as devastating to the happiness of a young wife and mother. The constant criticism, the devious manipulation, gradually ebbing away at his parent's marriage, until it disintegrated entirely and the old woman took control.

James could still see his mother's face as clearly as the day she left, her deep set green eyes twinkling with the manifestation of a happiness which had long since deserted her. It was the physical contact he missed most. A mother's hug, a soft kiss and the smiling pinch of a cheek at a naughty schoolboy prank. Her abandonment affected him deeply, and extended into adulthood. He thought of her in every quiet moment, every lonely silence which fell upon the Rectory. He wondered where she stood now, whether she had built herself a new family, one without the crutch of a conniving old woman. He understood her reasons for leaving, but could never forgive her for escaping without her first born son. They had a special bond, he and she and he felt that she had cast off the protective cocoon of motherhood too easily, and abandoned him.

She must have known when she left, that his grandmother's attention would fall upon her grandsons. James knew it on his thirteenth birthday, when the old woman had presented him with a leather bound bible wrapped in cheap paper when he had asked for a football. And he knew it when he was fifteen, when she had dragged him from a rugby match after playing truant from Sunday school. He knew it now, kicking his feet against the carpet, scuffing his uninspired shoes on the stone grating. She was his grandmother, and yet he would rather plunge head first over Auchobane's cliffs than remain forever beneath her, like his father and grandfather before him, beaten men. He was obedient to her but only to the point where their objectives diverged.

James had been surprised by Maggie Keiller on their first meeting. She was not the fierce monster his grandmother had vilified throughout his childhood. Nor was she the wild, frenzied woman that beguiled the villagers of Auchobane, fuelled by Church sermons. He had warmed to Maggie's independent spirit, her wise words, and one day he hoped, her sinful marmalade. Moreover he admired a woman who had strength of character enough to shun a village and live life on her own terms. He wondered if destiny had trodden a different path and his mother had happened upon Margaret Keiller, whether she would have found the necessary strength to remain in Auchobane.

As the piercing shrillness of her voice of his grandmother's Fife tongue cut through the sanctimonious air of the Rectory and with thoughts of an inspiring Maggie Keiller fresh in his mind, James felt he had nerve enough to challenge his grandmother. Thoughts of Dougie on the battlefields of France invaded his spirit and he felt himself at that moment to be ten feet tall. There would be no protection from her glare in the sterile Rectory. Bare, bland and colourless, it too had been beaten into its shell by that woman; but James held his head high as he opened the door to the breakfast room with an almost physical trepidation. His grandmother was a hard woman, with a complete absence of warmth and feeling. While others bore fond remembrances of their grandparents, his memories were swamped by fear and apprehension. He was not alone. He saw plainly how his father and many of the congregation cowered beneath her, and lately he felt his presence under greater scrutiny as she sought to mould a new minister for her own personal McLintock Church. It was a role for which James had no interest in applying.

For the course of his life he had been her foot soldier, doing her will without question, merging her thoughts with his so that the two were indistinguishable. In his younger years it meant throwing stones and insults. He had done it out of misplaced pride and because he simply knew no better. He had never challenged her insistence that the woman of Rose Cottage deserved nothing but disdain. As he grew in height and years, her manipulation increased in turn and while stones were no longer thrown at Rose Cottage's windows, his inability to contest his grandmother's bidding remained. Her orders to work with Dougie were met with compliance and he trod those steps to Maggie's door with his grandmother's intentions ingrained in his heart, proud that he had been entrusted to her confidence.

It was somewhat unexpectedly then, that he found himself standing before her with a courageous heart ready to defy all that she stood for. He had found his voice, later than most, lain amongst new friends who fought a war and asked for nothing.

"Well?" Mrs. McLintock snapped as the young man entered the room. "Where have you been?"

James shrugged his shoulders.

"Out", he replied, nonchalantly.

"Dinnae get smart with me laddie, fer you'll never be as smart as the Lord Himself", Mrs. McLintock replied. "You're nowt but a grain of sand in his eyes. Now out with it, or I'll force it fae ye."

Mrs. McLintock picked up a belt she habitually kept by her chair. She had no real use for it now that the boys were too old to be placed over her knee, but she still felt that the threat of physical discipline could be a useful tool to expedite her cause; all in the Lord's name, of course.

"I've been running deliveries with Mr. MacGregor", said James shuffling his feet. "'Twas you who asked me to be Dougie's lackie, remember?"

"Dougie is it now?" replied Mrs. McLintock with a wry smile, "As thick as kin are ye?"

James said nothing. It was not his intention to involve Dougie in his plans.

"Aye I know where you've been", continued Mrs. McLintock, "But I want tae hear it fae your own lips."

James cast his eyes heavenwards. Did God really have any interest in the minutiae of his day?

“McAdam’s steading… the old Mill… Mrs. Dagleishs… the School out on Carruthers road”, said James, counting residences off on each finger as he went along.

“Aye….” said Mrs. McLintock, waiting for the one familiar name she sought.

“And the old cottage on the cliff”, finished James.

“What cottage would that be?” probed Mrs. McLintock.

“Rose Cottage”, replied James.

“And what news?” she snarled. “Is that heathen woman dead yet?”

Mrs. McLintock’s face contorted with the syllables of her words, making her appear as though she were the woman more fit for the grave.

“She isnae”, said James.

“And the lassie? How long is she still stopping?”

“I don’t know.”

“How no?”

“I didnae ask.”

Mrs. McLintock was taken aback by the ineptitude of a relation she had hoped held dependence.

"Didnae…or wouldnae?"

James shrugged his shoulders, surprised by his own insolence.

"You're fit fer nowt. Just like your father."

Mrs. McLintock's voice dripped contempt.

"What's that ye have there in your pocket?" asked Mrs. McLintock, taking her walking stick and prodding the offending article in question. The jar chimed, revealing itself.

James took out the small pot.

"'Tis a wee present fer you, fae Mrs. Keiller", he replied, his eyes glistening with the lies he told.

"Oh aye? Can I have a wee look?" asked Mrs. McLintock, reaching out, demanding the inoffensive article.

James dutifully handed across the shiny jar of liquid. He knew instinctively that he wasn't to see it again.

Mrs. McLintock held the jar up to the light. It really was a pretty little pot and the liquid was as clear as the sea blue on a summer's day in the rock pools. But the devil comes in all guises, including attractively coloured jars which can momentarily lift a mood. With dangerous thoughts brewing, she quickly opened the latch on the Rectory window, placed her hand and the jar outside in the chilling Northern air, and casually removed her grip so that the jar fell inevitably to the ground, smashing into a million tiny pieces on the hard surface below, the glorious liquid seeping out onto the paving stones, coating them in a warm orange hew.

“I'll not have the devil's handiwork in this house”, she shouted, her voice dancing with the rush of her own power and supremacy, delighted that she had destroyed something so intimate to that woman. She was contented also that her strong authoritarian hand still grasped tightly around the starched collars of the McLintock clan and so it would remain until her grave, and ideally beyond.

At the sound of smashing glass, Mr. McLintock and his other son Ewan rushed optimistically into the room, but to their disappointment found Mrs. McLintock quite well, if a little giddy from castigation of her grandson.

She acknowledged the underwhelming appearance of her son in the doorway, an action which seemed to aggravate her temper.

“The sermon this week is the devil's temptation”, she directed him, rallied by the war against heathen marmalade. “I want a full hour of it! There's nae time fer Sunday rest when there's a God's work tae be done!”

“Yes mother”, the Minister replied deferentially.

“And you”, she continued, now directing her wrath onto her other idle grandson Ewan, “should pay more attention tae your grandmother. That could've been a rock against that window, I could've bled tae death afore you'd come running.”

Ewan, the younger of the two brothers and by far the more indulged, hung his head sheepishly, but his impish grin remained.

Throughout her chastisement of her clan, Mrs McLintock could think of none but Maggie Keiller. She saw the woman's smug satisfaction in the window pane, her conceit in every flame which escaped up the chimney pot and it made her blood boil.

She turned back towards her first grandson, her voice shaking with wrath.

"You're never tae set foot in that evil woman's house again."

"But it's my job", James replied.

"Not anymore."

James studied his feet profusely trying to assimilate the derision of his grandmother, filter out what was worth fighting and what should be left.

"'Tis God's will", continued his grandmother. "If you're tae walk in your father's boots one day, you'll need tae learn not tae question the Almighty. 'Tis nowt but the devil's work which goes on in that cottage, yer father knows it, and yer grandfather before him knew it. God rest his soul."

The late, great Mr. McLintock of course knew no such thing, being concerned primarily with bookie slips and the public house opening hours, but history is written by those who survive to write it, and Mrs. McLintock had rewritten her husband into canonisation many years ago.

"I'll not be a Minister", replied James, fixed intently on a tiny fleck of grass wedged firmly in the sole of his shoe so as to avoid his grandmother's piercing eyes. "I'd rather be a cow mucker."

"You", replied Mrs. McLintock, "will do as yer told."

Ewan sniggered, a happy audience to the downfall of his elder sibling.

"And I'll no give up my job with Mr. McGregor", replied James, examining the contours of the blade of grass as it twisted back upon itself in its confined position. He must have acquired it on the journey down from the cottage. How could it become so completely stuck, so as to appear as though it had always formed part of his shoe?

"He's a good man, and I like helping out."

"Dinnae backtalk your grandmother James", chastised his father, with rather less firmness than perhaps was due, proud of his son's impertinence.

"She can ruin yer life, but she's no having mine", concluded James, and it was done. The words sounded odd, less significant once expelled in the cold evening air. He had expected some great cataclysm, some magnificent transformation to occur, but there was none. Instead, his grandmother, for an uncommon moment, was open-mouthed at her grandson's insubordination.

"You're a disgrace tae yer grandfather's name!" she exalted, with a surprisingly venomous power for one so frail in years.

James felt the insignificant sliver of grass in his shoe was due its freedom for its part in the great uprising, and so he took it and himself, quite calmly, out of the room, and the Rectory entirely, in search of a suitable position for it to return to the wild.

"You're going straight tae hell", shouted Mrs McLintock, leaning forward with her gaunt Protestant fingers pressing into the arms of her hard wooden chair. "You're no grandson of mine."

The chair rocked unsteadily with the violence of her anger. She turned to her son.

"This is your fault", she hissed. "You're a weak man and he takes after his father."

The floor creaked beneath her fury as her mind began to whir at how she might punish both the Keiller woman's heresy and her grandson's impudence.

Meanwhile James had found himself, not for the first time that day, stomping back along the grass track that led up to Rose Cottage. He stopped at the Leap, equidistant between the cottage and village, and stood casually at the cliff edge, the front of his shoes peeking over into oblivion, the heel safely wedged into the soft earth. He watched the sea lap affectionately against the rocks some fifty meters below and felt the sudden urge to jump - a curiosity more than an inclination. Common sense prevailed as it always did and he sat down upon the damp ground, his feet dangling liberally off the tufts of grass.

He had lied to his grandmother about the marmalade and it gave him immense satisfaction to have quietly deceived the Auchobane oracle. He had proved to himself that with some degree of imagination and an excessive amount of nerve, she could be tricked like everyone else.

The gannets were flying low that day. James watched them take their deathly plunges into the depths of the dark ocean and reappear a few moments later, sometimes with an unfortunate fish pinned tight inside their bills. His future was something of an abyss. He was a McLintock and that in itself had steered the course of his life. But fuelled by his grandmother's unforgiving words and the ease with which she had rejected him, he felt an overwhelming desire to push further the boundaries of his bravery. He felt compelled to push the knives of his rebellion a little deeper and shatter the frozen depths of his grandmother's heart. Maybe then she would turn her judgement inward and find more lacking there than in any other person she sought to chastise.

Emboldened with a new found fire for retribution, an idea struck him now. Not contented to rest at the day's already momentous confrontation, James was convinced that he could rile his grandmother even further if he were to step out with the young Keiller girl at the New Moon dance. There was nothing remarkable about her person or her silent moping to register a chord of interest, but he knew that he would set tongues wagging if he were to arrive at the dance with a stranger. Auchobane was an intimate place, where an unfamiliar face was as much headline news as a wartime offensive or a political blunder. Moreover, if it were to be known that she was a Keiller, the locals would be intrigued tenfold. He would parade her past the Rectory, perhaps invite her in for tea - a Keiller under the roof of the Rectory - his grandmother would turn in her grave, if only he could place her in it.

With such a captivating thought buzzing in his head James bounded from his precarious position upon the cliff edge, and placing his hands deep into his empty coat pockets, continued his amble along the grass track and the remainder of the pathway which led up to Rose Cottage.

Inside that place, unbeknownst to James, a curious marmalade conversation was being conducted.

“An aphrodisiac?” exclaimed Isla, peering into the jar, searching in vain for some kind of mood enhancing coagulation.

“Aye”, reiterated Maggie.

“It’s only jam” said Isla, thinking this was another example of the nonsense proffered by her unworldly relative.

“Less of the jelly lassie”, replied Maggie, gently chastising.

“But how?” asked Isla, “how is it an aphrodisiac?”

“Just is”, replied Maggie, “‘tis no rhyme or reason to it. Sometimes things are just ‘so’.”

Isla peered further into the jar, continuing her scrutiny but without success. Maggie smiled at the inquisitiveness of youth.

“Shall we try it?”

Isla shook her head.

“Have ye the fear of it?”

“I’m not … scared,” Isla retorted nervously, “It‘s only marmalade.”

James’s knock on the door of Rose Cottage at that point was a fortuitous one. Even Maggie was curious to discover whom fate had deposited at that moment on her doorstep, and she opened it with interest to find an awkward looking James standing in the breeze.

“Back so soon laddie?” asked Maggie forthrightly, winking at a horrified Isla. James shuffled his feet. His plan had seemed straightforward on the cliff-tops - he would beat confidently on the door, exchange some idle pleasantries, and be about his business. But that business had seemed less daunting with distance, and James now felt less assured than he had done in his mind.

“Well - have ye a tongue in your head?” continued Maggie.

“I do”, James replied scratching his temple awkwardly, longing for escape and the opportunity to engage both his words and his head.

“The marmalade’s no ready”, Maggie continued, “if that’s what your after.”

“Aye”, said James, clearing his throat, but the words came shakily, “I mean…I know it’s not ready. I mean I’ve no got the labels anyhow.”

“So I see”, replied Maggie folding her arms and staring down at James’s unoccupied hands. “So what is it you’re wanting then laddie?”

James lent forward to Maggie and whispered in a low voice as close to her ear as he felt safe to approach.

“Could I have a wee word with your friend?” James asked, his face turning seven shades of crimson as he spoke.

But Maggie had not finished with the boy.

“And which friend would that be?” Maggie asked, toying with their scarlet visitor.

“The lassie”, James mumbled at his feet.

“Speak up laddie”, replied Maggie.

“The lassie”, he came again, clearing his throat.

“Do you mean our Isla?” persisted Maggie.

“Aye.”

“The very same Isla that’s sitting just over there, no ten feet fae the end of your nose?” continued Maggie.

“Aye.”

“Well then. You’d best stop inside”, said Maggie stepping aside and turning around to her young charge. “Isla, this laddie is wanting a word.”

It was Isla’s turn to be bashful as heat rose involuntarily in her pale cheeks. Her heart violently increased its speed, not because she had given this local boy any consideration since their first meeting, but because of the unexpectedness of his appearance. What did he want with her? Why was he here? With a history already brimming with a catalogue of errors, she was loath to admit any more.

She was not alone in her anxiety. James, equally fearful, remained fixed in the open doorway. And so Maggie found herself, for a few moments, mediator to two silent protagonists, reluctant to protect Isla from a life which was progressing without her and hesitant to push the boy too far lest he should baulk completely and be halfway down the path to Auchobane before she could bolster his fragile pride.

"Well, shut the door", she continued breaking the uncomfortable silence which resonated around the small room, "you wasnae brought up in a byre."

James duly stepped into the warmth of the kitchen, regretting his decision to come up to the cottage in this unannounced way, but there was no going back now. Best get it over and done with quickly and be back down that overgrown pathway, bouncing his way down to the village with relief in his step. He couldn't go home, not until the cover of night and the safety of an empty chair by the Rectory window. There would be some respite until early morning and his grandmother's penitential prayers, longer no doubt on account of his troubled soul.

As the rest of his day, and night, played out in James's mind, Isla looked at him with a fearful anticipation which was slowly beginning to turn to annoyance. There was nothing he could say which could be of any interest to her and she could not understand why he was so obstinate as to think otherwise.

"Say your piece", said Maggie, seeing Isla's patience wane.

James took a deep breath and extricated his nerve.

"There's a New Moon dance down in the village on Saturday", said James, eventually stumbling onto the reason for his visit. "Would ye care tae go with me tae it?"

Isla was dismayed. Not particularly by the dance itself, although the thought of close physical contact with this local boy was less than appealing, but more with the idea of having to engage in some kind of rural ritual where she would become the focus of the evening's entertainment. She grew angry at James's selfishness. No doubt, he had assumed that she would simply agree.

"No", she replied firmly.

James's once ambitious head dropped desperately low. The black clouds returned. Every chastisement, every demoralising slander thrown in his direction was reiterated tenfold, ringing out in his ears, accompanied by the mocking laughter of his peers. James was not considered conventionally attractive. Singled out for ridicule first for his name and then for his uninspired appearance, James dwelt within a public circle of scorn. When it came to the opposite sex, he was not naturally adept. Generally he thought too much for action, and often talked himself quite completely out of any engagement. The New Moon dance would have been his first successful foray into Auchobane's sporadic social scene; but it was not to be. Rebuffed, he turned to the door and his trudge back to the Rectory and the receipt of his not inconsiderable punishment for his audacity.

"Is that it?" asked Maggie, despairing at the lad's poor showing at courtship. "Are ye no going tae try and change her mind?"

"No. She's said her piece."

Maggie shook her head. In her day, there was a great deal more courage.

"I won't change my mind", exclaimed Isla, resolute in her firmness against this charmless local.

"Ye dinnae need tae dance", replied Maggie.

"I prefer tae stand myself", added James.

"Sounds really exciting", replied Isla sarcastically, the thought of engaging with a room full of drunken villagers as unappealing as the thought of spending tedious hours with this gormless boy.

"''Tis what ye make of it", replied Maggie, seeing for the first time, something of her niece in the young girl. She felt disappointed for the lad, and disappointed in Isla. Life's opportunities were precious and transient, she was disheartened to see them so effortlessly squandered without due consideration.

"My mind's made up", Isla retorted, turning her back in a blatant display of rejection.

James for his part began to feel some relief. The unexpected scorn with which his offer had been rebuked made him feel lucky to have escaped from an evening of condescension with this English girl. It was a price too high to pay for infuriating his grandmother. There were other, less personally aggravating ways he could do that.

"You'll have some marmalade tablet afore ye go", said Maggie as she rummaged for her safely stored sweet. "There's always time fer tablet."

Isla sat back in her chair, arms folded defiantly. James milled about the doorway, feet tapping nervously.

"Sit yourself down laddie", continued Maggie, pulling out a chair at the table.

James continued to hug the doorframe and his escape route.

“Consider it recompense fer that jar of marmalade ye took on your last visit”, replied Maggie.

“You stole a pot of marmalade?” asked Isla.

James looked down at his old boots, muddied by the day’s hike up the cliff track and several months of unwash. The blade of grass which had come to his rescue while defying his grandmother, was now gone. No doubt deserting its foreign situation for a more natural landscape, taking the opportunity to float effortlessly away to offer strength to another meek soul.

“Sit yourself down”, said Maggie softly, as she placed a tantalising plate of tablet down on the table. It was a beautiful caramel colour, cut into eight neat square sections, and arranged haphazardly on the little white dish which accentuated its attractiveness. They shimmered in the sunlight as if coated with an effervescent gold, a treasure of the most sublime kind.

James was tempted by their attractive, appetising nature, and having just sacrificed the stolen marmalade to his grandmother, he felt he deserved this sweet reward. He pulled out a chair, scraping it loudly against the wooden floorboards, and sat. Not a second later and the first slab of tablet hit his tongue. With delight he felt the succulent sweetness dissipate incomprehensively in his mouth, oozing with sugary warmth, coating his throat and melting slowly down into his belly, warming it with a fire usually reserved for the cheap whisky he siphoned from his father’s hidden reserves.

Maggie beamed proudly as the young man’s face lit up with the glorious marmalade. His smile had the effect of illuminating his weary face, his frown lifted and the tense hands which held on so tightly to his errant flat cap loosened their grip and the hat floated gently to the floor. His youthfulness returned as his mood lifted, and the clear pools of his large green eyes seemed deeper than eternity.

James was unable to speak while the tablet dissolved gloriously in his mouth, awakening his taste buds. He was fearful lest opening his mouth would invite new sensations inside, and he wanted to hold on to this perfectly exquisite flavour for just a few moments.

Maggie picked up the plate and offered the remaining squares to Isla.

"I know what you're trying to do", whispered Isla, their recent conversation on the aphrodisiac qualities of marmalade fresh in her mind.

"'Tis only jelly", replied Maggie, teasing.

"No thank you", said Isla firmly.

Maggie shook her head sadly and placed the tablet back on the table much to the delight of James, who took the opportunity to secure a second piece, and a third and fourth for the journey home.

"I'll be on my way. Thanks fer the tablet".

James sprung to his feet, his mouth crammed with the divine confectionary. He managed admirably to stand despite the heaviness of pockets now overflowing with Maggie's delicious squares of golden sugared sweetness. They'd steer him through a difficult evening, and he was determined that his grandmother should not find these specimens out. He could see her now, contorted with anger in her hideous chair, recounting the evilness of her first grandson, delighting in the numerous excruciating punishments she could dish out for his indolent behaviour, and contemplating which one would resurrect the devout religious values desirous in a Rector in waiting. James sighed heavily.

Maggie put a hand on his shoulders, ushering the brave young laddie to the door. As he crossed the doorstep, she took his arm with a firm grip.

“Old folk survive on remembrance but youth lives on hope. You hold fast tae that hope laddie; it‘ll be its own reward.”

James set off back down the slow, lonely path back to his subjugation. He had failed to persuade Isla to join in his impetuous rebellion, and her rejection weighed heavier on his mind than it should have done.

“She’s too big in her own head”, he thought to himself, kicking the small rocks on the pathway closer to oblivion on the cliffs. He popped another square of tablet into his mouth, and the world soon seemed a little brighter.

Maggie watched James go, sorry for his failure.

“You wasnae right tae turn the laddie away”, Maggie said, with enough meaning in each of her carefully chosen words for Isla to feel a twinge of self-doubt.

“It was only a dance”, Isla replied.

“Was it?” said Maggie. It was so much more.

Step 12: Gently Cook until the Peel is Tender

Isla awoke with a start. Through the thick blackness of the kitchen, she heard a distinct sound. She listened in the darkness, and it came again, a rap…rap…rapping from the direction of the window; a methodical, insistent sound clearly discernible above the gale which raged across the cliff-tops. It was an ominous sound which filled her with fear, and she rose tentatively from beneath the protective covers of her chair, her feet at once discovering the cold. She tiptoed to the window in the vain hope of arresting the fearfully rapping, prepared to force back the gusting winds which contested the cliffs and menaced the sea. Surprisingly she discovered the object of her anxiety to be nothing more than the old oak tree which grew stubbornly in the front garden of Rose Cottage, its branches outstretched and beating a tune on the unimpressed pane.

As she scolded herself for her melodrama, she noticed a strange disturbance on the horizon. Within the vividness of Isla's dream, it seemed as though those foreboding cliffs were rapidly advancing towards the cottage. She peered through the glass at the swiftly diminishing earth, crumbling from its existence, approaching like an indeterminable wave. She watched as the soil gave way before her eyes, vanishing into the sea from which it had clawed for centuries, swallowed up by a thundering swell pounding the rocks beneath. Isla was paralysed by fear as this growing chasm of earth moved closer. It had reached the cottage gate, its posts fragmenting and falling away from their stoic position where they had stood for many years, the garden threatened by a violent march of erosion, moving fast and unabashed. . It seemed that the enigmatic oak tree tapped on the window pane not out of idleness, but with a more pressing agenda. The tap... tap... tapping of its branches, offered salvation from the disappearing earth which surrounded. This aged oak tree which had stood for generations, safeguarding the cottage and all who sought refuge within it. Its branches were strong and numerous, they tapped gently but with confident insistence upon the glass, calling out to her to jump to the safety of its foundations and escape from a premature death. As the ground beneath her buckled and the earth disintegrated to dust, she lunged towards the reliable tree. As she did so, the old oak floorboards of the cottage were torn from their beds, the stone walls with which they were once so intimate, themselves gave way and the roof caved in as though made of cardboard. Isla grasped tightly to the great oak's branches, clambering onto its steady beams and protection from a world which was dissolving around her. In her dream, the cottage was no more, nothing stood upon the cliff-top tall but the roots of the old oak tree. She climbed higher within its sanctum, from the outer reaches to the security of its inner core. As she clung to the secure trunk, her arms barely circling its immense core, she became aware of a sticky substance saturating beneath the mature ridges of the bark. The texture of glue, it oozed from the tree, clinging to her feet and then to her hands, suffocating them as she tried to manoeuvre around the branches. She tried to wipe it from her fingers, but it grew denser as she fought its touch. She recognised the consistency of marmalade - its taste unmistakable on her tongue. Panicking, she tried to extricate herself from the sticky liquid, but it would not let go of her. She wrestled hard and long until she felt quite weak from the exertion; then suddenly, quite unexpectedly, the marmalade released her. She fell for what seemed like an eternity through a myriad of branches, snapping beneath her weight as she fell further, grazing her face, scraping her hands and wrenching at the softness of her bare feet. She grasped hopelessly at the twigs as they flew past, trying to prevent an abrupt ending, but they came too fast as she plunged towards a deathly inevitability.

"Isla?"

A calm voice pierced the blackness.

"Isla?"

The voice came again.

"Isla, wake up…wake up Isla."

Slowly, Isla opened her eyes, her falling finally at an end. It was a September Scottish moonlight which lit the kitchen of Rose Cottage, poking through its shy kitchen windows - still sturdy, still strong. As her eyes became accustomed to their shadowy surrounds, the light offered her just enough grace to make out the features of the retired serviceman who knelt on the ground before her. She started at those large honest eyes which stared anxiously back at her.

"It's me lassie…it's Dougie", he replied, tenderly touching her arm.

"Dougie?"

Isla examined the room, the remembrance of her disturbed dream still fresh in her mind. The wooden floorboards were as they should have been, the walls were entirely intact and the roof still provided enough protection against an encroaching clime. The cottage was as it ought to have been, save for this one moonlit guest.

“Dinnae fret lassie, it were nowt but a dream.”

The sun had not yet risen, the day had not begun, and yet here Dougie stood in the little enclave of Rose Cottage, gently stroking her hand in the sharp cold air.

‘What time is it?’ replied Isla, rubbing the remnants of sleep from her blurred eyes.

“O-four hundred hours!” replied Dougie, beaming with excitement.

“Four-o’clock? In the morning?” Isla repeated.

“Aye”

“Why are you here?”

“Jars”, he replied.

Dougie was making about as much sense as Isla’s falling dreams from marmalade trees.

“Can’t it wait till morning?”

“Oh no”, Dougie replied, “it cannae wait!”

With that he bounded to his feet and performed an impromptu jig around the kitchen table in the highest of spirits. This night-time sortie had reawakened in him memories of comrades and heroes born on the adrenalin plains of Northern France. Tonight he stole once again across enemy fields; risking his life with every heartbeat. This new operation, the stealthy delivery of marmalade jars up to Rose Cottage, rekindled the dramatic life of an old soldier, and he was eager to prove that he was an officer still up to the job.

Maggie appeared at the bedroom door, sheathed in the glow of a paraffin lamp which resided next to her bed for emergency situations such as these unpredictable early morning calls. Wrapping the worn, old cardigan she habitually wore through winter and summer together, tight against bones which seemed lately perforated by every early morning chill, she set the kettle to work and produced a jar of 1956 from inside a faded yellow cup.

“What’s going on?” asked Isla again from her clouded corner.

“The bairns have arrived”, smiled Maggie, placing three steaming cupfuls of tea on the kitchen table, along with the resplendent jar. She took a spoonful of the golden marmalade and stirred it into her black tea, the flecks of peel rising to the surface like little life-savers.

“Wee little treasures”, winked Dougie, “of pure Black Isle glass.”

Isla picked up a mug of the hot warming liquid and hugged it tightly against her shivering chest. It was the uncommonness of the early morning air when sleep should have been at its deepest which caused her to shake.

Dougie gazed across the ever altering horizon, noting subtle changes in the shadows, sensing the imminent arrival of their witching hour.

“Almost time”, he said examining the muddled dullness of the sky optimistically.

Instinct drove Maggie out through the doorway, inadvertently admitting a burst of approaching new day as she did so.

"I'll fetch Hamish so."

Isla shuddered and clung desperately to the warmth of her tea.

"Who's Hamish?" she inquired hopelessly.

The silence which defined those uncommon hours brimmed full in terms of character and personality. So completely unlike any quietude which reigned during daylight hours, it assumed its own voice, one of urgency and vitality and impossible to ignore. For Isla, the stillness became suddenly significant and she dared to utter words she would have baulked at in a fuller light.

"Dougie", she began. "Can I ask you a question?"

Dougie stopped and turned as if sensing the seriousness of Isla's tone.

"I'm not one fer knowing the world, but I'll call a spade a spade", he replied

Isla took a deep breath.

"Is Maggie well?"

Her question overflowed with unspoken intent.

"Now there's a spade", replied Dougie tapping his fingers on the kitchen surface.

The old soldier was of an age embarrassed by talk of a personal nature, preferring to set the tone of friendship in terms of the practicalities of life and the direction of it.

“She’s well and she’s no”, Dougie reluctantly continued.

“She forgets things?” asked Isla.

“We all forget things”, was all he said.

“But she forgets herself” replied Isla.

Dougie rubbed his forehead which crinkled under the strain of awkward questioning and the acuteness of a very personal situation. He sat down at the table and put his hands together as though he were praying to the heavens for strength. He withdrew for a moment, steadied himself, and began.

“A few months afore yourself arrived”, he continued, “I came up here with the food parcels as I do the first Tuesday of every month. There was a touch of winter in the air, and the snow had laid its first coat of the season. Well, as I’m tarrying along, I can see at a distance something moving against the white slopes at the back of the cottage. At first I thought my eyes had finally failed me - I’m not a young man, and a life in the army does some strange things to an old mind.”

He smiled a sad smile of age as he remembered berating himself for the onslaught of a premature dementia.

“But as I tarried nearer, I knew it wasnae my wits which had broken. Maggie was clambering in the snow, in nowt bur her night things, her bare hands burrowing with a fierce desperation. I ran to help her thinking there must be something down there, something she’d lost like. And so I started digging. But she pushed me away. And that’s when I saw her look.”

Dougie shook his head as he remembered the manic expression, the frozen eyes, the face paralytic with fear.

“It was not our Maggie” he said quietly.

Isla understood exactly. It was the face which had stared back at her on that misplaced summer morning.

“What was she looking for?” whispered Isla.

Dougie didn‘t reply, but his face was suddenly tinged with a great sadness.

“Did she know you?” asked Isla.

“She thought I was her Billy”, replied Dougie shaking his head.

“Billy was her husband?”

“Aye”, said Dougie. “Passed away in the great storm of 1929 after they were married not a year. He went to sea and never returned. She had begged him not tae put out, but he was a man of principal, and needed to feed his family through winter. So he went, and the waters took him.”

“She called me Morag.”

“Billy’s sister” said Dougie. He paused. “Has she said owt of Angus?”

“No. Who’s Angus?”

“That was her bairn.”

“I didn’t think she had children”, asked Isla.

Dougie turned pale.

“The babe was lost just after Billy. Heartbreak took it, as it was told me. She had to bury the poor thing herself, next to her husband. You asked me what she was searching for that morning. Well it was the bairn. Kept calling out his name, saying that he was buried alive. Poor soul.”

Dougie was visibly shaken. The tragedy of Maggie’s life, alongside his own, weighed heavily on his shoulders.

“Does she know?” continued Isla.

“Know?”

“That she’s having these….”, Isla tried to think of a suitable term. “Episodes.”

“Episodes’, repeated Dougie approvingly. “No, I dinnae think so. She’s never said owt about it to me.”

“Should we tell her?” whispered Isla.

Dougie examined his clasped hands intently.

“As I sees it, bannocks are better than no kind of bread”, replied Dougie. “She’s hurting none but her own self. As long as that’s the truth of it, I cannae see an advantage to be gained in telling her.”

Dougie leant over to Isla.

“I’ll let you in to a wee secret lassie”, he said. “Take your happiness while you’re living fer you’re a long time dead.”

He leant back on his chair again, satisfied with such profound advice.

Maggie re-appeared by the door, in her hands a dilapidated old red wheelbarrow, and all weighty thoughts of conversation disappeared.

“There‘s nowt so trustworthy in this world as an old friend”, she announced, gazing fondly at her loyal barrow. Her memories of it were bound with those of Billy. They had toiled the earth together, willing the land into fertile submission, forcing it to bear fruition and feed an anticipated brood. Time and fate conspired in that regard, but still the vegetables grew big and bold each year, long after their cultivator had withered and died.

“What’s the wheelbarrow for?” asked Isla.

“Tae help fetching the jars up from the village of course”, replied Maggie.

“That old thing?” Isla exclaimed with horror. “All the way from the shop?”

“Dinnae be daft” laughed Maggie. “This old barrow couldnae make it all that way.”

Isla breathed a sigh of relief.

“Hamish fetches the jars fae the leap”, continued Maggie.

“Fer the village, there’s Constance”, interjected Dougie.

“Constance?”

Dougie pointed towards a rickety old bike holding up the gate to Rose Cottage. Constance, as though overwhelmed by the thought of her impossible task, lost her footing against the gate and crashed to the ground. The basket once attached to her front handlebars, dislodged itself and made a bid for freedom across the grass.

Isla was appalled at the thought of these two elderly adventurers toiling up and down the cliff pathway with a variety of makeshift transportation.

"But…you can't", she cried.

"Cannae is as cannae does."

"We could do with an extra set of hands", added Maggie optimistically.

Isla hung her head low. With the advancing dawn, the brightness of this bold, new life was blinding and its air invaded Isla's lungs like a poison. Isla felt her throat tighten and her vision narrow. Black spots grew organically in front of her eyes, impairing her vision where she knew objects should be. Voices spoke to her but their dullness moulded into one inconceivable drone. She closed her eyes and tried to focus on each and every breath, as though it might be her last and she ought to savour her final moment.

"I can't."

Isla retreated back into the safety of her chair and the warmth of her saving tea.

"There you go again", said Dougie as he prepared to brave the elements, 'cannae is not a word fer a young lassie like yourself to be using quite so prolifically."

And with that the two souls retrieved their companions in arms - Hamish by the door, Constance at the gate, and made their way steadily down the grass track to begin their clandestine task, treading carefully on the mildewed grass which sparkled underfoot like a starry blanket. Together they trod the worn pathway which led in the peacefulness of early morning, to the sleeping sea and beyond. The stillness of the air was breathtaking. The breeze arrested its habitual aggravation of the Auchobane cliffs, and the sky assumed a deep crimson hue, streaking across a tranquil horizon, in anticipation of another day.

Maggie gazed upon the skyline with distrust. The years and more particularly her own personal history had marked her with an inherent suspicion of a beautiful dawn. The day which had taken her husband had started in such a way, and a sense of foreboding grew in the pit of her stomach lest such a tragedy ever be repeated.

"Storm coming?" asked Dougie, seeing the anxiety in her face. Maggie said nothing.

Every year since Dougie had first fulfilled her order for Seville Oranges, Maggie Keiller had created a batch of marmalade. For all of those years the jars in which this magical liquid was stored were also provided for her by the resourcefulness of her army friend. The retired soldier may not have received the respect he deserved from the folk of Auchobane, but he had many friends amongst the cottage industries thriving in the Highlands. Comrades in arms never forget, and the close friendships Dougie had forged upon those French killing fields had dispersed themselves across the country and taken with them a multitude of talents and skills, some inherent, some acquired. Ruaridh McLeod was one such soldier. A small understated man with thick rimmed glasses, his shiny receding hairline and emaciated shoulders gave him an unfortunate weasel-like appearance, but lurking beneath was a man with a generous heart. The years following Ruaridh's war were filled with rehabilitation of contorted fingers which had taken the full impact of an imploding grenade on the soggy fields of Neuve Chapelle. This incident had effectively ended his pre-war career, for he was descended from a long line of traditional butchers in the Black Isles - and so Ruaridh was forced to apply his talents to an alternative trade which might suit his now depleted tendons. Glass blowing had not seemed like the most obvious choice for the small man of carnivorous descent, but he found himself thoroughly satisfied with his newly discovered art, not dissimilar to the satisfaction he had once gained from a finely dissected Sandy Back. So when Maggie had lamented to Dougie the lack of sufficiently sturdy jars in which to store her precious consignments, he had instantly thought of his resourceful old friend.

In the early years, Ruaridh would personally deliver the glass jars himself, driven the necessary miles in a small green van owned by his first-born, Stuart. Stuart was a strong lad, six feet high and not far off the same again in width, so the challenging journey on foot up the grass track to Rose Cottage proved little or no more inconvenient than the car journey along the winding coastal road to Auchobane. But fate took Stuart's strength from him at an early age by way of a premature stroke and Ruaridh found himself unable to make the expedition alone. A delivery driver was dispatched to Auchobane, but the additional trip to Rose Cottage was too challenging for a stranger. Clearly the movement of such a weight as a hundred jars was beyond Dougie's agility, but his mind being more active than his body, he was soon able to construct Constance for the trip. Acquiring a large basket from the storeroom of the shop, he fashioned extra support by way of braces once used to keep his army uniform in place when rations were not able to do so. Twenty jars were lost in sorties before the optimum number of jars was calculated to keep both man and Constance upright and progressing along the cliffs to Rose Cottage. Taking pity on the old soldier flushed of face and short of breath when he finally arrived at her door, Maggie had remembered Hamish from Billy's wistful days of self sufficiency, and she offered to shorten the burden on Constance, and additionally on Dougie, by meeting them both at the Leap.

This had been their arrangement for many years and always carried out before dawn. Originally the timing of this precious delivery had been a matter of logistics - the hour at which Ruaridh and Stuart arrived at Auchobane from their long journey down from the Black Isles, married with the obligation to stop and politely sample Dougie's home-made whiskies, had caused the sun to set and reconsider its reappearance over the Easterly horizon before the final leg of their journey was even begun. Following the misfortunes which befell the McLeods, the daytime delivery driver appeared at a reasonable hour with no intention of sampling an old man's domestic spirits, but Dougie decided to respect tradition and consume the whiskies himself, in memory of two fine men who could no longer stop to call. When Dougie had finished toasting company, friendship, the war, long lost acquaintances, family, the Queen, the General, and the fine woman of Rose Cottage who made outstanding marmalade, the sun was once again peering expectantly across the calm waters of the North Sea. And so a tradition was born, as they are wont to do, out of respect and the unpredictability of habit.

At four am Maggie and Dougie had begun their amble down the grass track towards the village, Maggie negotiating the slippery path with Hamish and Dougie proving less than agile with Constance. Isla watched them progress, separating at the Leap, whereupon Dougie continued his trek down to the village and Maggie sat herself down near the edge of the cliff and wrapped up tight against the elements, relinquishing herself to her thoughts and to sleep.

In the hours that followed, Isla drifted on a wave of slumber, surfacing occasionally from its heavy swell, but with faltering consciousness, disappearing inevitably back beneath its weighty persuasion. She saw, or imagined she saw, Maggie appear in the doorway of Rose Cottage, arms brimming full with chiming jars each one carefully wrapped to protect it from harm, then reappear what seemed like a second later, although it must have been many more, arms burdened with yet another consignment. Isla's eyes weighed heavily the entire time, only lifting momentarily at the sound of clinking glass. As the sun grew in strength and brightness, Isla finally awoke from the oppressive sleep which had overwhelmed those busy hours.

The sight which confronted her was mesmerising. Throughout the entirety of the small kitchen was amassed an amplitude of shiny jars, each glistening and reflecting the bright sunshine, creating a clear brilliance extraordinary in power and strength. For the first time Isla beheld each and every white washed brick of Rose Cottage in all its lustre and noticed every shade and hew of the old oak floorboards which blazed with warmth. It was as though the cottage itself had awoken from a long sleep.

In the middle of this heavenly glow sat Dougie, slumped restfully in one of the chairs, flushed with the exertion of the morning's exercise. Despite the obvious exhaustion of an old man feeling the sudden burden of age, he still radiated with a contentment reserved for those who have experienced a moment of pure joy. It was the thrill of concealment which kept those seventy year old bones moving up and down that grass track hour after hour, in the midst of an early dawn when unsuspecting villagers slept soundly in their beds below. For those few hours, Dougie shook off the mantle of maturity and bathed deeply in the lifeblood of his younger self.

“Rise and shine lassie - a new morn’s begun!” Dougie announced, his red face flushed and energised.

“Is it over?” Isla replied with rather less enthusiasm, sleep dripping from her voice.

“Aye”, Dougie beamed, “new jars delivered, safe an’ sound.”

He patted a nearby jar with a gentle hand, from one journeyman to another.

Isla felt immersed in guilt. She had separated herself from their intimate happy group and gained little but disturbed sleep and the embarrassment of her lonely position. She had begun to absorb herself entirely in her isolation to such an extent that she now struggled to venture further than Rose Cottage‘s door. On those days when courage presented itself and she felt inclined to boldness, she found reason to be dissuaded by the cold sea air, or the rain soaked spray which rose up from its belly. The gate to Rose Cottage - and the world which lay beyond it - paralysed her with fear. Its questioning eyes, its biting tongue, were too imposing a reality to cope with under the burden of impending motherhood and the changeability of Maggie’s mind. Those were the excuses she clung to, which allowed her to hide within the thick white walls of Rose Cottage.

"How's that new laddie o' yours?" asked Maggie, as Dougie immersed himself in a slab of soda bread and the exclusivity of a jar of 1948 marmalade. A sizeable chunk, more condiment than bread disappeared into the mouth of a man who valued nourishment more than air.

"No idea", mumbled Dougie quickly, careful not to lose any of his delectable mouthful in the process. "I've not seen sight nor sound of him this past week."

"Not a word?" asked Maggie.

"Not a syllable", replied Dougie, "Strange business. But I cannae tell the good fae the bad these days."

"I think our Isla may have put the fear into him", said Maggie.

"Oh aye?" asked Dougie, always keen for a smidgen or two of gossip.

"Your laddie sauntered up here asking after a dance", continued Maggie, "but Isla set him straight."

"Spooked him did she?" smiled Dougie.

"Reckon so", replied Maggie.

Dougie laughed heartily, his stomach shaking with delight.

"Aye, he's awfully big behind his own door!" laughed Dougie, "I'll see him right. To be honest, I thought that his grandmother might have been behind it, but maybe no."

"His grandmother?"

“Did I no mention he’s a McLintock?” continued Dougie, as he cleared his throat trying to make his airways more efficient, coughing vigorously forcing his lungs to comply.

“Ye didnae”, replied Maggie, her arms folding out of habit at the mention of that name.

“Must…have…slipped my mind”, said Dougie, catching each breath as though it were trying to escape from his body without infiltrating his lungs.

Maggie’s eyes were alerted to Dougie’s sudden discomfort, constantly aware as she was, of the potential for devastation in a bright day.

“Are you well Dougie?” said Maggie, placing a comforting hand on his trembling shoulder.

“It’s nowt”, replied Dougie with an effortful countenance, “Just the… excitement of the day.”

He grasped forcefully for breath between each word, willing his lungs into operation, a pained expression belittling his optimistic face.

“I’m not as young as I used tae be, that’s fer sure”, he grimaced through the agony unfolding inside his aching chest.

Maggie’s concern was palpable.

“Fetch some water”, Maggie directed Isla with urgency and, taking Dougie’s hand, squeezed it imploringly, urging her friend to recover. He understood her anxiety and tried his best to resurrect bravery, but the pain growing deep and violent within the cave of his chest exposed something more sinister at work.

Tears welled in Maggie's eyes at the futility of their situation, as Dougie's breathing continued to labour. There was no time to fetch a doctor; it would be too late when he arrived. An ambulance would never make it up the narrow pathway to Rose Cottage, and the hospital was too far to even consider the journey. She knew her friend; she knew that if these were to be his last minutes, then they would not be ruined by wires and tubes, filled with fleeting consciousness and a myriad of strangers, incapacity and confusion. No, if it was his time, he would have it here, amongst friends, amongst familiarity and comfort, and as close as he could be to home.

Of course Maggie said nothing of her suspicions to Isla. The young girl had insufficient experience of death to recognise its appearance.

"The doctor", said Maggie as Isla placed a glass of water on the table in front of the dying man.

"But..."

"But no", said Maggie firmly. "Fetch him now."

Maggie's voice was calm but fierce. She recognised Isla's disinclination, but refused to allow these final precious moments to be wasted in debate. When death invaded, brevity was imperative.

She turned back to Dougie's face, furious that she had allowed herself to look away for even a second. His cheeks were tinged a deep crimson as he struggled to breathe, letting out a gasp, forcing into his lungs air which struggled to deliver in this final great battle of his enduring life.

"Go!" repeated Maggie to Isla, without deigning to turn her face away this time from her precious friend.

Isla read Maggie's tone. Taking the old cardigan from its hook on the kitchen door, she wrapped it tight around her young bones for protection against a world which would savage her. Quietly she opened the old, effacing door of Rose Cottage and confronted her fear.

She took a deep breath. And then she ran; too quickly for fear, too quickly for questions. She raced along the grass track as though it were the first time she had unleashed her newborn legs onto an unsuspecting world. They relished the task, unhindered by bumps or tufts of grass that threatened to arrest their urgency. She raced too fast for them, reaching the cobbled streets of Auchobane in what seemed like seconds, she stormed through its streets like a Kansas tornado, veering wildly, and sparing no-one. Past the rectory where Mrs. McLintock judged her flock; past the Church where James scrubbed the candle wax from the sanctified floor, part of his exacting penance; past the grocery store where Dougie had fulfilled his very last delivery, and finding the old doctor's house, she finally stopped for breath much to the relief of the unborn child which had taken the journey inside her.

Meanwhile, in the deathly hollows of Rose Cottage at the sacred table around which two old friends sat holding their goodbyes, Maggie's grip intensified, grasping the familiar hand which was slowly slipping from her forever. She willed it to stay, but knew he had to go. It was his time. She had come to accept that she could not change fate, it would come and he would go. But she could help, in her own small way.

Maggie picked up a small spoon which lay next to Dougie's tea, half drunk and growing cold. Maggie gently dipped the spoon into the 1948 marmalade - a breakfast fit for a king, a reward for the many years of friendship. Retrieving it slowly, so as to not disturb the flecks which flashed within the heaped portion, she held the spoon aloft, and dipped her finger into the sweet syrupy texture. The finger she then placed upon those lips from which the life was draining steadily, those eyes screaming for the pain to end, and behind them fear for what lay beyond.

She rubbed the beautiful marmalade gently on his lifeless lips, and around the inside of his mouth, hoping to stimulate for one last time the tongue that would taste no more - a fond farewell, a thank you for all that went before. In those eyes, between the fear and trepidation, she saw, or at least, she hoped she saw, a gratitude for this little saving grace, and as his head slowly bent forward, the air extinguishing from his chivalrous frame, she gently caressed and cushioned it from the hardness of the wooden table, stroking the few thin, grey hairs of a man who had once fought in a war.

It was some time before the doctor came. The hours, if they were hours, passed quickly. Dougie had left not long after Isla did, and Maggie felt his body grow gradually colder, life relinquished forever. His spirit lingered for a time, amongst those empty jars stacked high in anticipation of their fulfilment. Perhaps he lamented a vintage not of his time, a marmalade he would never taste, or perhaps he stayed to say goodbye, to a place full of fond remembrances, and comfortable conversations. And then Maggie felt the chill as he crossed to his long lost comrades in the field, and to Morag, Billy and Angus before him. She longed to join their intimate party, but was comforted in the knowledge that it would now not be long.

Isla entered the room quietly, followed some time later by the old doctor who had struggled greatly up the grass pathway to Rose Cottage. Isla would have carried him if she could, but he would not be rushed. When they finally came into view of the cottage, Isla had rushed ahead, where, standing in the doorway, she found the little room encased in silent reflection, two old souls bent together on the table, one no longer of this world.

With the setting sun, the pallbearers took Dougie's body back to Auchobane with far less ceremony than it was due. There were no military honours for this old soldier, just the quiet salute of friends. Constance stood where he had left her by the gate, the only guard of honour as he passed through the garden of Rose Cottage for the very last time. And down the grass track with a nod to the sea which had been his companion on each of his deliveries laden with provisions.

Maggie walked behind the plain, wooden coffin, betraying no mark of the man contained within, until the Leap where it continued on its journey without her, to the village where few would welcome it home. She stood for a while watching its progress along the track to the embrace of the houses which stood on the edge of the village, until it was swallowed up entirely by the red sandstone and flint and she could see it - him - no more.

Isla saw her return back along the pathway, taking each and every step slowly, with thoughtful consideration, her arms wrapped close against the autumnal weather, so close they pressed against her frame and she had to fight their intimacy for breath. The winds riled her - toying with her hair, trying to shake the woman, but she refused to be moved, only stopping for a moment by Constance, remembering the man who had stood there before dawn.

She did not linger long; she would not allow herself the indulgence. She returned to the home where she had lost a friend. Isla stood by the door aimlessly, ignorant of what to say to lift her spirits. With youth she had also an innocence of death, having yet to experience the loss of a loved one, or the passing of a friend. Isla's loneliness was self-inflicted, self-gratifying, and more importantly, one which was unlikely to be permanent.

"Well, that's that", declared Maggie as she entered the cottage and closed the door.

Isla looked with pity on a woman trying to bear it all but found nothing to say of merit or comfort.

"He went with his dignity, not like my Billy."

Maggie stopped and thought the remainder of her words rather than spoke them.

"Billy was your husband?"

"He was", said Maggie, "but the sea took him, many a year ago."

Her tea stewed in the large, steaming mug on the table where she had lost her friend.

"You miss him?" continued Isla, curious to get to the heart of the man, and the woman who loved him.

"The same as I did the day he was taken", replied Maggie, her eyes gazing out towards the deep black ocean which had destroyed him.

Maggie took a sip of her tepid tea. She had begun to feel the exhaustion of her early dawn excursion, and married with the day's events, it drew a surreal veil over her thoughts and feelings.

She rose from her seat and Isla watched her seeking out relief in her routine. She saw the beginnings of grief in those eyes which brushed a surface or wiped down a table.

Maggie felt devastation at Dougie's departure. His passing seemed to amplify each and every one of her previous agonizing goodbyes, as loved ones left her, one by one. Rose Cottage would be a sadder place for his leaving, just as it had been with Morag and Billy before him. Maggie recognised that she had become a broken version of herself and considered that her greatest loss may not have been her husband, but her own self. In the days that followed her first bereavement, she had tried in vain to busy herself, first with the tedious, then with the marmalade. With Dougie's passing now, she lost again her enthusiasm for life and wandered aimlessly searching for meaning. She retreated further from life, and more importantly, from the preparation of her newest batch of conserve. Isla awoke the next day to find all the beautiful new jars removed from the kitchen to the outbuilding where they would remain, destined never to fulfil their marmalade duty.

Step 13: Extricate the Pectin from the Muslin Bag

For many weeks Maggie's introspection continued and Rose Cottage was a more subdued place for it. An occasional word was said, an irrelevant comment made upon the weather. The moroseness cast upon them by the death of their friend resonated in the glum clouds which trundled overhead. Maggie played out her grief privately, remembering each of the years which Dougie had spent at her kitchen table, recalling the good and bad, and on the whole, simply missing him.

Her lengthy silences also influenced Isla's mood. It was almost eight months since her youthful infatuation had taken her innocence. With her tousle-haired boy she had momentarily soared to new heights then plummeted to such depths that she felt she had pierce the earth and arrived in a kind of hell. Yet here she was, alive and in a perfectly acceptable kind of torment.

She remembered clearly how she had watched him from her window for weeks, distracted by his appearance. She had tracked every movement of his teenage angst. She had watched him rebel against the limitations of adulthood and rile against authority, disdainful of the rain which clung to his dishevelled hair, and Isla's insulated glass. As they stood under the same dark sky, conjoined by those rain droplets which encased them both, she had felt a connection to this rebel with a disturbed soul.

He caught her gaze and she was instantly penetrated by those deep blue eyes. Her heart danced with the thrill of discovery, he had unlocked an intangible passion, a fire longing to be ignited beneath the dullness of her comfortable life. It was a fleeting glance, but she felt they had finally connected and she relished in the joy of their commonness.

She was a young schoolgirl stirred by a thrilling future she had invented and grown frustrated for. She saw the path unfold before her, paved with hourly excitements. No longer would she be subjugated by a hateful mother, with her suffocating social aspirations and idealistic ambition for her daughter.

"What you looking at?" The loudness of his voice, at such an intimate distance made her jump. His curtness, his jarring tone and unfamiliar accent shocked her, jolting her back from her desperate dreams. This was not the extraordinary encounter she had dreamt of through every claustrophobic classroom minute, nor the profound language she had bestowed upon him. Gone were the romantic words and his absolute understanding of the intimate pain of her daily life. This was not the poet and philosopher she had designed him to be. Isla blushed.

“I seen you”, he continued. “Watching me from the window.”

Isla’s cheeks flushed a shade deeper. It was impossible to explain the whimsical feelings she had divined for a boy who looked just like him, but with a tone and soul a thousand times better.

The dreary raindrops trickled down his leather jacket, forming rivets and inlands; it was a curious landscape. He was growing bored with this quiet little schoolgirl, and let his lost blue eyes wander from Isla, to the cigarette he struck into life with casual care.

“Don’t say much, do you?”

Inside Isla roared with eloquence. She breathed in his confident exterior - the cigarette, the detachment. The banality of her own nature irritated then frustrated, as she heard her pathetic words outside herself, then detested herself still further for having uttered them. Sleep had been her salvation. When she slept, it was impossible to think, and although the dreams were sometimes dark, they were involuntary, dictating rather than discussing. The unconscious state was a welcome placation, it soothed her soul. She relished the darkness, longed for it, urged the setting of the sun, and willed the moon to follow. But with the tousle-haired boy, she would have no need for darkness, no need to dream of a better Isla - because she had arrived; and the adrenalin of expectation at her imminent self-revelation raced quicker than any of the droplets streaming down the boy’s cavalier chest.

He saw the eagerness in her eyes. It represented opportunity.

“Let’s go somewhere.”

In the painful moments which followed Isla grew a lifetime. They were brutal minutes in which she became a woman. He seized her hand and she dared not look into those cold eyes, lest her unsteady courage would fail and her innocence would be found out. Instead Isla allowed that strange sensation of skin on skin to stifle any rational thought which dared to rise. He said nothing, perhaps he knew that words would break the spell he had cast upon this little girl.

His breath was nauseating. He held her tight out of necessity rather than desire. The labouring continued for what seemed to Isla a brief kind of eternity. Thoughts were strangely absent; until eventually his grip loosened, the elusive climax attained and his chore complete. He withdrew from her, his brief headiness forgotten, her value at an end and he lit another cigarette. It was over, their physical connection broken, and with it Isla.

After such a significant event, she had returned home to a child's bedroom, filled with childhood things. Everything was unfamiliar, every memorable toy and trinket, different suddenly. She had yearned for the onset of adulthood, and here it was in volumes. She buried her head into one of the perfectly pink cushions which adorned her bed, screaming her loss into its superficial reaches, crying from the depths of her heart at the passing of her virginity, and the manner of its bereavement.

The confusion which filled those first few days of new-found womanhood was intense. She felt compelled to be reunited with this stranger, to find meaning behind the amputation of her innocence, something which explained her easy compliance to such a deflowering. It was this driving notion which overtook her, which saw her rush from window to window at the appearance of any stranger passing on the street below. But he had disappeared. In his absence, she read upon him the words she longed to hear, gave him action where there was none. Hour after hour, day after day, she stalked the streets, veering from her mission only to fulfil the obligation of routine.

It was two weeks before her anxious frame felt the rush of alleviation. There he stood, a solitary boot resting awkwardly against the cladding of the wall, the cigarette drooping ambitiously from his mouth and his hair rustling in the wind which rushed down the alleyway he inhabited.

She stopped, surprised by the abruptness of his presence. Every day she had passed that same spot, indistinguishable from others which occupied a tiny modicum of this uninspiring world. That today it should reveal her heart's desire, that it should be chosen for such an enormity, rendered her speechless.

The tousle-haired boy glanced at her with apathy.

"What?"

"Nothing", replied Isla, finding her voice, but not her emotion.

"Good."

His voice was confrontational, daring her to challenge his indifference. But she had neither courage nor desire to react to his threat.

"Because you're second hand now."

He smiled derisively, sneering from the corner of his mouth. It made his face appear ugly and Isla could see his teeth, black and chipped, stabbing through his devious, broad mouth.

"You're used."

He walked up close to her now, menacingly, with a swagger. Isla felt instantly small. Her eyes lowered, laden with tears.

"You didn't think I liked you..." he whispered quietly in her ear, his breath dripping with the bitter taste of alcohol.

He resounded with a large, cutting laugh which echoed loudly in Isla's ear. The vanquisher admonishing his victim, raping and pillaging her mind as he had done her body. Isla shook with a wretchedness and self-loathing as she absorbed his words. Her heart was broke.

Perhaps it was fear of her mother's paralysing judgement or the chronic days of fatigue and nausea brought on by the seismic events unfolding in her uterus, but Isla successfully avoided the reality of her impending confinement. Ironically it was on that final morning in London that Isla had finally gathered enough courage to confront her mother with the truth of her situation. Her blossoming figure had begun to necessitate such action and an impasse had been reached which forced action in her. She allowed herself to entertain the fantasy that her mother might delight in her new maternal role. Her mother was deeply ensconced in her middling years, framed on either side by the trough of youth and maturity. She had lingered for a lengthy time at her manipulative, middle-aged summit, clinging to its sharp edges with her manicured nails but a newly acquired title of grandmother might encourage the retirement of her mantle and the adoption of a new, quieter life.

It was with such vain hopes that Isla had descended the stairs to breakfast that morning, easing herself into one of the colourful chairs which guarded the large kitchen table of their townhouse. Opposite her sat the familiar face of her mother, instinctively judging her youthful face, and with each belittling look, Isla's optimism sank.

"We're going on a trip", began her mother, her words floating over condiments at the breakfast table.

"For how long?" Isla asked, protectively clutching her stomach where an innocent child lay.

No answer was forthcoming. Isla had lived her life in darkness, without responsibility, without self-determination. It was only when she made her way to Rose Cottage that she had the opportunity to set her own course. Isla remembered the coldness of her mother's stare. She was strangely calm and composed that particular morning, safe in the knowledge that she would soon be purged of an inadequate daughter. Soon society would forget that a child had ever dared to taint the crisp, clean life which Kirsty Keiller wore so well. Her falseness was repugnant to Isla, whose eyes remained firmly fixed on the blandness of her morning tea.

"Fine", mumbled Isla between the carefully timed bites of toast. "Don't tell me."

And so the closing words were spoken, the final exchange made, before her mother dealt her most comprehensive blow. It was a long and easy journey into the wilderness of Scotland and the arms of a strange new relative. Was is punishment or a lucky escape? Isla mulled it over as she watched the sun disappear over Auchobane's pink cliffs.

She placed her hand on the door handle to Maggie's bedroom. It was Maggie's sanctuary and out of respect for her privacy Isla had refrained from crossing the exclusivity of its threshold. She did so now, hoping to find a placated Maggie safe within the confines of her sleep. But an uncomfortable voice inside her doubted it was so.

Maggie's bedroom was small, in keeping with the general style of Rose Cottage. It was dominated by a large, absorbing bed, enveloped by a hand-made floral quilt. A small window allowed in a modicum of fresh air, enough to disturb the powdered smells and musty scents of a well-worn space. In general the room was stoically neat, each trinket in its place, undisturbed. On the face of the bed lay the only indication of discord. Where Isla had hoped to find her piece of mind, she found instead an austere tin box and its contents scattered amongst the sentimental bedcovers. They represented sixty years of memories, all poignant and affecting to the individual tied irrevocably to them. A love letter, a wedding band, a collection of old photographs which told the story of a life. Isla picked up a black-and-white photograph and examined the welcoming eyes of the young man who studied her in turn. This was the intangible Billy, who still preyed heavily upon Maggie's uneven mind. When she thought she was alone, Isla would see Maggie smile at an empty corner, or speak to an empty chair. She knew it was Billy that she talked to, or imagined there. But she said nothing; she let the old woman have her dreams. Isla returned Billy's photograph gently to the bed, respectful of the man for whom adoration was an absolute, humbled by a union which transcended generations.

A second print now fell from behind the first. It was the image of a young girl, with faded face and loyal curls, all wrapped in a pristine, prim white dress. Smiling dutifully for this new, modern contraption, mystified by its ability, fearful of its potential, her teeth were boldly crooked and her freckles unfashionable, but her features were pleasing and the general appearance was one of simple, natural beauty. There was something familiar too, as Isla gazed into those encouraged eyes, as though she had stared into them a million times before. Turning over the photograph, she found her answer - written in simple ink were the words 'Kirsty Keiller, spring 1946'. Her mother the child was a paradoxical image. Isla had only ever known the vacuous grown-up, the adult whose cutting comments and actions haunted and shaped her dreams. Isla was loath to contemplate her mother in this childhood form. It was to admit the possibility that good lay deep within that cold exterior. The adult representation of her mother was a far more palatable enemy to revile, so Isla buried her mother's photograph beneath some less notable artefacts adorning the bedclothes.

The voice of disquiet was rising once again within her at Maggie's absence. Leaving the inner sanctum of Maggie's bedroom, Isla rediscovered an unlatched cottage door, fearful that she would find again a trance-like Maggie by the gate searching eastward for her lost love. But to her relief, the gate was unoccupied and no wistful Maggie clung to its bolt.

Isla ventured into the small but perfectly formed garden which encircled the cottage. Daylight was declining and the long autumn evenings were drawing to their inevitable close. The slopes behind Rose Cottage were becoming engulfed by the murky shadows of dusk, into which they would soon ebb entirely. During her many months at the cottage, Isla had never walked amongst the maze of shrubs and climbing roses which formed the bulk of the garden's belly, but today she crossed its small, worn pathway with purpose, examining every corner and bed, desperate to discover Maggie. But as each hidden enclave was revealed, she found none but the most delicate of blooms, exalting unseen, trumpeting untended.

Having uncovered every secret of Rose Cottage and its scented surrounds, Isla found herself full circle, standing by the old, red wooden door through which she had first passed what seemed like a lifetime ago. Isla felt overwhelmed by her loneliness, standing helpless in her isolation. She found no solace in the stirring landscape nor in the fresh wind which blew in from the sea, dripping with the residue of its salty air. Its dramatic vista held no heartbeat, its dynamic seemed irrelevant. As she stood upon that deserted cliff top, she realised that this must have been Maggie's life. She must have stood small and insignificant against the magnificent backdrop of the infinite North Sea. There were none to hold her close, none to whisper words of consolation, none to displace the dark clouds which gathered.

The longer she lingered incapacitated, transfixed in the vacant confines of Rose Cottage, the more desperate the situation was becoming. The horizon was dimming rapidly, the sea resounding with an ever fortifying strength and the shadows were growing longer against the cold, wild grass. Soon she - and Maggie - would be engulfed by the absolute darkness of a Scottish night, and all would be lost for the many desolate hours of obscurity. She scoured the depths of the eastern horizon for some sign of life, just as an agitated Maggie had done so intently only weeks before.

For the first time she noticed a piece of paper fluttering amongst the roses. The wind ravaged at its easy corners, pressing it hard against the thorny bushes. She carefully removed the note from its pinned position and read it through twice - first for information, second in astonishment and disbelief. Scrawled in a thick, dark hand it read 'Down in the caves waiting on ye Maggie' and it was signed '- your husband, Billy'.

Isla's eyes darted in the direction of the harbour and she ran as close as she dared to the edge of the cliffs. Her eyes, softened by a horizon, blurred the lines between wistful imagination and its blunter relation. What she saw, or what she thought she saw, was the faintest movement, a fleeting dancing amongst the rankness of the rocks. She looked intently at this faint anomaly of shade against a backdrop of saturated blackness. It was exactly what she had feared all along - Maggie in all her distraction, casually treading amongst the sharp sea pools. Each jagged rock anticipating its opportunity to consequent a fall, against innocence and the bewilderment of lost love. Isla's heart plummeted.

Step 14: Discard the Remaining Pips

That slippery grass track, over which Isla had once soared with speed in search of a doctor for Dougie, now seemed the most impossible of paths. Before she had negotiated the protruding boulders quickly, now in dusk and with eight months of pregnancy she found her passage frustratingly slow. Growing angry at the impediment of light, she scraped bone against stone, groping for a balance which was repeatedly elusive. She stumbled awkwardly, lashing out at the wind which arrested her desperate motion, it too an obstacle to her speed. She made the Leap after what seemed like an eternity. The dark shadows which lined the route seemed bemused at the urgency of her mission, an apathetic audience. Isla gave them little notice as she forced the fear from her heart and buried it deep in the queasy confines of her stomach.

Eventually, the sparse pockets of lights which marked out Auchobane finally appeared close enough to touch. It was a breathless Isla who found relief on the hard pavement of this unfamiliar world but she continued, without direction or reason. The streets once occupied with villagers during daylight hours, were now bereft of any signs of life. Her pursuit of support, some greater strength to save Maggie, had engrossed her so completely that she had forgot that she had not an idea of where to find such assistance. It was this sudden realisation which eventually forced her to come to a stop.

She looked around at the small plain houses which in return studied her suspiciously, their rectangular windows framed by thick set curtains designed to support an inwardly directed life and resist a dangerous, intrusive world. Arranged in a fixed line down either side of the street, the houses clung together defensively to form a barrier against the onslaught of a sceptical Sixties modernity. Clad in their bulky sandstone, they stood to attention, uniform and lacking in the kind of character and warmth so abundant at Rose Cottage. In the early darkness Isla inferred from their coldness an inherent distrust for strangers.

As she felt her hopes wane, the distant strains of a Celtic lilt wafted down the desolate street in which she stood, turning her lamenting spirit. It was foreign kind of melody, a basic composition telling tales of generations. She followed the pipes and fiddles to a garishly bright Church Hall. It was an ominous, grey building whose heart and soul had been acquired for the evening by the residents of Auchobane. Peering inside its daunting doors, she watched the dancing hoards making their way around the sparsely decorated four walls, parading up and down reverberating wooden floorboards, many having consumed more than their share of the home-brew supplied.

Isla stood just outside the entrance to the hall, her bright curls hugging her forehead with the exertion of exercise, her clothes wet from the spray of the sea air. She watched the energetic young souls continuing their abandonment beneath the cheap lighting, beaming smiles and weathered faces. She watched them easily twirl with inhibition and wished for a flicker of their uncomplicated lives.

Inside the hall James languished in the shadows, watching the progress of his peers with circumspect derision. The more he had dwelt upon it, the more he had taken the refusal of the English girl to heart. The futility of his rebellion had struck him, as upon his return to the Rectory his grandmother had begun to trail his every movement with renewed vigour. He was not permitted to laugh, to smile and on occasion, to breathe.

He felt suffocated by her scrutiny and had grown increasingly reflective and despondent. The opportunities provided him by the Leap seemed ever more lucid and enticing. He felt he would linger longer there next time, and give its argument ample reflection.

“Harlots, the lot of them”, snapped Mrs. McLintock, her body contorted with disgust.

Normally the self-appointed despot of Auchobane would not have condescended to attend such a frivolous event as a local dance, but feeling her flock and more importantly, her influence over them, to be threatened of late, she had made an exception in the name of their salvation. Truthfully, her grandson's indolence had unnerved her more than she cared to admit to those who offered their respectful pleasantries on that dark autumnal evening. But Mrs. McLintock was a resourceful lady and following the rebellious turning of her grandson, she had taken steps to ensure that the recent admission of Mrs. Keiller's marmalade into the Rectory would be the last. She sensed a portentous evening ahead, one which would finally see an end to Maggie Keiller and she smiled inwardly in anticipation of the heathen woman's demise after so many absent years of recompense. She felt supremely justified in the actions she had taken to effectuate this downfall, believing that her deeds had been and would continue to be, endorsed by the Lord himself.

The irony of his grandmother's unexpected appearance at the very dance where he had hoped to present a Keiller on his arm, was not lost on James. How he would have turned her daily palpitations into something more sinister, if only the girl had acquiesced to his plan. But destiny had spurned him once again, just as the girl had, and his mother before her, and his self-pity now gouged a little deeper into his soft, outer layer.

James disregarded his grandmother's snide remark, in much the same way as he had disregarded the patronizing lecture into which she had launched after his return to the Rectory on that day of rejection by the English girl. Her homily was necessarily strewn with fervent biblical citations and inexorably ended with his eternal damnation in the excruciating depths of hell. James felt that this latter excursion could not be any more daunting than his current one. His infliction was not of a physical kind, but rather manifested itself in a perpetual circle of introspection and self-disparagement. It was a downward spiral of critical examination which spun to a vortex of despair. His rejection by the girl – by that pretty face and those appealing eyes - was simply another rung on the ladder of his melancholy, its height protruding ambitiously by the day.

It was with this gloomy disposition that James stood and watched the other villagers find their happiness on a Saturday night in September. The hall was hot despite nature's early warnings of a hard winter, and the few windows which deflected the grey blandness of the authoritarian stone, had this mark of happy humidity stained on their glass. He gazed with envy on their easy pleasures, uncomplicated and unconstrained. No darkness moved through the compartments of their hearts, no wounds had ever been inflicted on them by an absent parent.

His thoughts were always of his mother, her face passed involuntarily through each and every memory he had acquired since her departure; as though by her association, she would know him instantly despite the missing years, when their eventual reconciliation came.

Just as his heart sighed, the door of the Church hall burst open, and an alarmed Isla stood frantic within its frame. Her eyes were frenzied, her hair dishevelled, her entire appearance screamed with a distraught air. Moreover to all but James, she was a complete stranger.

"Please! Help!" she cried, her voice ringing out in stark contrast to the frivolous atmosphere which enveloped the room.

The music stopped at this dramatic interjection and the room at once assumed a foreboding silence. Blank faces turned to stare at this interloper, this outsider who had imposed herself on their jovial mood and looked to spoil their merry evening. Their gaze was followed by the obligatory hum of conjecture, as neighbours dissected this unwelcome outburst and vilified its wild, discourteous owner.

Exposed, Isla stood naked before them in all her neediness, petitioning their good Christian values for decency and humanity. She had plummeted to the same depths of humility as the day of her rejection by the tousle-haired boy, standing before the townsfolk as she had before him, relinquishing all pride.

"It's Maggie Keiller. She's lost down on the rocks."

"We dinnae know of any such person here and we dinnae take tae strangers bursting into our hall of God and disturbing our worship" shouted Mrs. McLintock, her voice piercing through any expectation of help. “Take yourself off and leave these good people to their business.”

The hall resounded in agreement with the old matriarch.

Isla stood fixed in the doorway in the company of despair, the blackness of her fading expectations behind her, bewildered by their prejudices, exposed to their fearfulness and the easy repudiation of all her hope.

“Maggie Keiller”, continued Isla, her voice beginning to tremble. “From the cottage up on the cliff. Rose Cottage.”

If Mrs. McLintock was surprised by Isla’s persistence, she hid it well from her parishioners whose curiosity was increasing along with their whispering.

“That woman is no friend of the God fearing folk of Auchobane”, replied Mrs. McLintock. “And neither are you.”

Sounds of approval rose at her words.

“But she’ll die….” Isla shook with despair, the cold and fear.

James simmered in the shadow of his grandmother, frustrated at the influence she held over her flock. They congregated against the fear of a new world order and its foreign morality, imbuing his grandmother with the power she craved. Here was the full manifestation of their distasteful prejudice, directed towards a young girl who came to them for help and who was rebuffed for no other reason than that she was a stranger.

"Call yourselves a Christian people?", he exclaimed, lifting Isla's despair. "Shame on you."

He walked with a purpose up to the Isla.

"I'll help."

"You'll do nae such thing", interrupted the shrill voice of Mrs. McLintock.

"If ye want tae stop me, it'll take more than spiteful words", James replied.

The old woman's eyes narrowed with hatred for this man who happened to be kin.

"'Tis no matter. The Keiller woman's as good as dead now", she sneered.

Not a soul moved.

"There was a note", said Isla handing him the piece of paper gathered by the clambering roses.

As James read it, his heart raced with fury, beating ferociously within his chest at the recognition of the penman's poisoned hand.

His grandmother stood proud and tall, her frame lifting with delight as he approached.

"Did you write this?" challenged James, throwing the note at his grandmother's feet.

The corners of Mrs. McLintock mouth curled with satisfaction.

"What if I did?" she boasted. "The sooner that Keiller woman joins her husband in his watery grave, the better it'll be fer everyone."

She looked round the room in expectation of approval from similarly minded Church folk but they looked at her with a pity she had not anticipated.

"You've sent an old woman tae her death on the rocks", James continued. "Awfully proud your God will be in the taking of a helpless life."

"If our Lord reckons she's worth owt, then he'll save her fae the sea", replied Mrs. McLintock. "If no, then she'll be no worse off dead than she is alive."

"You best start your praying that He's on her side", said James, taking Isla by the hand and pulling her away from the prying eyes of Auchobane's residents.

In the newness of the cool night air, Isla looked at James with a simple gratitude, feeling a little bit less alone. The path to the harbour was a steep and precarious one. Steps had been carved into the cliffs to accentuate a natural lie, but with the heavy boots of generations of fishermen the sturdiness of the steps had gradually worn down into an unsupportive slope. The path's surface was still coated with the remnants of a high tide, and it struggled to shake off the damp sheen in the cold autumnal air. Isla felt her footing fail several times during their descent, scraping her fingers off the pebble dashed walls, desperate to maintain her balance.

They happened upon the harbour quite suddenly. James surveyed the dim outlines of the boats as they sloshed in the ample wash. Beyond the harbour wall however, the wind was stirring to a storm which would soon prove too much for any man.

"Tide's full in", said James, noting the spray of the waves against the height of rocks which sprouted organically on either side of the harbour.

"She'll have made the caves by now", he continued, seeing fear in the young girl's eyes. His optimism was feigned, it was an empty hope and he knew it. What chance had a sixty year old woman against the power of an ocean?

"'Tis some luck that it's the new moon", he added, continuing with his improbable theory that all was not lost until determined so. "The neap tide is the only time the caves dinnae flood."

James began to clamber over the rotten wood and frayed rope which formed the graveyard of the quayside, reluctant to rest in the face of this watery foe, lest his fearfulness should take root. He struck out towards the harbour wall. Several times his footing failed as in the dark shadows as he missed where bow broke and stern began, but with his breath shortening, eventually he could make out the slippery surface of the outer edge of the wall.

Given her physical incapacity at eight months pregnant, Isla followed tardily. Should she fail to recover Maggie, abandoning herself and her unborn child to a similar fate might not be the worst course of action.

"Go back", James urged on finding his heroic actions matched by those of this young girl.

"No", Isla replied defiantly, fearful of remaining safe when all those around her danced with their demise. She would not wait by the water's edge for the resurgence of a day which proved to be lonelier than the one which went before. What joy could be found in selfish security while others perished courageously?

“This is no place fer a girl in your condition”, he shouted again.

But his words fell on stubborn ears. Isla paused momentarily to appease him but as he turned away to continue on his journey, she resumed, fuelled by abhorrence for the restrictions of her ’condition.’

James grasped onto the green algae which had made its home on the harbour wall and peered over the safety of its edge at the abandoned fury being unleashed beyond. The fortification afforded by the wall was a sound containment of a sea which raged like a flooded battlefield across which he now considered his route.

Auchobane’s caves were protected by an efficient layer of rock; their entrance was secreted deep within its folds, hidden from the naked eye. James looked upon the endless field of serrated stone, watching the pattern of the waves which thrashed upon their sharp surfaces. With every rousing gust the rolling train of the ocean ploughed towards the caves, each soaring wave giving way to the next, until they all crashed down remorselessly upon the shiny surface of the well worn cliffs. His journey would be fraught, but with little to lose but his own way, James carefully removed his shoes to take advantage of his feet’s natural grip.

Isla meanwhile sat clinging to the mast of a small, wayward boat in the harbour, watching as James, betraying little of the fearfulness she was certain he was feeling, climbed the sheltered face of the harbour wall, and was instantly exposed to the tempestuousness of the outer storm. He paused for a moment, and then he was gone.

Engulfed by anxiety now not just for Maggie but for the man she had sent to retrieve her, Isla cowered in the protection offered by the harbour. She closed her eyes and prayed for a calmer dawn, death or restitution, wishing for respite from her current ordeal.

The power of the sea was staggering, yet simultaneously thrilling to a docile man such as James. Here amongst the havoc of the storm, had never felt so alive. Fighting through pools of frozen water and across stone which sliced his bloodied feet, he thought of his mother and how proud she would be at his bravery. Rising from the multitude of rocks, the cliffs themselves now afforded him little improvement in shelter. It was not until he had travelled deep within the caves that he found some respite from the violence of the rising storm.

Inside the caves, the blueness of the rock pools seemed to shimmer, being drenched with sparkling salted droplets stolen from the world outside. Light skipped frivolously in the air creating a kind of ethereal grotto or dreamland. James sensed that mother and son could reunite in such an unearthly place, that she could appear from around a corner, as easily as she did in his dreams, but a piercing cry soon woke him from his reverie, echoing through the cave and out onto the currents of wind where they stirred Isla from her self-pity.

James followed the urgency of this shriek to an area deep within the cave where he found Maggie. She was huddled with the distraught appearance of a child, clasping her flimsy nightdress, damp from her course across those sodden rocks. Fear permeated her eyes, and wounds were clearly visible across the bareness of her well trodden feet where sharp stones had taken more than their allocated pound of flesh. She had also acquired a cut across her forehead and a trickle of blood now fell unhindered down the curvature of her forehead compounding her distress. As James approached, she baulked, jolting backwards and hugging the protective rocks.

"Billy!" she cried, "Is that you? I got your note. Oh I knew you'd come. I knew it all the while."

"'Tis no Billy", replied James, intentionally coddling his tone with calmness.

"What! Who are you? What do you want?" she cried, leaping to her unsteady feet, pressing against her already broken skin.

"I've come tae fetch you home Mrs. Keiller", continued James.

Maggie's eyes flashed with anger, a furious defensiveness rising inside that fragile frame.

"I'm not leaving", she snapped, protective of that precious but uneven memory, "I'm not leaving without my Billy."

She looked through James as though expecting that her long lost love would reappear at any moment, providing her with deliverance. James turned around, so ardent was her gaze, but the cave was empty save for two lost souls. No ghosts materialised.

"There's no one there. There's none coming."

"Lies!" shouted Maggie, every syllable loaded with frustrated aggression. "Lies and untruths…I know your kind, you're fae the village…you've nae time fer strangers."

Maggie paced the uneven floor of this damp, new habitat, her mind racing across the decades, and differing versions of herself. James watched the deterioration and longed for the persuasive powers of his peers - a clever word, a few gently cajoling lines – to pierce her delusion but wits had always been his downfall.

By the mouth of the cave, a gust of wind caused a shower of tiny rocks to release themselves and tumble disobediently downward until a mass of stones lay transposed upon the ground.

“Billy!” cried Maggie, rushing past James towards the cave entrance where foreboding washed upon the rocks.

Maggie scoured every inch of the vast, empty ocean, but none reflected the image of her drowned love. Confusion ebbed and flowed in the pathways of her mind, voices whispering stories of better days and newly discovered truths. Their murmurings were louder than the roaring backdrop of a howling wind and a thundering sea.

“I cannae see him”, she continued, sure that it was her eyes rather than her memory which deceived her. She implored this unexpected stranger to restore her hope, but he looked at her with a pitiful gaze.

“There’s no one there Maggie.”

She filtered out his realism, examining the rolling horizon.

“Billy… Billy!”

The sound of her despair reverberated around the cavernous tomb, as she clambered out further onto the watery floor, struggling for sound footing, insensible of danger.

“Billy!”

James's heart raced with each unsteady step she took. He watched the old woman dance with death, oblivious to its morbid crescendo. He tried in vain to grasp her arm, but it was too far from his reach. The bitter sea soaked through Maggie's threadbare nightclothes, quietly anticipating a new conquest. James edged ever closer, shoring his step against ledge and rock, but each time he move nearer, Maggie lunged forward again, convinced of a boat and a lost husband upon the waves. With each distracted leap and thwarted triumph came frustration and an increase in the speed of his pounding heart.

At the third attempt, Maggie finally lost her footing and succumbed to an aggressive current which caught her by surprise. Slipping hopelessly down a rock face, lined with the remnants of shell and sand, she scraped against their coarse edges and disappeared from his view.

James watched her perish with muted disbelief. He had failed.

"Maggie!"

Isla grabbed at Maggie's arms as she slid down the perilous slope. The fear which had enveloped her at the harbour wall had been conquered, temporarily. She had found her mislaid courage, enough to challenge the impenetrable mountain of water, and had cautiously made her way through the pools of sea and spirit, to arrive at this opportune moment. She now formed her own impenetrable barrier between the old woman and the sea, as secure as any harbour wall.

Maggie looked at Isla with the bewilderment of one who had expected angels at her heels.

“Morag! What are ye doing here? You’ll do yourself harm.”

“I’ve come tae fetch you home Maggie”, Isla acting her part with fierce determination, transforming herself in front of Maggie’s eyes into the wistful beauty of her grandmother.

“But Billy?” replied Maggie, her eyes streaming with the dismay of her situation. “He’s no here. He’s no come back tae me Morag, he’s no come back!”

The spray of salt water from the advancing waves, the anxiety of her heart and the grief of her loss, rolled over Maggie with more devastation than nature’s tides. The tears which burned her cold cheeks were nothing compared to the hurt which blazed within and she ached with the realisation of her love’s demise. Her body folded and she sank down into her own watery grave, a broken woman. Distraught, she reeled helplessly amongst rock and sea life, her body numb to its effects, as she exhaled the years of their union, mourning and grieving. She clutched her vacant womb, rolling with the resurgence of a shattered mind and the loss of the child which had haemorrhaged from her forty years ago, and took with it her heart. Amongst the darkness of the pools she saw again the image of its lifeless form. Gently she leaned over and caressed the surface of the water, oblivious to all but the reflection of that perfect child, untouched by this world, the untarnished face of her dreams. The cold, cruel rock on which she sat lay as steadfast as its occupant, immersed in this very personal vision. She touched gently the tiny, premature fingers of her child, perfectly formed. There was no life there now, it slept the longest sleep and she longed to lie next to it and sink with it into restful slumber. They would sleep together for all eternity.

Isla touched Maggie's hand as it lay delicately floating across the surface of the black rock pool. The lucid image of her stillborn son dissipating with the interjecting ripples of reality. Maggie watched her beautiful boy fade back into the darkness leaving none but meaningless water.

"Maggie?" whispered Isla.

Maggie had begun the journey back, but lingered longingly on familiar pathways. James clambered down into the pool. He lifted the frame of this fragile woman in his arms and elevated her from the depths to which she had descended. Carefully they trod the precipice between destruction and deliverance, a quiet convoy of broken souls across the rocks, steadily beguiling nature. No words were spoken on the return to safety, too great the tragedy of those hours, and too dramatic the recovery from them. None would see the night end with quite the same perspective as they had seen it begun.

Nature appeared to renounce its crusade, the angry sea abating, calming slowly with the dawn, and the promise of a new day. A crowd had gathered at the quayside, this new, young stranger who had interrupted their evening, too intriguing to disregard. The dance had been temporarily abandoned to witness the downfall of the Keiller woman from Rose Cottage.

Mrs. McLintock stood amongst them in all her splendour. She had commanded an advantageous position by the jetty waiting patiently for God to take his vengeance and she anticipated at any moment the appearance of a lifeless body or three by her feet. It was regrettable that her grandson should be amongst them - she would mourn the loss of his youthful life, but such a lesson would be invaluable in the coercion of her erstwhile flock. An unpleasant taste of liberalism had stained their intimate community but the bitterness of death would soon stamp out its cause.

It was therefore a disappointed Mrs. McLintock who watched her grandson re-emerge over the harbour wall conducting Maggie Keiller to safety. As he approached, she ground her teeth and prepared her attack with an indignant tongue.

“Put that woman down”, she snarled as they came within earshot.

Maggie was thankfully unconscious in James’s arms, the strain of her nocturnal activity had overwhelmed her and she rested out of necessity rather than choice.

“I willnae”, replied James.

“She’s evil”, shouted Mrs. McLintock.

Isla looked into the eyes of the embittered old woman, staggered that someone could be so consumed by hate for a stranger.

“Not as evil as the woman who sent her tae her death”, James replied. He had strong words for his grandmother and was in no mood to be swayed by her now.

“I’ll tell ye once more”, Mrs. McLintock hissed, her eyes fierce. “Put her down.”

James stood tall.

“No”, he replied again, standing resolute on the quay, a quiet Maggie in his arms, an obstinate grandmother his only impediment. This was not a confrontation planned and mulled over like others before it, and his previous causes seemed suddenly as futile as his anger and any fearfulness in his grandmother’s reckoning. He could have spoken many words, chastised, bled retributions, but it was all in vain. His grandmother was intractable. Her mind was as fortified as the harbour wall, and she would never admit the error of her ways. To hope to convince her with logical argument was naïve and so he passed by her without a word.

Mrs. McLintock by comparison was less reflective. Blind in her resolve, convinced by her own rhetoric, she was determined to protect her own sterling reputation amongst her flock.

"You're not a McLintock", she hissed, venom spouting from every corner of that thin, miserly mouth. She had raised her voice to ensure that every one of her audience could hear her castigation.

"You're no grandson of mine."

James looked into those cold, unmoving eyes and allowed his tongue some freedom.

"You can keep your name as well as your religion", he replied. "It's not a Godly life you lead, but a judgmental one, sitting on your grand pulpit with a head bigger than a cow. They've no respect fer ye", he continued, looking at the crowd of villagers transfixed by this very private matter now made public.

He'd seen their faces many times before, each Sunday forlorn and distant as the Church bells rang out, mechanically making their way to the same pew, repetitively droning the same response, and returning to their lives, unfulfilled and unaltered.

"'Tis only the fear that keeps them here. Well, I've not the fear of you."

He bustled past their stunned silence, followed a loyal Isla, shadowed in the protection his bulk afforded against their inquisitive glances and critical stares.

But Mrs. McLintock could not allow the final word to pass in challenge to her own. As the exhausted party turned towards the coastal path and their refuge in Rose Cottage, she called out to her grandson with calculated malice.

"You always were your mother's son."

Step 15: Add Sugary Sweetness to the Orange Mixture

Maggie was returned to her familiar bed in Rose Cottage; rest the only remedy for her mental anguish. The physical torture of her spiralling grief had been too much for her mind and body to bear. She had not raised her grieving eyes during the long journey back from abandonment at the water's edge, not even briefly on that meandering track up from the village under the gaze of expectant stars. The doctor had been persuaded out of his comfort to examine the patient, but it seemed that nothing could be done. It was a complex disease of age with a suitably complex name. His manner was as dismissive as his advice and he soon trundled back to his living grumbling his frustrations.

The silence of Maggie's room became an added persuasion to Isla's own weariness. She found her respite upon the colourful quilt at the foot of the bed. A healing stillness enveloped the walls of the bedroom, far from the angry words unleashed upon their names by Auchobane's scandalised villagers. It was moments, probably seconds before Isla too welcomed enthusiastically her sleep and for hours she rode dreams of things to come, things which had passed, and things which might have been.

James remained in the kitchen, beyond the convalescence which was taking place in the small bedroom. While their exhaustion had resulted in a peaceful slumber, his adventures had encouraged the exact opposite. Reeling from his grandmother's manipulation in the name of religion, he lamented how he too had once been intimidated by it and how she had deluded a village riddled by fear. That one woman could direct a multitude was bewildering. There may have been a wholly virtuous intention in the beginning, but power had so utterly corrupted her authoritarian spirit that all it held now was hatred. James paced the small kitchen for many hours with the sun rising as his witness, conquering the resentment which welled inside him, with forgiveness and reason, then liberating his heart. He absolved her of severe words, her often acerbic actions and her insidious intent. He forgave her all but the vociferous assaults upon his mother. Those were not his to forgive. Once his peace had been made, he too eventually found his solace and abandoned himself to the brief intoxication of sound sleep.

In this way passed the encompassment of a day. No noise emitted from beneath the old, tired roof of Rose Cottage, no air retreated from its shutters and no outside life interrupted their delicate sleep. It was an indeterminable hour when Isla lifted her head. She was stirred by the inconsistencies of Maggie's breathing, as it laboured temporarily before relinquishing once again to another cerebral adventure. Maggie's eyelids flickered with the commotion of fast dreams, as her subconscious played out the anxieties of her past and Isla was sure too that she saw an impression of happiness submerged within her hollowed cheeks.

Rising from where she lay on the edge of the bed, Isla found James resting his weary head on the kitchen table; his face tinged a deep red from the imprint of his hands. As she went about tasks notable only by their triviality, he stirred and opened his eyes.

"What time is it?" he asked, as he began adjusting the muscles in his neck which had been contorted for some hours. He ached with the sudden ramification of his exertions. His legs in particular still felt encumbered by the heavy watery load which had beaten down upon them. His arms had resigned all ambition and hung limp by his side, their recent consignment from dark cave to cottage had extricated all strength and they now embraced feebleness. He felt by degrees, much older than his age, as his body refused the youthfulness demanded of it.

Isla looked out the window at an unremarkable skyline, grey and uninspiring in contrast to its recent nocturnal display. That it should be transformed so absolutely from the desperate version which had threatened their destruction seemed impossible, deceitful even.

"I think it's evening, but I'm not sure", she replied, eyes fixed on a doubtful horizon anticipating a metamorphosis.

'I should go', he began, thinking to rise from his seat, but his body rested firmly in its preferred position.

"Home?" asked Isla, looking at this chivalrous boy with different eyes.

Home. Truthfully in the throes of his rebellion, James had failed to consider the practicalities of his impulsiveness. His outbursts towards his grandmother now seemed reckless as he considered briefly the possibility of returning to the Rectory. He would never be admitted, not after such public defiance. His father might have argued his side, but he would easily be overcome. He thought of where he might find refuge - with friends, acquaintances, then strangers, finally settling on the latter as the only real opportunity.

It was an awkward silence, which sat softly in the corner of the room. A journey commenced as strangers had concluded with something more intimate, but neither knew if this was a permanent or temporary change. They both considered a bold admission, but the courage to articulate such delicate words seemed more unconquerable than the physical impediments placed before them by Mother Nature.

A sudden cry from the bedroom brought to an end their mutual unease. Isla was the first to reach her, pale and limp as though the very lifeblood which had travelled through her had suddenly departed, and left but a shell, ready to die. Quiet with remorse, Isla sat opposite the tired old woman whose face reflected a monotone of grey. Maggie's vacated eyes were half closed, lacking any desire to behold her common surrounds. Her thoughts, her landscapes, were inward now. Isla sat immovable, watching and waiting for what she knew to be inevitable.

"I'm almost gone", Maggie whispered to the young travellers.

"You've just had an episode, that's all", replied Isla. "You need to rest."

"Dinnae feel bad fer me lassie, I cannae wait tae go", said Maggie. "I've been too long fae my kin."

Isla squeezed at the lined hand within hers.

"There's only one thing left to settle before I go", she continued. "The marmalade. Promise me, you'll make a go of it."

Here she grabbed Isla's hand, determined and with urgency.

"Use the Keiller book. It will help you find yer way."

Maggie lay back, her breath shortening with this last exertion, but with a sense of pride in her young charge, who had grown from child to woman in the shortest of time. She saw the fading of fearfulness in Isla's eyes, along with, she hoped, a mother's influence.

"There's not much of your mother left in there now", whispered Maggie, her eyes calm with the knowledge of one who rests a little nearer to her final destiny.

Isla's cheeks tinged a faint pink. Many months ago that colour would have been a deep crimson, but her rehabilitation was almost complete. She felt that the bond between mother and daughter had been now been severed and that the regret at this loss, would not be hers. She had many memories ahead of her, not least that of her own motherhood, whereas her mother's life was fast accelerating to its tedium.

"You cannae change her", continued Maggie, feeling that at the end, she ought to impart what knowledge she had acquired, to those with life left to use it. "She is what history made her."

"You don't need to find excuses for her", replied Isla. "She doesn't deserve sympathy."

"Sympathy, no; but understanding", continued Maggie. "Fer a part of what she became was my own doing. I should have listened instead of speaking but I'm no different from other foolish women of my time. What did I know of her story?"

Maggie shook her head remembering the young girl she had failed.

"She's had more heartbreak than most, your mother. She buried it deep and ran far away, making herself brand new so that the wee girl of her childhood and my memory is lost forever."

Maggie handed Isla the black and white image which had lain before on that homely quilt. Isla took the photograph from her and looked again at the young girl with spirited curls and uninhibited freckles, standing in her Sunday best on a hillside a lifetime ago. Of course her mother had existed as a girl, had lived through the same age as she; but Isla was determined not to give her voice and reason. For Isla, it was infinitely easier to retain her bad opinion if it held no shades but black and white.

Why Maggie chose that moment above all else to resurrect her niece's past, she couldn't say. Perhaps it was the intimacy of her home at the end which released those thoughts again, or perhaps it was a type of last confession, to ensure those dates and times did not pass with her unsaid, but had opportunity to set their own course. Whatever the reason, Maggie determined that the girl had maturity enough to hear the facts and reconcile within her own mind whether her mother deserved compassion.

"That wee girl had the fire of the Keillers inside her", continued Maggie. "Some said she had too much, some said it was that which drove her into the arms of your father."

"My father?" asked Isla, her heart leaping at the image of this idolised, distant character, for so long banished from her mother's lips. This was the first anyone had dared utter a word of him in her presence. "You knew him?"

"Our paths crossed only once."

Maggie shook her head, remembering their first and only encounter. "He was a fierce laddie, in size and spirit."

Her brow furrowed as she recalled his intimidating fists.

"Sixteen she was, and in no way accustomed tae the world, having been spoiled as an only child. So when this new laddie took a shine tae her, she was lost to him fae the start."

"So she loved him?" asked Isla.

"Aye she did", replied Maggie with a sigh. "She let him beat her black and blue, she loved him that much."

Isla's eyes widened with this shocking revelation. Never in the course of her young life had she even guessed at the story which had played a hand in the formation of her mother's character. If she had, this would not have been the tale she would have written for her.

"She was right tae leave him", continued Maggie. "She knew that if you'd survived the birth, he'd have beaten you too."

As Maggie recalled a little, more breached her mind like a long repressed flood.

"She saved yer life, by giving up her own and fleeing far fae him."

"To London?" pressed Isla.

"Aye. In the end", replied Maggie. "She tarried here a while, but tae my shame, I didnae help her. My words drove her further away, as far as London where she found her freedom but too late tae keep her soul."

"She never said anything to me."

"Sometimes it's not what people say, but what they dinnae ye have tae heed", replied Maggie. "Now ye know why she hates those hills with the only heart she has left. The wee girl in that photograph doesnae exist anymore. Your father killed her, just like that poor McLintock woman."

James's ears enflamed at the mention of his family name. He looked up at Maggie but she avoided his look with resignation.

"There are too many secrets in Auchobane", she shook her head with dismay. "Too many."

She steadied herself in the wavering old bed in which she lay.

"Some say the real reason he didnae follow your mother all the way tae London is that he'd set his attentions on the new Rector's wife. He took a fondness tae her at Church and, as I understand it, she was flattered by his admiration as things were not so easy under her own roof."

James understood the intimation with respect to his grandmother.

"As it was told me, she met him one day at the Leap, and well by some accounts he sent her over the edge fer spurning his advances. She wouldnae leave her bairns. Nowt was ever found of them both save fer some bits of clothing and a wedding ring."

James's face ran white.

"She was a good woman as I heard it."

Maggie felt she was right to say what had been hidden from them both for so long. If they were to make their way in the world with honesty, they would do so with the truth. She had equipped them with knowledge. Whether they had the strength to live with it, was another question.

Isla allowed some pity for her mother to embed itself in her heart and although she could not forgive the woman her crimes, she understood a little more the motives for them. Kirsty Keiller had lost all faith in humanity, and with it, affection and love were lost too. There could never have been any hope for a child's love. Isla's only regret was that she had not known her mother's history sooner. It might have been her own salvation.

"She's dead?"

James's voice shook with trembling emotion as the hopes and dreams which had rested within him for years, shattered in the space of a moment.

Maggie was quiet and calm, recognising in him the desperate motion of eyes which had lost all meaning. She had experienced such despair, a long time ago.

"My mother is dead?"

Words seemed redundant, their content a rhetoric which could never be fully understood by a brain in revolt.

"These fifteen years past", continued Maggie.

Fifteen years! Fifteen years of expectation that she would return at any moment. Fifteen years of constantly anticipating her appearance - around a doorway, in a street, a shop, every bus and new boat which anchored at harbour. The dreams, both day and night, of a triumphant and emotional return, filled with love and regret, and most of all untenable joy, all evaporated. The expectation that she had spent these barren years, in constant wrenching from her sons, curious of their growth, their characters, and the day when she would hold them close once more, disintegrated. The physical contact he so yearned for - a mother's hug - would now forever remain unfulfilled. His heart broke with the pain of it all.

"It's a lie", he shouted, the hurt unbearable. He made to stand, but Isla persuaded him back onto the edge of the bed.

He hung his head. The expectancy was part of him. He had grown with it, carried it with him through difficult years. His thoughts, his actions - those recent exploits upon the rocks, had all been for her. Now none of it made sense. Sitting in that cold, empty room, it had all been for nothing. His loss was absolute, devastating. He sat outside himself, feeling the world traverse without him, and not caring an ounce for it. Let it go. Without her, what else had he to live for?

Maggie saw the struggle to reconcile the reality of a mother who would never again embrace the expectant child within him. His eyes darted back and forth with each and every new distressing recollection which had once formed part of his truth.

Maggie rested her hand on his. He looked disgusted at this pitiful attempt at conciliation. Her words had wreaked this devastation, had obliterated his idealised, familiar life. Built on endless tearful evenings following even more tearful days, he had focused on her when all else had failed him. Now, in the space of a moment, that once sound fortress had crumbled to sand. Without the anticipation that one fateful day there would be reclamation of all that had been lost before, there was no reason, and no desire to lift his soul out of the dismal mood into which he was now irrevocably sliding.

“But she is still alive”, Maggie continued. “In here.”

She tapped his chest gently, but he recoiled and scoffed at her token attempt to lift his mood.

“She’s always been here”, said Maggie. “Whenever you needed strength, or hope and she’ll be there still, until the day you die. You can see her whenever you care to. All you have to do is close your eyes.”

James’s eyes focused a little straighter now, but the thought of her was nothing to the expectation of her physical presence.

“I lost my Billy too”, she continued. “But when I need him he’s there. And is no everyone can say that about their kin that‘s living.”

She squeezed his hand. The warmth of her well worn skin seemed to reach deep down into the very depths of him, and wrap his heart in a loving embrace. He was riddled with self doubt, not only in himself, but in those who had indulged his extensive daydream. They had treated him like a child - true he was one in the beginning - but fifteen years of deception was unforgivable, and he hated them still more for their betrayal.

With an old mind, slowly withering, Maggie leant back on her familiar pillow which had rested her thoughts for more years that she would have liked. Nearing the end now, she felt nothing but relief - that the long wait was over, that she would take no one's secrets with her to the grave.

"I'd like tae be buried on the hill", she began.

They looked at her with surprise.

"Next to my Billy", Maggie continued. "And to my wee bairn so that we can be a family at last."

Maggie closed her eyes. They were coming to her more clearly now. She could see Billy's eyes, as real and true as forty years ago and she felt a surge of youth within her as the shackles of age removed themselves from her. It was the happiness of those early days before the storm came.

Isla watched as a new wave of joy washed over Maggie's face, erasing the lines of so many years. She saw the smile which told her that Maggie had found her family again.

His hand reached out to hers, and Maggie took it with an overdue enthusiasm. It was warm; it was loving. It was home. He pulled her to him, and whispered gently in her ear. "I've missed you hen."

The light was beautiful, and from it came her son - a little boy, the image of his father. He knew her too, and ran to her as though he'd missed his mother for as long as she had missed him. Her heart was mended with the joy of their reunion, it was the happiest she had ever been in this life, but it was hers now for all time.

Isla knew that she was gone. Maggie's breath laboured with the ecstasy of her overdue place in the heavens, and then it stopped. The peacefulness of her passing was comforting, and Isla could feel nothing but contentment that she was gone to a place she had longed for an eternity.

Isla sat with her for an hour, holding the hand which now held no life. The smile remained even when the breath was extinguished and Isla placed both hands upon her chest, then she quietly made her way out of the room.

James was unable to bear the loss of his mother with the same composure as Isla had accepted Maggie's passing. He felt overwhelmed with anger at the duplicity of the adults who surrounded him. Their knowledge of his mother's death and their decision to deny him such information was unforgivable in his mind; worse than the actuality of her death.

Here was further ammunition against his grandmother. He recalled the naivety of his childhood loyalty to her and his blind admiration for every word of seeming fact which ushered from her mouth. In light of her lies and deception, his devotion seemed gullible or at least, misplaced. He could not hate his mother - her death was at the hands of a man into whose arms she had been driven. His grandmother was wholly and entirely to blame, he concluded, as he passed through the rusty old gate of Rose Cottage, kicking every wayward stone forcibly from the pathway as he made his way back down to the Leap.

He stood there longer than usual; trying to imagine the final moments of his mother's life and give closure to them. Those images were badly formed and lacked focus and he began to wonder instead whether the place he chose to sit and swing his boots idly at the cliff edge had also witnessed the final moments of her life. He imagined her falling - sometimes alone, sometimes in the company of the man who had pushed her.

It was only as the shadows of dusk began to wash over the waves rolling beneath him and the imagined bodies which floated on them that James left the Leap and started out down the remainder of the grass track to Auchobane. His ramblings now were without purpose or direction. Although devoid of any idea as to where he would go, he nevertheless felt he ought to walk there with conviction, as the newly enlightened adult that Maggie had moulded of him. It was important to embrace this notion of confidence from the outset, so that others would know that they could not pull the wool over his eyes in such a blatant manner as his grandmother. He did not want to return to the Rectory, not now, not ever - but with time and just the right amount of bribery, he hoped to persuade his impetuous younger brother to fetch some of his things. Theirs was a complex sibling rivalry. James, as elder brother had the more vivid memories of their mother. Where James remembered detail, Ewan held only vagueness. It was something which James felt was often to his brother's advantage. Ewan cared less for her because he remembered less just how wonderful she was. He missed her less and therefore his pain was not equal to the suffering endured by his brother; or so James imagined. The thought struck him as to whether Ewan would even care about her death. The animosity between the brothers had been fuelled by the attention heaped upon James by their grandmother. In Ewan's eyes, James was obviously the favourite and as a result, his grandmother's control interjected little with his own indulged life. Ewan was a popular figure amongst his peers. His confidence rebounded with such standing and he had little to rebel against during turbulent teenage years.

As James ambled down the grass track to the village, he wondered whether his grandmother's lecturers on moral fortitude would now be directed towards Ewan. If she had resigned herself to the loss of an elder grandson, might the younger not prove equally as useful? And what reaction would this new focus conjure up in Ewan? Would it transform him into a less selfish being? James concluded that his brother would either relish in the departure of an idolised elder brother and bask in the consuming attention which would now be solely his; or he would realise quickly that this spotlight was a vicious luminosity which would penetrate his life, his actions and most notably, his whereabouts, and he would bolt for the hills as swiftly as a guilty parishioner past the caustic glazing of a Rectory window. Having experienced the unpleasantness of this intensity for many years James felt some culpability should Ewan's reaction turn out to be latter. He could never wish such animosity on his worst enemy, or even a brother.

James's feet continued to propel him forward and downward aided by a steep gradient. It was only when he looked up and found himself a hundred yards from the mouth of Auchobane, that he took his errant feet in check. Before him stood the glowing red sandstone of the outer village houses, burning brightly in the evening dusk like a smouldering fire. They reflected a scarlet horizon as the sun set many miles away. The scene was not dissimilar, James thought, to the crimson hues found at the fiery gates of hell. He half expected his grandmother to appear, wielding horns and firing sulphur to complete the compelling vision. Instead the sun completed its hasty retreat; the houses resumed a more sedate charcoal tint, and the flames once brilliant, expired. James resumed his journey amongst the newly found shadows which suited him better. He felt himself move from house to house unnoticed, invisible for once to the inquisitive eyes of

Auchobane, and their covert lace curtains. In an evening light, the cold, unfriendly houses of the village seemed new and foreign despite their familiarity. He crossed empty streets and dark pathways, the omnipresent Rectory diverted, until he found himself at the tired green door of Dougie's old grocer's shop.

Reaching above the wooden frame, paint flaking like its disintegrated owner in his grave, he found his reward - a key. Opening the lock he entered into a different kind of cave, one no soul had happened upon for many months. The store retained its musty smell, exacerbated by the dried products which still stacked its shelves. Through the encroaching darkness James felt his way along the stale ledges to the door at the back of the shop and the pokey stairway which led up to a private life.

Dougie had lived alone with his decorated memories ever since returning from a military life which destined him forever to tread this world alone. Army years spent roaming amongst treacherous graves which reached out and took friend after friend had marked him with a determination to see out his personal battles in solitude. For Dougie, it was clearly a very private war. His endeavours in the poppy fields of Northern France were only one chapter of the hostilities he was fated to endure. His small flat above the village store became a respite in this lifelong battle. It was his haven, his safety from the imaginary bullets and the bombs which rebounded on the streets below. Inside this quiet place he found solace with his thoughts and memories, exorcising them from his recollection, finding comfort and relief in their physical depiction - a photograph or a medal.

As James reached the apex of the narrow stairway, he carefully opened the door into the old soldier's sanctum, as though he expected in some way to find Dougie's ghost casually loitering there. What he found instead was the blank canvass of an exposed wall repapered with a more meaningful, personal mosaic. The pictures of his lost comrades, clippings from commemorative newspapers and letters from those who were allowed to leave those bloodstained shores with their lives, but not their minds; adorned the plain, incongruous walls, creating the most beautiful, dedicated mural to wonderful friends.

On the back of the single chair was slung Dougie's loyal armour - his old green soldier's coat, waiting patiently for its owner to return and relieve it from its resting place. On the table lay a crimson ribbon adorning the stem of a quiet medal, its lustre faded and frayed around the edges. The cross itself bore an inscription which simply read, 'V for Valour'. James examined its delicate history and muffled honour - the date '26th April 1916' inscribed upon its back, along with the name of its recipient 'Douglas Stuart MacGregor, Private, 2nd Battalion Argyll and Sutherlands.' James felt suddenly humbled by the magnitude of the man he had occasionally walked alongside and replaced the sacred cross with as much delicacy and respect as he could modestly offer.

James had never been heroic. He may have done heroic things, but they were never undertaken out of selflessness. Even his exploits amongst the threatening caves had been self-serving. It owed less to a desire for the wellbeing of the old woman of Rose Cottage and more towards proving that he was not the subservient incapable boy that had been impressed upon since early adulthood. It was rebellion, pure and simple -

maybe years too late to be considered adolescent, but impetuous nonetheless. There was no higher morality at play. It was self-serving. He baulked at the idea of selflessness and in Dougie's reverent home, surrounded by the lost faces and words of true courage and heroism, he felt instantly inadequate and embarrassed by his own presence.

The sharp moonlight had begun to perforate the industrious cloud cover, enlivening the faces of young soldiers in old photographs, who contemplated their new, uninvited guest. A few of their kind had been graced with a picture frame, and James examined one of them for familiar features. Their impish, jovial countenances betrayed a close, easy friendship which he could never hope to achieve. James found familiarity with difficulty. Such relationships were rare and James had touched upon them only fleetingly during his life. His mother's disappearance had not only been cataclysmic from a personal perspective but it had set the tone for all future relationships. Fear of abandonment being a powerful deterrent, he found it impossible to trust that the object of his friendship would not also eventually forsake him.

Despite the military façade, the faces of the soldiers beheld an innocence more of their age than their experiences. Their intimate knowledge of death in all its excruciating glory had somehow not dulled their enthusiasm for life and its drudgery. They stared out from the confines of a grainy photograph, whose format was not advanced enough to preserve the austerity they deserved, fixed in a point in time when hope sprang from muddied fields.

James's attention was drawn to the tall man standing at the edge of the happy group. Something in his eyes restored his comfort and forgave his intrusion. His physique was proud and statuesque, and a green army coat adorned strong capable shoulders. Despite his youthfulness, and a body riding high on unrelenting vigour, James recognised the birth of an old man from within the spirit of that time. Dougie's appearance may have waned but his hopefulness and vivacity had endured; and it was that essence of the man which James found instantly recognisable.

The moon became consumed once more by a clouded sky, and the light degraded to such an extent that the venerable faces of soldiers dissolved into the shadows of the photographs from which they had emerged. The darkness prompted a gentle wave of tiredness in James, as the span of a day and most of a sleepless night gushed over his furrowed face. The temporary aches of early evening returned and he rested his legs in the worn wooden chair and his head upon the sturdy writing table on which the dimmed array of wartime memorabilia were displayed. He coddled his head on its proficient surface, hands outstretched to form a token pillow between his browbeaten skull and the unforgiving wood.

James's dreams came fast and deviant, the product of a strained subconscious. Transposed through pathways deep within his mind, he found himself wandering a nightmare, weighed down in a heavily sodden field, each step requiring the exertion of an army just to move an inch. As he stomped through the dampened earth, deep chasms began to form more frequently around his feet, until he stood fearfully encased by a dangerously excavated battlefield, the countless graves of missing soldiers lingering at his feet. He stepped carefully, negotiating those tombs with markings indicating lack of vacancy, alongside the empty breaches of those waiting to be filled. Exhausted from physical demands, he stopped to consider his strange surrounds and became aware of a presence at his back. Turning he saw a pallbearer, unmistakable save for a thick green army coat. As the man approached, he saw a comforting face form with soft distinction.

Dougie stood as clear as any man, and placed his arm gently upon young James's shoulder.

"Mind the cavities", he guided, nodding nonchalantly at the chasms which sprung organically from within a sodden ground. "They're a fierce abyss."

Dougie produced a silver shovel which had a crimson ribbon tied about the handle, and began to dig, filling with one of the gaping holes with soil while another sprung immediately from the earth just as one chasm was replenished.

"Looks like hard work", replied James, watching his forlorn friend toiling hard against the ground for no reward.

"Life or Marmalade?" asked Dougie, smiling and lifting his head, happy to engage his young companion in idle chatter.

It seemed like an odd remark, given their situation.

"Same difference", Dougie continued with aplomb, "cannae have life without marmalade, cannae have marmalade without life!"

He put his hand into his old army coat, and pulled out a jar of marmalade.

“Look at those stars”, he beamed, holding the jar up to the light. James was dazzled by the brightness. “Each one a perfect soul”, he whispered into James’s ear, “swimming blind in a sea of darkness.”

He sloshed the liquid around disturbing the flecks as they bumped against the glass.

“Good tae mix it up, eh?” he continued. “You’re in here somewhere.” He tapped the glass fondly. “And so is that lassie of yours.”

He lifted the lid from the jar and peered inside.

“She’s not my lassie”, replied James with defiance.

She was not his, and he was not hers - their paths had simply crossed with the practicalities of their own objectives. He didn’t know her after all - their mutual misadventure hardly formed a basis for friendship or something more.

“Is she not?” Dougie replied, “well that is a tragedy.”

Dougie began to dig once more, depositing dirt all around as the hole which he created took form. After a few momentous shovels, and perhaps a foot in depth, he stopped and took in hand the jar of marmalade. He threw it into the dirt and began to fill the void of his newly dug grave.

“What are you doing?” cried James, seeing the old man’s pride and joy slowly disappearing beneath the coarse earth.

“There’s no life in there now,” he replied. “And no hope.”

He pressed a small wooden cross into the ground by way of a marker. Etched onto the frame was written 'Keiller Marmalade RIP'.

He then took his shovel and slung it heavy across his shoulders, and lifting his dishevelled frame, paced off in an arbitrary direction, continuing his journey in pursuit of a new resting place. James let him go, contented by a reunion with this familiar face, but perplexed by his message.

When he opened his eyes from this disturbing dream, the warm rays of a morning sun had emerged and were caressing the writing table which he had acquired as his pillow. The old room seemed less intimidating in a new light. Old pictures assumed their easy reality, their meaning dismissed with a broken morning, a little further from their day, a little longer in the grave. James rose and loitered by the window, watching as the villagers resumed their insidious lives. Did they once have hopes and dreams? How did they die? Was it a gradual withering or a rampant flood one day in spring? And did they miss them? Did they even know that they were gone? The consideration that there might be nothing beyond Auchobane and its daily tribulations was enough to destroy his spirit. He clung resolutely to the hope that something greater lay in store for him around some indeterminate corner.

With this thought of a higher prospect, vague recollections of his dreams returned. James remembered Dougie's words about the girl and made some attempt at trying to understand his meaning but he eventually concluded that he could infer a thousand theories, and talk himself out of any action. Instead he made his way down into the shop, thinking that some sustenance would aid not only his thinking, but also his weakened digestion. He rifled through the many cardboard boxes and nondescript bags until he achieved his nourishment.

Step 16: Increase the Heat to Fuse the Ingredients

In Rose Cottage, Isla sat in careful study of the cover of 'Mrs. Keillers Recipes for Marmalade' at the kitchen table. She had stared at the stained, weathered cover for over an hour, with some notion of acquiring the passion of her ancestors. But with every passing minute her thoughts muddled and she began to realise that the enthusiasm felt by Maggie for marmalade, did not exist within her. She struggled to find within herself the same joy they had felt for this conserve, and while she appreciated the historical significance, their legacy and meaning, it brought her no closer to actually opening the pages of the book and absorbing their lives. Her downcast eyes began to tire and so she rose to invigorate her enthusiasm with a change of outlook.

Standing by the window, she noticed that James had reappeared by the wavering gate of the Cottage and was leaning casually against the flimsy fence, which threatened to give way and deposit him into the flowerbeds. He cut a forlorn figure, his head hung low, in deep contemplation.

She opened the door and he eventually made his way inside.

“Where is she?”

“On the bed. Wrapped in her quilt,” replied Isla.

“What are you going tae do with her?”

“Bury her on the hill like she asked.”

James looked at Isla. Eight months pregnant, he knew she would have taken the shovel in hand and dug the hole herself. He wanted to help, not just for her, but as a kind of recompense to Maggie, for having the courage to tell him the truth where others didn’t.

“I’ll do it”, he said looking beneath his dark eyebrows at her.

Isla allowed him this burden and he spent the day and most of the evening, digging a grave next to the overgrown resting places of Maggie’s husband and child.

With each foot of soil, his anger retreated a little, his frustration being distracted by his physical exertion. By the end of the day, when his arms could swing no more, he found that he had discovered a greater acceptance of his loss and a strange peacefulness settled within him.

That night, they sat together waiting for the dawn and the time at which they would return Maggie to the earth from which she and her forefathers had sprung. Clasping mugs of hot tea next to the stove which staved off the first broach of winter, they spoke not a word.

As the Eastern sun broke over the still North Atlantic Sea, they were roused by a loud, confident knocking on the roughened door of Rose Cottage, stirring both from their quietude.

Isla opened the door, and instantly regretted her impetuosity.

"Hello darling."

Kirsty Keiller stood upon the doorstep, as she had done months before. The reality of her presence, the first since her abandonment of her daughter, stunned Isla momentarily. Perhaps she thought that her mother's regret would have permeated her glossy exterior and that her guilt would have manifested itself in a poor complexion and an extra line or two on an otherwise impossible shiny face. But the contrary appeared true. With the removal of her daughter she now had opportunity to erase ten, nearly twenty years of undesired motherhood and she had embraced her rebirth with urgency. She appeared before Isla more immaculate than the mother who had furnished her daughter with sleeping pills and deposited her amongst the isolated Auchobane hills.

"Aren't you going to invite me in?" she slithered, pretension stifling the pure air, like an intoxicating gas. Her voice was all false cordiality and disinterest, and she feigned the supplanting of a kiss on Isla's indifferent cheek.

Never would her words betray the actual thoughts which swarmed inside that perfectly coiffed head and never would she display true affection in public or in private. This apathy was in itself, a relief. Isla worried that her capacity for forgiveness and her desire for the unconditional love of a parent would somehow cause her to remain in this self-afflicting circle of maternal disappointment. She was anxious that, in the presence of her mother, with the offer of reconciliation, she would renege and fold in upon herself for one last chance of affection. But thankfully her apprehension she now found to be unsound and as she faced the object of her anxiety, she found no warmth lurking there.

"What do you want?" replied Isla.

Her mother smiled with pitiful sarcasm. This little girl, easily manipulated, appeared to have acquired some gumption. She found her attempt at self-assurance laudable but laughable.

"Is that any way to greet your mother?"

She pushed her way inside the small cottage, still a menacing force and a bulk to be reckoned with despite the reconditioned armour.

"You obviously haven't acquired any social graces since I saw you last", she continued with an easy cutting remark, one of many commonplace against her daughter. "But I suppose I didn't send you up here for etiquette."

Never comforting with praise, hardly deigning to pleasantries, Kirsty Keiller cut an imposing figure, and despite Isla's transformation, she knew that she would eternally be the incompetent child in her mother's eyes. There would be no respect, regardless of the magnitude of her accomplishments. It was as though her mother extracted her own superiority by sapping conviction from others, draining from them the confidence she needed to bolster her own frame.

Isla's felt her poise creak beneath the old wooden floorboards on which they stood, feeling at any moment that they might capitulate entirely and throw her into oblivion.

Kirsty turned towards her daughter with glee in her eye.

“Is it true? Has the old woman finally gone to her grave?”

“Not quite”, replied Isla pushing open the door of Maggie’s bedroom where her body lay, lifeless, waiting for burial. Kirsty strode into the room, and pulling back the homely quilt which protected her shell, stared at the pale, hallowed out lifeless face in front of her. She examined each line and livered hand, seeking confirmation that Maggie had, at last, passed.

“She looks even worse dead than she did alive”, replied Kirsty, her mind assuaged, leaving the room and shutting the door behind her. “Get rid of her.”

“If you mean bury her, then yes, we were just about to”, said Isla. “She wanted to be laid to rest on the hill, next to her kin.”

“She’s dead”, said Kirsty, reaching for her address book. “She doesn’t have a say in the matter.

“It was her last request to be buried here.”

“I’ll have someone come and take the body away,” continued Kirsty, thumbing through her considerable book of contacts.

“The grave’s already dug”, interjected James.

Isla looked at James, his voice heavy with reason and responsibility, contrary to her own invisible protestations.

“And who are you?” sneered Kirsty, casting a judgmental eye on this unimpressive young man. Her opinion formed in those first few seconds, she had decided that by association, he must be ineffectual too.

“James McLintock.”

James stood to his feet with the object of exerting some kind of influence with his ample physique.

“How quaint, one of the dim-witted locals”, Kirsty replied, her eyes glaring intimidation, her voice raw with its natural dialect buried for a Southern clime. “Well claw me, James McLintock and I’ll claw thee”.

She paused, daring him to challenge her immeasurable authority.

“If you sleep with dogs, you’ll rise with fleas”, Kirsty continued, delving into her armoury of insults. “My daughter has neither beauty nor intelligence. Her honour is muck and she has no fortune. In fact Mr. McLintock, she possesses no redeeming qualities which mark her out as being anything but ordinary and even within what I imagine to be a limited village society, even you could do a great deal better.”

Tears welled deep within the ducts of Isla’s expectant eyes but she fought them back. A year ago she would have folded, accepting her mother’s words as truth and sought solace in self-destruction, but her education at Rose Cottage and the wilds which surrounded it, had given her strength to persevere.

"As James said, the grave is already dug", continued Isla. "It would cost money to have someone come up here to fetch Maggie, when we have everything we need to bury her."

Isla had hit at the root of the woman.

Kirsty sat down at the table and lit a cigarette.

"Throw the woman in her hole then."

She blew smoke in James' direction, enveloping his face in its musty haze. It was her subtle way of suggesting that he'd best get on with it.

"Let me know when it's done."

Happy to have opportunity of extricating herself from her mother's caustic presence, Isla returned to Maggie's bedroom and wrapped her relation a little tighter in the warm quilt which had been her blanket for forty years or more, while James fetched Hamish from the garden. Kirsty viewed their actions with amusement.

"A wheelbarrow?" she smiled sarcastically, sucking on the end of her cigarette, dripping with the stains of her bright red lipstick. "A suitably undignified end"

James placed Maggie's body in Hamish and wheeled her from Rose Cottage for the very last time. Down the stone pathway and through the red, wooden gate, they passed - a very humble and unusual funeral cortege, but somehow fitting to the unconventional woman they bore. Hamish was more of a friend than any with heart could be, with Isla and James the only pallbearers left to take the journey with her. On the other side there would be a crowd to welcome her home.

The wind that morning toyed with the body and its bearers on the steep incline to the make-shift graveyard Maggie had built all those years ago. Two very old crosses were joined by a newly constructed third, and James and Isla guided Maggie's body down into her resting place beneath it, with as much care and attention as she had given her own kin.

"Should we say something?" asked James, picking up a shovel, and placing it poised in the mountain of earth next to the grave.

"I don't think there's anything to say", replied Isla. "She is where she always wanted to be."

James nodded and began to replace the disturbed earth. Isla watched as the colourful quilt turned to muddied brown and eventually disappeared. There was a sense of finality to it all, and it was only now, as she looked back at Rose Cottage, and the trail of cigarette smoke emitting from its new visitor, that she began to think of what was to come.

"If you'll pardon me for saying so", began James, patting the last of the earth flat against its undisturbed neighbours. "Your mother is some kind of old whinbuss. You couldnae gather berries there."

Isla stared towards Rose Cottage. Her feet were reluctant to follow her gaze and she stood steadfast in the gusts blowing in from the North Atlantic, even as her mother came to the door, to check on their slow progress.

“Courage doesn’t always roar”, said James, turning around to meet her fear. “If Maggie had treated us like bairns, we’d never have been any wiser or grown any older.”

Isla sighed as she looked at the cigarette smoke which was snaking through the thin window of the kitchen.

“Come on”, he pushed her gently up the path to the open doorway. “You’ll be ten feet taller with Maggie’s spirit on your shoulders.”

Isla trundled with great reluctance in James’s footsteps. Whatever courage Isla held as she walked towards the cottage, instantly evaporated with the arresting vision of her mother with arms folded, waiting their arrival.

“Down to business”, snapped Kirsty with impatience as Isla crossed beneath the lintel once again. “Where is the money?”

“What money?”

Her mother was growing bored of conversation, her ennui displaying itself in her pacing of the square footage which formed the kitchen floor.

“The money Isla”, she pressed. “Where is Maggie’s money?”

“She didn’t have any”, replied Isla. “That’s why she lived like this.”

The small room, the functional furniture, all supported the notion of a woman of modest means, without wealth and the luxury of comfort.

“Because she chose to.” Kirsty rolled her eyes at her daughter’s naivety. “Maggie was a rich woman. She inherited a fortune from the Keillers and their awful jelly.”

“Marmalade”, corrected Isla.

“When Billy’s father died, the business was sold and the money was divided up between the children”, continued Kirsty. “Your grandmother squandered her inheritance in less than a generation, but Maggie’s money from her dead husband is still around here somewhere waiting for me to find it. And I will find it, if I have to tear this place apart and smash every one of these awful brown jars to get it.”

She picked up a nearby marmalade jar with visible disgust, recoiling at the unimaginably repellent contents.

Isla sat down next to James at the kitchen table, her hands holding close the Keiller recipe book bequeathed to her by Maggie, protecting the only treasure she felt was of any importance to Maggie.

“Wouldn’t she have told you where the money was if she’d wanted you to have it?” said Isla softly.

“Don’t be ridiculous, of course she didn’t want me to have it”, replied Kirsty, “That’s why I sent you.”

Isla was taken aback by her mother’s frankness. Honesty was not a natural gift.

“You were supposed to charm it out of her. You were the acceptable heir, young and stupid. I knew she’d never come round to me, she’s hated me for years, but you, you were a fresh flower, ready to snap that cheque up like a Venus Flytrap.”

“Maybe Maggie was smarter than you thought”, replied Isla.

“Or you were more useless than I thought”, snapped Kirsty, sneering from the side of her contorted mouth.

“I am what you made me”, retorted Isla, reminding her mother of her role in the creation of such an abhorrent individual. “I am my mother’s daughter.”

It was a quiet rebuke but one which her mother moved to quash quickly, as though she had expected such impertinence and had stacked high her vengeful rebuttals.

“No darling, you are all your father”, Kirsty replied.

Daggers reverberated against the cold white stone of the walls around Isla, their blades sharp and menacing, aimed undeviating at her heart. She felt a fury at her mother’s refusal to admit any culpability for her struggles. She had consistently eschewed any liability for her daughter’s failings, and had expected that she make her way in the world completely alone.

“Of course Maggie’s inheritance wasn’t the only reason you needed to be removed from London”, Kirsty’s mouth curled at the edges like a venomous snake. “Did you think I hadn’t noticed? The morning sickness, the lethargy, the mood swings? Who is the father of that child you are carrying - or do you even know?”

Isla recognised the increasing shrillness in her mother’s voice. Her intonation lunged between deep rage at her daughter’s attempt at concealment and fury at this contesting of her control.

“You would make me a grandmother? At my age?”

She would cut to the heart of any who dared cross her, even kin.

"I would be a social outcast, turned away from every party of the season. No, I had to get you out of London. Maggie's money was just a convenience."

Kirsty sneered derisively.

"'I will find that money and then I will get rid of this", Kirsty continued, waving dismissively at Isla's unborn child.

"What do you mean?" Isla's voice wavered.

"You're not keeping it" her next words of conciliation.

Isla placed a protective, fearful hand over her blossoming stomach, as if her mother were about to rip the child from her there and then.

"You can't take it", she cried. "I won't let you."

"Darling, you're only a child. You can't look after a baby", replied her mother. "You couldn't even look after an old woman. Look - I send you up here and six months later Maggie is dead. What if the same thing were to happen to that child? Could you ever forgive yourself? No, I will sort this whole ugly mess out."

"You're the reason there is a mess in the first place", cried Isla, unable to repress any longer the emotions which had so long travelled her thoughts.

"It's not my fault you opened your legs, darling."

"It's never your fault", mocked Isla, she too had amassed her own long list of accusations. "That I was so starved of love at home, I had to look for it amongst strangers."

Kirsty looked into Isla's wide eyes, which were frenzied with words she had wrestled with for years, now released with giddy adrenalin. She saw in her child the face of the man who had beaten her, sixteen years ago. This colloquial man who spoke with his fists was so far from her now that it might have been another's lifetime. This incidental father of her child was revived in the eyes of her daughter and playing at vengeance. She still hated that man but moreover she hated the woman she had been when she was with him – ineffectual, inadequate and weak. When she left him, she left that naïve, little girl and reinvented another, far superior version amongst the manicured set of London.

"But a stranger abandoned me, just like you" continued Isla, a cracked sentiment reverberating in her emotional tone. "He felt nothing for me. Just like you."

Tears rose once more in Isla's flushed eyes, but her willpower conquered them. She would not let them beat her, not again, not after the many months she had spent in this isolated wilderness. She had grown, and she would not allow their attempts to stunt her now.

Kirsty turned towards James, witness to this monumental battle between mother and daughter, her voice oozing saccharine.

"I am not monster James. I am just a mother, a mother whose only failing was in giving her child everything her heart desired and this James, is the thanks I get."

Isla almost choked on her mother's sugar-coated words. Did her mother remember a different child, one which existed only in her imagination?

"If indifference and coldness are the marks of indulgence, then yes, all of my heart's desires were satisfied."

She was absolute in defiance to a mother who had repetitively brushed her aside. Strength welled inside Isla, a sensation previously alien to her, the fortitude of years of rejection building to a confident crescendo.

"A perfect childhood?" she came again. "You were never even there!"

Her voice amplified with strength and volume - anger, rage and frustration concaving in on one another, merging, fusing to form an indistinguishable weapon of pain.

Isla's irrational outburst seemed only to confirm to Kirsty Keiller, her daughter's instability. An emotional child, prone to exaggeration and overly sensitive, her thoughts were warped by memories carefully selected from a coddled childhood; images which bore no resemblance to fact and the sacrifice of adulthood.

She persuaded herself that her daughter was channelling traits inherited from her father. Her overdramatic allegations further evidence that her child was not the confident, extrovert young woman she had hoped she would be. She felt vindicated in her decision to erase the girl from her life and protect that most valuable of assets, her reputation. If she had not that, then she was nothing more than the plain girl from Dundee, and nothing had been gained through those years of sacrifice.

"I look at you and all I see is disappointment", Kirsty replied.

Why Isla was surprised, she couldn't say. She had heard these words countless times in the conversations they had contested in her head. Perhaps it was the effortlessness with which her mother casually dismissed her daughter, which caught Isla off guard.

James lifted his head at the callousness of such a closing comment. Never had he imagined the spitefulness which could exude from a mother's tongue. The perfect vision of his own mother which he had constructed throughout a difficult teenage angst was threatened by such a display of maternal brutality. It forced his own examination of words he had bestowed upon his mother, and caused him to question that which his imagination had crafted.

"There is a car outside", continued Kirsty calmly. "Get in it."

Isla stood slowly.

"Stand tall", whispered James.

But Isla looked at him blankly, dejected and beaten.

"She's right", replied Isla, her words jarring. "I can't look after a baby."

Her hand slipped from his and she walked slowly from the cottage. She felt nothing but numbness at this final act of denunciation. Perhaps now that all had been said, the mental anguish would be at an end and she could find her own brand of restitution. She ventured into the dullness of the garden where the deteriorating roses seemed to mirror her own condition.

As she reached the gate of Rose Cottage, Isla's courage seeped through her fingers like the contents of an overly saturated marmalade. From the reflective corner of a dark anonymous car, the same one which had carried her to Rose Cottage all those months ago, Isla watched her chivalrous boy depart, his head hung low contemplating the revelations he had heard that day then she turned back towards Rose Cottage.

It had given her life, if only temporarily. Every indentation, every leaking slate, every cracked window, taught her a lesson. It was Maggie's home, but it had also become hers. Never again would a Keiller rise to the musical whisperings of the sea, or embrace its thunder on a stormy summer's night. Never again would a Keiller wander freely amongst the protective bushes, treading delicately by the roses and stepping carefully across its hearth. It was not just an old cottage Isla left behind, but the bond which had been created with Maggie, with marmalade and her Keiller kin. She imagined Maggie by the gate, consoling her, and urging her to courage. Isla smiled at her optimism and promised she would be strong, and do her best to keep her promise in regards to the marmalade. Then Isla turned away, clasping the Keiller recipe book tight in her hands and faced again this new impersonal world, from behind the dark windows of an ambiguous black car.

Step 17: Boil to Setting Point

Next to Isla, in the shadows of the dark car, sat a strange, stern woman. As Isla sank into the seat alongside her, the woman's nostrils flared nosily with expectation giving her the appearance of an inhospitable dragon. Her face encompassed a disapproving frown, amplified by lines burrowed deep into the folds of her forehead. She could have been her mother's peer, or closer to Isla in years, such was the premature ageing implied by her pessimistic outlook.

"Where is she sending me this time?" asked Isla, resignation dripping from her voice.

"Somewhere for girls in your condition" was the cold reply.

Isla clasped the Keiller book tight to her chest. She found herself staring out once more from the dark tinges of a car at the rugged beauty of a Scottish wilderness, which eventually dissolved into vagueness.

The self-satisfied woman, who sat next to her on this latest, dark journey, was a midwife from an era where women were for breeding and children for moulding. She revelled in the historic suffering of childbirth; an atheist in this new religion of painless birth and medical interference. In her clinical mind, a woman required nothing more than a leather strap and a strong character to do the distasteful deed. That Isla was little more than a child herself, mattered not. That the midwife had never practiced what she so ardently preached mattered even less. No more words were spoken by the acerbic dragon on the long and silent road from Rose Cottage, to their gradual re-emergence in a more sedate countryside, the location for a cold hearted hospital and Isla's new home.

For Isla's second exile, her mother had chosen an altogether more practical isolation. Compared with the wild outlook of Rose Cottage, this new hospital for "resting" girls, buried deep within Northumberland was noteworthy only for its blandness. It represented the carpet under which almost a century of misadventure had been conveniently swept and Isla's appearance at the antiquated residence was nothing more than a footnote in its repugnant history. A large house with desolate grey walls hidden far from judgmental eyes and the censorious glances of society's finest; it was a world away from the warmth of kin and whitewashed cottage walls.

It was approached along a long winding drive so that only those directed there by mothers of a similar persuasion to Kirsty Keiller would find its black door. The private hospital was the saviour of a multitude of matriarchs who bowed at the feet of social convention and offered up their daughters in return for their pride. As the latest of such sacrificial lambs, Isla stood before the ominous panelled door, and looked up towards the large, rattling windows, each and every one with curtains drawn, as though the house itself shut its eyes to the horrors taking place within its walls.

She was directed by her fiery companion through melancholy corridors, past doors locked shut. She saw no one as she was led to her own functional room, her cell for the remainder of her confinement. As the door was quietly bolted behind her, she could hear the desperate screams of another unfortunate inmate, crying out for an eternity or until suppressed by force or medical means.

Isla's days passed predominately in seclusion within the confines of her cold room, without windows, without hope. Her only visitor was a large, impenetrable nurse who bore over her twice a day, two small plastic cups in her unwashed hands. One filled with liquid, the other with numerous unmentionable pills. Isla viewed them, and their courier with distrust.

Comfort was marked by its absence, stripped from all of the rooms as a discouragement towards repeat offending. Isla conceded to its oppression for the remaining weeks of her internment, drifting on a frivolous bed of sleep, thinking little of her mother and the tousle-haired boy, but always of Maggie and Auchobane's cliffs. Days merged together as they had done once before under the roof of Rose Cottage, but her new confinement was the antithesis of those wistful days of spring. In hours of darkness she thought she could smell once again the rich pungent scent of the sea, and feel the touch of Maggie's lined hand. She dreamed many dreams of Rose Cottage during those short weeks, but never about the child which grew within her.

"Time for your medicine Miss Keiller", the forceful nurse bellowed.

The nurse took the pills, a rainbow of colours and effects, and forced them into Isla's reluctant mouth. She pressed Isla's jaw together until the pills were swallowed and placed the tepid water on the table, taking time to gaze upon her newly acquired prisoner with disdain, before returning to the more compelling curiosity of her crime novel. Isla looked at the oversized nurse negotiating herself back through the heavy door, back to her own delusions. The pills in Isla's mouth tasted bitter and reminded her of her mother, but at least they brought with them quick hours of sleep.

It was during this scheduled sleep that the pain of childbirth finally presented itself. It began in intermittent discomfort, but quickly rose to an overpowering, consuming ache which ripped out her soul and wrung it to the floor. Hour after hour through darkness and the dawn, the pain persisted, crashing upon her young body in bursts of varying time and strength. It seemed to Isla, unbearable and unending. The intensity of its sting shocked her, its extremity and its force, overwhelmed her. She tried to sooth her failing frame, caress it into submission but again it came - another surge of pain, and she buckled underneath its power. She thought of her adventures in Auchobane harbour, and wished for the physical hardship of its storm. It seemed a far more conquerable mountain than the one presented before her. Throughout the night she reeled, screaming with fierceness, crying out for a maternal saviour which had never, ever existed. She longed for a cessation, either by death or deliverance. Chastised by the menacing midwife for her lack of strength, denied the drugs which would have eased her pain, she willed the child after many hours from her broken body with eventual exhaustion.

When the elusive, writhing stranger, the product of such painful anguish, was finally placed in her trembling arms, she gazed at the boy with the same look of apathy that his transient father had given her only nine months previous. No trumpets heralded his arrival, no unbridled joy, and no parent's pride. Isla had expected she would feel different - instantly indoctrinated to adulthood, but there was no dramatic transformation. She was still the same, just tied irrevocably to this small bundle that now exhaled with a deafening cry.

Isla felt no initial mothering connection. She thought to say 'my son', but the words seemed strange - too real, too heartfelt. The child stirred now, with more desire, and more determination than before - his laborious exertions had only been of a physical kind, his recovery from them more rapid than hers. Isla viewed him from a distance, where his movements could not influence her world in deep disorder. As this new life unfolded before her and her body recovered from the shock of childbirth, a fearful loneliness embedded itself within her heart. It was fear that she would fail him just as she had failed Maggie, and fear too at her mother's fortuitous words and threats which were rarely empty.

Those first newborn hours trickled past in a daze of exhaustion. Isla relinquished all hidden glories in attending the child, lurching in nightmarish sleep while a nurse tended to the child's every whim and saw off his persistent cries with the disinterest of employment. During the darkness she feigned sleep, in the light, detachment. Peering from the safety of her self-constructed cage, she observed as others tended the boy. She sat on the edge of her simple cell bed, deluding herself that her indifference was in the interest of the child, but it owed more to her self-preservation. She watched his desperate wriggling for comfort and warmth, wrapped in a warm woollen blanket and yet it was the soothing swathe of a mother's heartbeat he craved most.

As the physical aches and exhaustion began to wane, Isla's thoughts turned to her future and that of her son. She could bend to her mother's imposing will and abandon him as she herself had been abandoned; or she could chose a different life for her child. One filled with difficult days, but with self-determination and a security she herself had never felt. In the landscape of an isolated hospital, renouncing her son and returning to an anonymous London seemed an even colder future than one surrounded by the wilderness of Scotland. She gazed into the darkness of small hours with wide eyes, searching for an answer.

The boy too was awake, and she stood over him, quietly observing. She found fondness in his vulnerability. Something in his look betrayed knowledge greater than his hours and he seemed to sense her presence, pulling at his covers more desperately, trying to remove another barrier to the mother who lay beyond. She felt an unswerving protectiveness towards him welling inside her and she suddenly knew their fate. She felt a thunderous necessity to act at that moment before the storm of her mother's scorn closed in upon them both and they were lost forever.

Raising him gently from the firmness of his cot, Isla hid him safely amongst the warm folds of her dressing gown, the Keiller book still tucked neatly in its pocket. She dressed in outdoor clothes which would take them unnoticed through the daylight hours should they succeed that far. As she had writhed in pain through those last hours of childbirth, she had noticed the makeshift wooden board which hid a window in her room. Its details had distracted her from the trauma her body was suffering, but she remembered now the disintegrating window pane, veiled behind casually constructed timbers. It was ironic that the room which bound her forever to another being should also bring with it the means of her escape, as she tore through the careless boarding to reveal the draft of an outside air. The window itself opened with ease and she tentatively lowered herself and her son down onto the leaf-laden earth. Turning her back on this home for restless girls, she faced a view offered only by the stars and began to trek her way towards a brighter future.

With the light of a new day came the dawning of Isla's first real morning of motherhood. It was a gradual turning of shades from the darkness of night to a multitude of blues and the final brightness of a day which brought unexpected certainty in the course of her future and that of her son. Just as her mother had stolen away from a destructive relationship with her father, so she found herself taking the same brave steps from a different, damaging life with nothing but a Keiller book and a newborn child nestled securely in her arms. Her mother would not recognise the parallel paths of their lives. She had travelled too far along her own superficial course to acknowledge anything outside herself.

Glancing down at the boy in her arms, Isla doubted he would ever understand the magnitude of their journey, not just in miles but in setting the course of his childhood and adult life. As they trekked further towards the dim glow of a nearby town, Isla could hear the approaching drone of its modernity or the hum of traffic across fields and valleys. They made for the local railway station and stood huddled in the doorway of the waiting room searching the horizon for the first train which would take them northward.

Above Auchobane's pretty harbour, James watched the boats leave before dawn, gliding peacefully across water unusually still for that time of year. His thoughts were filled with Isla, the effortlessness with which she had left his life. Kirsty Keiller had found no great wealth in Rose Cottage, and had been true to her word in tearing the place apart in her empty quest. He had stolen back to the cottage after she left, and put things back in their rightful place. He had stayed that night at Rose Cottage, and every one since. Perhaps he waited for Isla to return, or enjoyed its distance from the Rectory and his old life. Whatever the reason, he was contented in his new cocoon, far from the attention of inquisitive locals and far from an intruding world. He watched the gannets engaging in their daily deathly plunges from the cliffs, pursuing their prey with enthusiasm. He envied their fearfulness, their courage and single-mindedness in pursuing their desires without compromise and he determined that from now on, he would take a similar approach with his own dreams.

In a cold train carriage trundling through a sleepy countryside many miles away, a piercing cry ripped through the wooden compartment, startling all who slumbered peacefully, not least Isla. A brief glance of recognition flashed across her face and for a moment those heavy eyelids which had drifted easily with the gentle lilting of the train, lifted up their weight and surveyed their strange surrounds. She gazed down at the small bundle rousing steadily within his swaddling. His eyes were quietly urgent and directed towards her own. Her heart melted with the pureness of its plea. It was the unequivocal love she had sought from her own mother but was destined to be denied. The child offered it to her in abundance, without question, without condition. A tear came to her eye and her throat tightened, constricted with overwhelming sentiment; but then the cry rang out again, stronger than before, with increasing urgency and volume. Appeasing the choral child, Isla gently rocked it back and forth in the early light of day as slumbering fields flew by, soothing it momentarily, distracting it from its demands. Cradling the boy in unsteady arms, she was tracked by his large expectant eyes which gazed up at her with an unyielding, insatiable yearning for fulfilment. His feelings were of need, want and desperation. They were feelings so alien in the often deathly humdrum of Isla's days that she had forgotten that they once existed. His hunger was quickly appeased. A small trickle seeped from the corner of his mouth making a bold bid for freedom, allowed to remain unchallenged by the boy.

Sitting back in the musty train seat which had seen better days, consoling a now quietly placated child, Isla reflecting on his transformation from loudly protesting newborn to gloriously contented infant, and feeling just a pang of jealousy at his black and white life. Here was a clean slate without taint and corruption, a suitable beginning on which to construct a life. Isla longed to be able to turn the switch so easily on her own feelings, but fate had placed that key too high, or worn it through so that it no longer functioned. Too tired, too broken, words that defined her life now speeding towards its next chapter.

Isla picked up the old Keiller recipe book, the only other item she now possessed, and dismissed the cobwebs which clung affectionately to its ancestral cover. She carefully peeled open its rusty binding, and touched the yellow pages which belied its age. On the first page, written in a neat, but practical and steady hand, were the words, 'Mrs. Keiller's Recipes for Marmalade'.

She felt herself undeserving of this sacred world of good women and strong character and that would be an insult to them to even touch its hallowed pages. But it was not an accident which had placed the book in her care. Maggie had intended it for her, to embrace it and learn from its pages but Isla still felt unprepared and stared only at the first page, allowing it to remain exposed to the elements of a cold, clandestine carriage.

James meanwhile had opened another jar of marmalade and dipped a spoon luxuriously into its contents. It gave warmth to his chest, and distracted him so that his melancholy had not the opportunity to settle. He had expected to be awash in a deep depression - the loss of his mother, the departure of a girl he had unexpectedly loved and the small matter of the obliteration of his home-life - any one of these trials would normally have triggered Armageddon, but for some reason, sitting on the old wooden gate of Rose Cottage, staring at the gannets, ladling his spoon in the warm, orange jar, none of it seemed to matter. Perhaps the marmalade was special after all, or perhaps it was Maggie herself, pressing a comforting hand on his heavy shoulders. Either way, his mind was as clear as the visibility that morning and his heart as buoyant as the fishing boats which glided across the silver sea. He took himself further up the hillside to gain a greater vantage on his new kingdom.

Isla's thoughts raced faster than the speed of the old diesel bus which was now winding its way from the train station at Dundee through rural villages along the Fife coastline and on towards her final destination of Auchobane. Her thoughts drifted naturally towards her mother and how she was now in possession of the incongruous title of grandmother - one he was never likely to know or meet. Perhaps that was that the greatest gift she could give him. The tiny fragments of her old life casually floated from her, passing through her fingers like traces of dust, disappearing into oblivion. The child she would call Billy after a man she had never met, but had known intimately, gazed up at its young creator with a wide watchfulness of expectation. His look was deep and his innocence palpable, thrilled by simply the presence of his mother. His sincerity melted the young girl's heart and all thoughts of London and regrets were instantly swept away.

Step 18: Skim off the Excess from the Marmalade

A bright winter sun had passed through its highest point of the day by the time Isla reached the old wooden gate of Rose Cottage. She found the spare key where Maggie had left it, entwined amongst the thorns amassing by the door. Inside, each room seemed more barren than the next, ambiguous contortions and vague shapes slicing across their desolate spaces, their deserted walls seemed to resonate more with Maggie‘s departure. Isla stood in the doorway of Maggie's now vacant bedroom, the keepsake of a once enthusiastic occupant. She remained for a while within its frame, mulling over Maggie's sudden departure, remembering the final moments of a life which had ended there.

She placed the plain, hardback Keiller notebook which coveted the recipes of many lifetimes, on the hollow bed next to her sleeping newborn son. Maggie had tried unsuccessfully in those first few weeks of Isla's arrival at Rose Cottage, to convey the history of those whose blood ran through her. But Isla could not see past the mother who blocked her vision to greater endeavours and realised too late the greater meaning of the tales Maggie told and the words of wisdom she proffered over those beautifully warm, vibrant Seville oranges.

Isla sat on the corner of the comfortable bed and turned the first of the delicate pages of the handwritten Keiller book, her family's book. Page after page revealed new and informed recipes - each of them scribed in a variety of styles and to varying degrees of education. All with the same ultimate objective - that of setting out in degrees of detail, the steps to be undertaken to achieve the most sublime kind of marmalade.

The first recipe which Isla read was for an 'Orange Jellied Dundee Marmalade'. It was written in, what Isla assumed to be, old Scottish. The words were muddled by modern standards, often misspelt, and the grammar, extraneous; but in line after line, page after page, came the practical steps for boiling, steaming and preparing ripened Seville oranges for their transformation into a wholesomely consumable marmalade. At the end of the recipe was written, in very tidy and efficient letters, 'Mrs. Janet Keiller', and the date - 1797. This was the very first Mrs. Keiller and the very first Keiller marmalade, written in innocuous blackened letters on a simple stained page. Without this fervour, this enthusiasm for the creation of a conserve, Maggie's own passion would not have existed and there would have been nothing remarkable about the old lady of Rose Cottage. It bound them together, this involved process of boiling and chopping. It created something very remarkable and unique in each and every Mrs. Keiller.

With curiosity Isla continued to turn the pages of this extraordinary notebook. The next recipe was that of 'Pippin Marmalet' - an unusual conserve by Isla's knowledge, proposed by Mrs. Barbara Keiller. The date at the end of the recipe was 1810. Isla leafed through the fine pages, carefully browsing this most unusual account of the Keiller family, and the lifeblood of her history. The subsequent recipe was credited to a Mrs. Margaret Keiller, who described the necessary actions to produce a 'Transparent Marmalade' as first produced in 1840. It was succeeded by Mrs. Elizabeth Keiller's 'Grated Marmalade' of 1851, then by Mrs. Mary Keiller's recipe for 'Special Thick Cut

Marmalade' dated 1865, and latterly by Mrs. Catherine Keiller's 'Marmalade for Puddings' from 1890. They were enlightening and instructive pages of beautifully described, intricately detailed marmalades of all shapes and sizes, all designs and uses. As she came towards the end of the notebook, Isla carefully turned to the final recipe, she began to read Mrs. Maggie Keiller's instruction for 'Orange Marmalade'. The steps were simple, the language direct - a recipe for smooth Seville marmalade, twice boiled. Isla looked at the date - it was 1933.

The book was not just a fantastical insight into the annals of Keiller history, but a record of the life, language and passions of Keiller women throughout the centuries. As she read again through their varied accounts, Isla imagined each of the Mrs. Keillers hugging their large blackened pots, in their small bothies or kitchens, fervently peeling, cutting, boiling, for hours on end in their cottages scattered along the Dundee coastline. All interconnected through their passion for marmalade. The final few pages of the notebook were optimistically blank. No doubt the first Mrs. Keiller had high hopes for the extension of her family tree, providing as she did a book with so many pages, but it was not to be. The family name and passion could not exist forever, and Isla thought it ironic that the pots of Maggie's marmalade haphazardly strewn throughout Rose Cottage were likely to outlive Keiller history in terms of their longevity and existence. The book would come to a sad end, resting as it did, not in pride of place in some hallowed historical society, but hidden away in the dampness of an unremarkable Cottage by the sea.

Isla closed the notebook gently so as not to awaken the ghosts which lay within. As the pages settled back into their intimate positions, a piece of paper dislodged and gently floated onto the bedroom floor from its concealed location in the back cover of the book. Isla bent down to retrieve it from the worn-through rug. Straightening out the pristine white folds of a modern letter, Isla read a grateful reply to enquiry, thanking the applicant for their submission fee. She skimmed the pleasantries of the letter for further meaning. It spoke of a marmalade competition - for glorious conserves, to be held in the regal surrounds of Caird Hall in Dundee, with the glorious prize of a silver spoon and the accolade of the 'Best Marmalade of the Year (1970)'. Isla read the letter with a tinge of sadness that Maggie's submission to the competition would never to be realised. Those dreams and ambitions had been stolen from her and there would be no more awards for Maggie and her momentous marmalade.

Isla sat for a while on the edge of Maggie's bed. She felt peaceful in this quiet world; reassured that to have conceded to the barbed embrace of her mother would have been a greater solitude. She looked again at the piece of paper which had fallen from the recipe book. It was then that she noticed something strange. The letter was addressed to her and not to Maggie. The entry to the competition was in her name, not Maggie's. She read the letter twice just to be sure. Maggie had taken some secrets with her to the grave after all, but sitting on the edge of that fortuitous bed, Isla decided that if those overdue happy days would not find her then she would seek them out. The disappointments of a young life would end here and, at least for Maggie, she would try to reach the stars.

She rose from the bed with greater confidence than she had sat there and returned to the small kitchen, resolving to ingest as much as she could from the book's fortuitous pages to create of her own recipe for the competition. When she had arrived at Rose

Cottage she had no knowledge of marmalade. To find herself some months later employing her time and energy in creating one, was unexpected. She reopened the notebook and did what anyone would do with a history book - she started from the beginning.

James stood leaning awkwardly over the chair, ignorant of the prologue unfolding around him.

“I didnae think you’d come back”, said James with a smile.

Where else could she go? There was no other home - not in name, not in spirit.

“This is my home”, replied Isla. “Our home.”

Why should it not be? If her mother’s only desire was the financial reward offered by an old woman’s inheritance, she was welcome to it. All she asked for was the modest four walls in which she sat.

James peered over Isla’s shoulder at the letter which was demanding her concentration.

“What have you got there?”

“Hope”, was Isla’s cryptic reply.

James read what words he could while arching over her engaged body. Their sentiment seemed less of a revelation to his eyes.

“A marmalade competition? I don’t understand.”

“It was a gift from Maggie.”

Fearing ridicule James remained silent in the expectation that all would eventually be revealed. It was a technique he had hit upon during school when his name alone had been enough to incur the wrath of teachers and peers. It seemed ill-advised to invite further mockery through imprudent questioning.

In contrast, Isla's thoughts had become enveloped by marmalade. If she could produce a conserve with even a drop of the magic contained in Maggie's wondrous condiments, then perhaps there was a chance of a prize and if fate was on her side, some reward which would support them in the beginnings of this new life. Independence from her mother gave heady hope. It was an idyll, a dream and in Isla's experience such fantastical thoughts never took flight. She stood up with a purpose and handed the letter to the perplexed young man who now leant upon the weathered surface of the sink. Speed was of the essence, she felt, as to produce enchantment may take considerable time and so she ventured out into the expectant garden in the direction and discovery of the old outbuilding which nestled in the delights behind Rose Cottage.

An old corrugated shed stood amidst the glorious unruliness of the cottage garden. It had an appearance of being hastily constructed in the space of an afternoon. Overrun and improved upon by wild ivy which clung to its sides and forgave its unsightliness, it had imbedded itself within the heart of the garden greenery to such an extent that its position was not immediately apparent to an explorative Isla. Despite its flimsy appearance, it had withstood the same natural abuse as the cottage itself and had stood tall against the infinitesimal storms which rolled in from the sea. Isla unhooked the rusted lock and with a proclaiming groan, the thin metal door swung open on its hinges and revealed its inner glories.

The beam of light which leapt forward through the open doorway enveloped the long lost contents of the shed and it suddenly gasped with life once again, glass glistening with delight at its beholder. Since Dougie's death, the resplendent jars had waited patiently for their deliverance and here, on this most benign of days had come their reckoning. They exhaled with delight at their prospective return.

Isla was blinded momentarily by their enthusiasm and glorious brilliance. Stacked neatly in square trays, they formed a pillar of radiance waiting to be unveiled. Isla gently touched one of the outer jars. It rang with delight at this living interaction, giddy with expectation in its purpose.

"You're going tae enter one of Maggie's marmalades in tae the competition at Dundee?" asked James, appearing at the door and suddenly blocking the only source of light which had aided Isla's delightful rediscovery.

She carefully removed a tray of jars from its delicately stored position.

"There's near fifty jars in the cottage", continued James, standing to one side. "Why not take one of those?"

"Because I'm not going to enter one of Maggie's marmalades into the competition", replied Isla, stacking a second level of glassware above the first. "I'm going to enter one of my own."

"You know how tae make marmalade?" James folded his arms, surprised by Isla's ambitious determination, or astounding naivety.

"I'll learn", was her indomitable response, in an unwavering tone with gritty inflections.

"But the competition is in three days", replied James hoping to dispel this misplaced enthusiasm. He could sense failure and sought to navigate Isla from a disastrous course.

She said nothing, refusing to admit any fragment of doubt which could thwart the precious rebirth of hope within her heart. She spun round to face him, eyes barely visible over the not inconsiderate weight and height of three stories high of glass jars. She had embraced wholeheartedly the stubbornness of her Keiller ancestors, and stood shoulder to shoulder with each of them, an army against nonbelievers.

"It can take years tae fashion a good marmalade" continued James, intimidated by this unexpected wave of resoluteness.'

"I don't need to make a good marmalade", replied Isla, her words at once appeasing and confusing the anxiety of this man who stood in her light. She brushed past him out into the blinding starkness of a day.

James made negligible inroads into an offer of help with her heavy load as Isla flew past him. He followed, with chivalrous intention of saving any jars which may make a big for freedom from the girl's unsteady hand.

"I just need to make a perfect one"', Isla concluded, her eyes now proficient to arrest a potential exchange with the back wall of the cottage.

James stopped abruptly, his hopes for her abandoned.

“Before she died, Maggie gave me the Keiller marmalade book”, continued Isla, over the sound of a rising tide and reproaching gannets. “It contains every recipe for marmalade, ever created by a Keiller woman.”

“Well, I suppose that’s something”, James started again and tracked Isla and her heavy burden as they rounded upon the front of Rose Cottage.

“But I’m not going to use it”, Isla exclaimed with force, disappearing with her pillar of glass, inside the dark, depths of the cottage. “I’m going to create a recipe of my own, because I’m a Keiller.”

James, finding himself on the breach of the cottage door, stopped to consider his path. He had a clear choice. He could walk away and allow her to fail alone, or he could follow her inside with the hopes of persuading her out of her nonsense, before time, and her faith, faded. If he followed his heart, he would have leapt through that doorway without fear or question. If his head ruled his thoughts, he would be back in the Auchobane before sunset.

Inside Rose Cottage, Isla was frantically exploration the gluttony of bric-a-brac which rested within those bothy walls. What Isla sought was every year of marmalade - on congested cupboards, and sacred shelves, behind bedraggled bookcases and inside vacant vases, she hunted for her prize. Some were obvious, others required some ingenuity, but after an hour, perhaps more, she had covered decades in conserves.

Isla placed each of the jars on the kitchen table. They covered its surface in warmth, effusing the room with their welcoming glow. Glass upon glass lifted an ambiance like a field of candles or the brilliance of a glorious light. With awe, she beheld these marvellous marmalades, conserves which contained not only the shallow mouldings of a fruit, but harboured the passions and the spirit of Maggie's resplendent life. They were the heart of the woman, her hopes, her desires, her soul, and together they rang gloriously like the trumpeting of angels.

James passed quietly through the doorway, drawn in by the brilliant light effusing from the cottage as natures own glow faltered.

"Is that them all?"

"Every last one."

He crept closer, mesmerised momentarily.

"How many?"

"Thirty seven."

She handed him a spoon.

"No", he shook his head. "This is fer a Keiller."

Isla took back the implement and began with the first marmalade. Nothing rivalled the taste of those magnificent orange morsels. The fruit was exquisite and matured, a sugary delight, the flecks of peel dancing upon the tongue and sweeping with the sunshine of Seville. Isla's mouth warmed with the promise of the smooth conserve as with every spoonful of marmalade, she was thrown amongst the orange groves of the Mediterranean. With every drop, a new wave of happiness and she danced inside to a glorious tune.

James watched Isla's brow lift, released from the weight of her difficulties. He was confounded that a simple mixture of fruit and sugar in just the right quantity and combination could relieve the physical exertions of a hard life. He waited for Isla to return from her delicious travels, but she was still far away on her sensuous journey, still accommodating climes too exotic for explanation. Her eyes dimmed as she basked in the sunlight of a beautiful day, surrounded by a bountiful nature too exquisite to comprehend. It was some time before she resurfaced from her tremendous exploration, one which she found herself transformed utterly by, and wonderfully so.

She carefully placed the spoon transposed across the rim of the final marmalade and looked up from her expedition, a new, more subdued being.

A patient James had succumbed to sleep, his head against the comfortable chair, passing an unremarkable night which came and went in shadows and stillness. When he awoke the next morning it was to an industrious kitchen and a mountain of citrus fruit smothering every available surface within the room and beyond. The smell was invigorating - sharp, pointed, but fresh and feisty.

Isla stood patiently peeling, the floor gradually acquiring an orange hue with the mountains of disregarded flesh which floated downwards from her busy hands. Instinctively he rose to gather up the deserted ends, coercing them together, amplifying their peaks.

"Don't!" exclaimed Isla suddenly. "I need them!"

James immediately released his citrus load and they fell back upon their heap, their conical twists bouncing merrily off the floor with enjoyment at this entertaining game.

“There’s pectin in the peel”, she continued with frantic authority. “That makes the marmalade set.”

James was reproached by the abruptness of her tone and the dark circles around those manic, but beautiful, blue eyes.

“Have you been up all night?”

James peered at the new rawness of those porcelain hands, stained with blood where the peeler had excavated deeper than the fruit. Isla’s weariness was reply enough.

“Stop. Just fer a wee while” he continued with touching concern at those self-inflicted wounds.

“There’s no time”, replied Isla, her fingers continuing their work like a fever.

James placed his large hand on hers to arrest the erratic to and fro of the peeler against skin and fruit.

“Just fer a wee while.”

Isla put up token resistance to the repeal of her repetitive motion, but James’s hand held firm and the effect was liberation to her tired fingers.

The peeler disentangled itself, in a long overdue release and dropped to the kitchen floor. The implement removed, Isla’s hands remained fixed in their contorted position, the constancy of many hours not easily shaken. With their movement broken her will ebbed, and Isla herself slid to the floor like a piece of dismembered peel, slumping amongst them like a suitable sibling. Her head fell forward, pressed upon by unsustainable weights and her eyes drooped wearily with exhaustion. Her fingers reborn, she placed her head and her abundant strawberry curls into them, their natural home.

James sat next to her amongst the conical skins which bobbed between them like a bright orange sea.

As Isla's tears trickled then stormed, and her shoulders reverberated in sympathy, he sat quiet and still, waiting for this temporary downpour to abate. It did wither after a time, her head lifted and her eyes opened.

"I thought I could do it", she said quietly.

Isla shook her head at the magnitude of her task. She was just a girl after all, sitting in a kitchen - without lovers, without friends, without kin.

"Mother was right."

James understood the maternal weight which sat on Isla's shoulders. In truth, he had born a similar burden of his own. He longed for an unconditional maternal love, to be held close, without judgement, without question. It was the stuff of dreams.

As this enchanting girl was unable to raise her head to meet his eyes, James lifted it instead. He had been taken aback by the depths of his own feelings at her departure. Surprised by the unexpected desertion of a girl he had warmed to; his initial reaction was to recoil with shame at his own rejection but he saw after a time that it was not he that she had abandoned, but her own self. He had underestimated the magnitude of Kirsty Keiller's influence over her daughter and he had, to his own disgrace, offered Isla too little support to fight her corner. His words and actions might have helped her find her courage, but it seemed she had discovered it by herself, lurking in the depths of a maternity hospital. His joy at her return was intoxicating and he was certain now that he was lost forever to her transfixing blue eyes.

"I didn't even like him", Isla's voice trailed off, her thoughts drifting to the tousle-haired boy for the last time. His person, along with any affection, had faded and any images which persisted now were due to her stubbornness alone. A consuming need for love, channelled to a stranger in the absence of a more intimate source. Now, with her newborn son Billy and this comfortable, local boy, she felt she might have found what she had desired for so long.

Beneath the old dresser, in a corner almost hidden from view, sat a jar of marmalade. In its position, Isla had easily missed it during her search of the Cottage, but it peered out now from its concealment, a gem from the first batch of marmalade in 1931. It reminded Isla that the lows of her life were not exclusively hers and that others had suffered beneath that same roof.

"Maggie never questioned my past and never judged my actions", Isla began. "I need to believe in her and the marmalade. I need believe that I can win that marmalade contest, or else I've failed her and I've failed myself."

James examined the bumpy surface of one of the multitude of oranges which dressed the floor. Its vividness was exciting, the whiteness of the pectin a suitable accompaniment to its brightness. It was as though the inner and the outer had conspired together to produce a perfect altercation.

“We’d best get on with it then”, he replied, rising from the floor. “If we’re going tae win that prize.”

He offered a hand to Isla which was quickly taken, and together they set about the production of a conserve with expectation and the bond of youthful love. Hours were filled with bubbling, gurgling liquids, brimming with the scent of citrus in varying degrees and the smoke of an almost ready marmalade. With graduations of success and failure, conserves were born and dismissed with equal regularity as perfection eluded the innocent inventors. Rose Cottage waited expectantly, watching with interest its occupant’s distraction. Half-set jars sat on every surface, a spoon ladled here and there where tasting had been made, a saucer or two where the marmalade had failed in its final set and now sloshed like the stormy North Sea with every breeze and direction.

“It’s no use”, cried Isla as she tasted her umpteenth marmalade and slumped in a chair.

James languished his spoon by the latest jar which Isla had swiftly dismissed.

“It’s not that bad”, he replied, squinting with the excessive tartness.

He looked at an exhausted girl beaten by her own ambition. Her head thumped against the table top sending the half-empty pots chiming. He laughed at their merry harmony. Isla smiled at the idiocy of their situation. Surrounded by pots and steaming pans, the room filled with a stickiness which clung to their clothes and hair. It could have been tears which followed, but instead it was fits of laughter which embraced the heavy household. With liberation came mischief, as Isla placed her hand inside a pot of rejected marmalade and smeared it across James’s cheek. He reciprocated with a coat or two of a too sweet variety. Isla retrieved a spoon and launched her offensive in the form of a ladle of marmalade which missed its target entirely and hit against the whitened surface of the stone wall, imbuing it with a splodge of orange. James failed to duck for the second attack, which landed squarely on his shirt. Encouraged, he responded by firing the entire contents of a tart marmalade onto Isla's head, increasing her fits of laughter which buoyed her strawberry blond curls and her brimming blue eyes. She wiped the liquid from her face and distributed it readily down the arm of her afflicter. Sensing that a line had been breached between innocence and something more profound, James grasped Isla's porcelain hand, and place a long anticipated kiss on her sweetened lips.

Isla was startled but she did not disentangle herself from him. Her mind raced with remembrances of a previous embrace, a far less tender one, and one she had confused for passion. This was different - more familiar, less intense. While his lips pressed against hers, a thousand doubts were born within her mind. It was a moment he may have taken for affection, but she was less secure. It came to an end after a few seconds, and he stood back, in search of assurance.

Isla looked at him, but said nothing, unsure of what she felt or thought. James's deflation increased with every second she spent in interpretation of her own feelings. They sat in silence, covered in marmalade.

As if the cogs had finally found again their rhythmic routine, Isla stepped forward and planted a reciprocating kiss upon his brave lips.

"Needs more sugar", she announced with a smile.

Perhaps the marmalade was an aphrodisiac after all.

There were only a few crystals left, a drop of rosewater, half a cinnamon stick, some saffron and an ounce of musk. The exquisite box of exotic ingredients which had sat for an eternity beneath the sink was now heavily depleted from their marmalade endeavours. Isla unleashed the entirety of these few remaining elements into the pot which stewed above the fire. It was the last of the oranges, the final strands of peel, and now the residual ingredients, all consumed within this mystical brew. If this final batch of conserve proved inadequate then there was nothing more to be done. The competition would be lost and so too the trust of an old woman who had overflowed with warmth and history.

Isla watched the substance bubble for a time then, as the heat slowly dissipated, it calmed and the process of infusion began. A magical intermingling of ingredients commenced and a new, glorious scent was born, providing the foundation for an elusive spirit and with it the possibility for a fantastic marmalade.

The course of such conception was a delicate one. Their previous failures had prepared Isla for an inevitable downfall. It was with some trepidation that she approached the cast iron pot, two hours after releasing its potential.

Removing the lid, she peered deep inside the glowing chasm. The liquid was serene, resting after its monumental invention. Its aroma enveloped her and the room - it was powerful and rich. The rush was intoxicating as she drank in its heady delights. Reaching for a spoon, she delved it desirously inside the orange formation, and watched as the flecks of peel danced upon the flash of steel, consuming and taming its cold heart. The light flickered from those errant orange chips, the tantalising expectation of a fruit, now utterly transformed. She abandoned the spoonful to her lips and the now experienced taste buds which lay beyond.

The glorious carousel of flavour unleashed upon her soul was enough to calm Isla's fluttering heart which had feared that all was lost. What she found, was delirium. In great abundance with mesmerising flavours as the accumulation of ingredients fused to form their enchantment. She smiled a joyous, liberating smile. From the clutches of exhaustion and weariness, she had discovered absolute pleasure. Here was a kind of nirvana.

Seeing the exorcism taking flight in young Isla's eyes, James took the spoon from her hand, and obtained a morsel of his own. Nothing could have prepared him for the intensity of flavour and ethereal journey on which he now found himself. His spirit lifted as he traversed the Indian Oceans, and rushed clearly through those Caribbean hills, finding himself in glorious Tuscany, with poplar trees brushing gently in summer fresh winds. Finally he landed by an orange grove, with citrus scents overwhelming all physical sensations, toying with his taste buds, awash with moisture and succulence.

"It's…."

"Perfect", concluded Isla.

Step 19: Transfer to pristine Glass Pots

As this new marmalade dissipated on their tongues, the adventurers returned to the practicalities of Rose Cottage. The hot pan was emptied with exuberant care of all its delicious contents, repackaged into perfectly small encapsulations, labelled and stored for its significant journey to Dundee. They numbered ten in total, and sat upon the table, awaiting their great undertaking. Although the darkness came, it arrived with little determination, a full moon offering enough light to stir the contents of the jars and its creators, with restlessness and intermingled dreams.

At an early hour the next morning, James took the tray of jars and placed nine of them in Hamish, the old wheelbarrow, and the last one he placed next to the baby, who grasped the importance of this innocuous jar in his newborn hands. All three made their way down the grass track to the village, navigating every bump and turn which threatened to usurp them.

James had remembered Dougie's old van, hidden beneath an old sheet behind his shop, where it had been retired with the same pride as one of his comrades in arms. His companion for years when no soul could be roused for the job, the two had ventured across hills and valleys in pursuit of their noble employment. James had discovered it one day, while distracted by other inflictions and thought that Dougie would approve of its use now to support their means of escape.

He removed the cover with aplomb and opening the driver's door, he found the ignition key as expected, hidden beneath the seat where Dougie could always find it. Turning the key, it reawakened a dormant engine, enlivening that which had slept too long. The cobwebs reverberated, shocked by the reinvigoration of their homesteads, but the mechanical heart of the vehicle roared its delight at rediscovery. The engine hummed merrily with contentment, like a purring pet lying dizzily on a temperate lap.

The jars were shut carefully in the back of the van, wedged tight between old boxes to soften any adventurous corner or sudden arrest. Isla and Billy joined James in the cab, a contented resting place for a few hours. The thrill of this new adventure preoccupied them such that they failed to perceive the faint movement of those back doors, groaning as they swung open again at the request of a dangerous hand.

The subsequent sound of smashing glass pierced the vulnerable containment of Isla's heart. With every piercing crash, her hopes, her dreams, the recently resurrected faith which dared to hint at a distant clearing of the dark clouds of depression, all disintegrated with that desperate noise. The image of a smiling Maggie faded like the promise of a beautiful day. Isla's head weighted forward as the heaviness returned, she was beguiled again by an irrepressible fate.

James rushed from the cab, knowing that it was already too late to save all the jars, but he soon realised that even a singular rescue was in vain. He found an exuberant Ewan by the van doors, wilfully and enthusiastically bearing down upon the tray of marmalade pots with the destructive force of a large stick. His eyes flashed with giddy glee as he saw his brother approach, and he increased the vigour of his destruction despite none of the jars having survived his initial onslaught. James grabbed the wooden implement and forced Ewan to the ground, wrestling the stick from his hands, and fending off the fists which rose against him in a fury. It was a rare opportunity for Ewan to give physicality to his frustration and his hatred for an elder sibling who drained all interest and affection from those around him. He revelled in the arrival of his day.

“What are you doing?” cried James with bewilderment at this act of pure loathing from his brother.

A satisfactory smile presented itself on Ewan’s young face. His eyes were wild with excitement, delirious with adrenalin at the hurt he had exacted upon his brother.

“Why?” came James again, ignorant of the strength of jealousy his brother held against him. He felt nothing in return, had no deep festering desire to unleash similar blows against his younger brother. They weren’t close, it was true. Their characters were dissimilar. James had always felt that his brother had equipped himself better for the world. Ewan was at the heart of Auchobane’s youthful promise, surrounded by friends, accepted easily and readily by all. He appeared unaffected by the emotional struggles which wreaked havoc on James’s personality and Ewan embodied a popularity which his elder brother could never hope to achieve.

From the shadows, a small figure slithered unnoticed, smugly satisfied at this pitting of brother against brother. Her walking stick was swiftly dispatched into the cushioned ribs of her eldest grandson in support of the younger who remained pinned to the ground.

“He was doing as he was told”, said a familiar voice. “He’s a good laddie, no like his brother.”

James looked up and was confronted by the lined face of his calculating grandmother.

“This was you!”

“Course it was. You didnae think I’d let another Keiller marmalade triumph, now did ye?”

She laughed with the volatile release of her revenge.

“‘Tis only marmalade”, replied James.

His grandmother sneered.

“You’re soft, just like your mother”, she replied through teeth which ground their disdain.

“I know the truth of her now”, replied James, his moment having arrived. “But it took a Keiller to tell me.”

“Oh aye?” replied Mrs. McLintock. “The truth was it she told ye? Did she tell ye your mother was a disgrace tae this family? That she disrespected your father and the Lord? That she was no good, a jezebel and a loose woman without a moral bone in her body?”

“There’s nowt but poison comes fae your mouth”, said James, angry that his grandmother should slander for the memory of his mother. He turned to Ewan.

“She’s known all this time that our mother was dead”, he continued. “Dead these fifteen years but she’s never said a word of it tae you or me.”

Ewan looked at his grandmother for some kind of reassurance. He found none there.

“Aye, I kept it from you”, she replied without guilt. “‘Twas fer your own good so that her sins wouldnae turn you bad and all. She took a depraved, immoral path and she got what she deserved.”

“What she deserved was a life without the interference of a manipulative old woman who wanted tae rule her husband and village afore him. She deserved happiness, and that’s what she was looking fer at the Leap when she was taken. The Lord himself knows she was never going tae find owt at the Rectory. I was old enough tae remember how you treated her, how you whirred away at her with a snide comment and a nasty remark. Nothing she ever did was good enough fer you, and you always let her know it. Then you played our father for a fool, so he turned against her. I cannae fault her fer wanting tae leave, I‘ve been wanting tae do the same ever since she did!”

“Well, there’s nowt stopping ye now”, Mrs McLintock muttered bitterly.

“Aye but there is. There’s a sanctimonious old woman who can’t abide the happiness of others” he continued, surveying the devastation at the back of the van. “No without wanting tae destroy it. Even something as wee as a jar of marmalade.”

“’Tis not about the jelly laddie”, cackled Mrs. McLintock. “I couldnae care a speck fer it.”

She prodded the remnants of glass jars now scattered about the body of the van, as if to emphasize her apathy at their harm.

“What then?” asked James, mystified as to the workings of the old woman’s mind and the thoughts which festered beneath her thinly set eyes.

“Humiliate me in front of my parishioners will ye?” she slithered. “This is not the Lord’s retribution, ‘tis infinitely worse. ‘Tis mine.”

“There’s more of the devil in you than any Keiller”, shouted James, standing not an inch from the end of the old woman’s nose. “Aye, this may be your retribution but your day is coming an’ all. But it’ll not be with St Peter, it’ll be at the burning gates o’ hell!”

James had never felt closer to unleashing some kind of physical force upon the old woman, but he stopped short, fearing that it would make him no better a person than she. Instead he slammed the van doors shut with such a force as to shake all who sat within it. He stormed back into the cab, and drove off without saying another word. Ewan looked at his grandmother. She appeared taken aback, for perhaps the first time in her long and severe life. But she recovered in moments, disregarding her grandson’s arguments as the voice of a child and determining that they ought never to see each other again.

Not a word was spoken as the van sped unwieldy through the village streets, out of Auchobane and along the winding road towards Dundee. It was only when considerable miles and minutes had passed that the arguments which swam around James’s head began to wane.

“That’s it then”, Isla spoke quietly.

Her mood had plummeted faster than the gannets which dived from Auchobane’s cliffs. Pessimistic at heart, she had relinquished the unfamiliar hope which had settled within her, surprised it had lingered there so long.

“Not quite”, replied James.

Isla looked at him. Surely it was all lost. The jars were destroyed, their glass shards still rattled around the back of the van with every unbridled corner taken at speed.

She followed James's gaze down to the baby, who slept, sucking intriguingly on the lid of the shiny jar he held tightly protected within his small hands.

The old van continued on its journey, bouncing a little higher on the uneven surface of the road, tilting with abandon at every enjoyable swerve, as the smiles of anticipation returned to grace a vista.

The beautiful wilderness of Fife and the red cliffs of Arbroath made Isla feel less anxious about their journey as the shades of Dundee became less intimidating passing along the eternal beaches of Carnoustie. They drove inland, trundling through green fields which struck a contrast against the rock pools and dynamic cliffs which had formed the coastline of Auchobane. The menacing waves of the North Sea were replaced with tranquil shades of emerald and jade which lifted her spirits as they sprung their way along the winding roads which hugged each and every hillside enthusiastically. Hope bubbled throughout the countryside around Dundee, brimming from beneath the rusty roof of the old van, extolling the raw beauty which framed their view. Isla thought of Maggie amongst her rose bushes. Perhaps it was the approaching fulfilment of her dying wish, or the impression of their wild surrounds, it may even have been the remnants of the marmalade which still lingered on her tongue. Whatever the reason, Isla enjoyed the recollection, and smiled at this lucid vision.

She saw again the gentle persuasion of a woman who had given them the gift of knowledge and in return had asked for very little. Isla remembered the wistful movement of Maggie's mind, how it wandered freely through her history - from the young woman with excitement and enthusiasm for a life before heartbreak, to the older Maggie, transformed by her desperate reality and associated sorrow. Her private moments of delusion were a more understandable mirage than their hopeless journey to Dundee with nothing but a single jar of marmalade.

Caird Hall stood resplendent, steadfast with its ghosts and chequered history. Its splendour was of a different kind to the London townhouse which had formed Isla's childhood. The van came to an abrupt halt beneath trees which had been contorted by aggressive storms some years back. Isla's courage ebbed as she came face to face with the reality of their task and she began to feel inadequate at their coming, and intimidated by what they hoped to achieve. It struck her, standing in the shadows of this great building, that this was perhaps her greatest act of immaturity. In her mind it had seemed so simple. The marmalade was produced, and yes it was glorious, but in these grand surroundings, its glory seemed suddenly mediocre.

"It's very impressive", said Isla, gazing up at the formal cornices.

"We're all Jock Tamson's bairns", replied James. "We've as much right as any to be here."

Isla caved to the uselessness of her legs, and sat down on the great granite steps, hanging her head so low that she could see each glistening piece of grit, wonder how it had come to be there, who had laid it down, and how many had travelled across the surface of those individual stones.

James sat down beside her, a comforting large hand placed between the blades of her back. His touch was strong and determined and her racing heart subsided a little. His support was unfaltering and she thought if she could not be strong on her own, then he would have strength for both. There might be good days, often bad; but they would not have to be endured alone. She had been carried on a wave of curious enthusiasm, had believed that the impossible was possible. She had embraced the fervour of Maggie's passion. It was an unusual state for Isla, for whom life was always half empty, if occupied at all. Here on the grand steps, surrounded by an intimidating metropolis, she drifted back into that familiar, warm embrace of despair.

"I think we'll be back in Rose Cottage by dusk with nothing but a lesson on how the world works", she whispered, first in her own mind, and then to the paving below. She laid her head upon her hands, balking at the power her pessimism.

"There's nae heart without hope, and nae hope without heart", replied James.

The white clouds which dotted the undulating horizon seemed transfixed by the conversation beneath Caird Hall, and as fellow competitors passed by, curious at the party which had gathered there, Isla considered the blurred line between bravery and folly.

"Let's get on", said James, pulling her up out of her stupor. She let him raise her and her hopes and they passed up the steps and into the great hall.

Step 20: Cover the Pleasing Pots with a Protective Lid

The information board at the front of Caird Hall may have detailed the formal proceedings of the day, but it concealed a multitude of emotions for those who followed its direction through hallowed corridors and beneath glorious pastiche. Faded shades of history lurked behind leaden doors as they trekked past in convoy through curtained openings. Finally they arrived at the heart of the building and the Mirror Room where the reflections of nervous entrants echoed a thousand times around the ornately crafted mirrors which adorned its walls. It was a glorious gathering place for curious historians and many more with a humble pot. A small queue of hopefuls had already begun to form at the far end of this majestic hall, where a sturdy table had been erected to receive their precious offerings. Isla and James added their number to the burgeoning crowd.

"Just the one jar?" asked a cold voice with more condescension than surprise as they reached the head of the queue with their single pot of marmalade.

A clip-board was produced as an authoritative hand created some decisive marks on a piece of paper, furiously scribbling as though dictating a government bill. Isla froze under her interrogation as reality rung round the hallowed hall with every shrill tone from this austere mouth. The sudden urge to abandon her cause rose swiftly once again, as it always did when she found herself faced with fear of exposure. She longed to remove their insignificant jar and rush from their imposing surrounds, forgetting every nonsensical notion of a prize from her mind; but the marmalade had long disappeared onto the judging table which was now brimming full with promising entrants.

This judicial woman's piercing green eyes bore through Isla from behind turtle rimmed spectacles. Inferring a convenient answer from Isla's silence, she scribbled neatly on her paper, ticking each and every one of the boxes as dictated by culinary regulation.

A smaller lady now appeared at her shoulder with hair extending ambitiously upward and outward, a full foot from the top of her head. Rampant in the extreme, it expanded in all directions to create a kind of halo around a rotund face fond of jam tarts. Her appearance suggested a successful navigation through the storms of this life, without flurry to arrest her sails or swell to break her bough. Isla wondered whether her breeze was as free as she presented it, or whether she were merely overcompensating for a vessel which had sunk entirely, and she now waded in depths too great for her comfort.

This lady looked approvingly at Isla's submission.

"What a bonnie wee jar!" she squealed at a pitch uncomfortably audible, with a grin of mischief.

"I havenae seen a jar of its kind fer many a year", she piped, her eyes dancing like the playful grey hairs on her head. She picked up the jar and tapped it, the peel within swimming at her beckoning.

Her colleague sighed at this display of informality from a fellow judge and removing the jar from her hand, placed it back in the clearly designated area, attaching a number to the lid.

"Name?" she snapped, reaching the finality of her long list of formality.

"Keiller", replied Isla.

The severe woman looked up from her notes with surprise, her right eyebrow rising to an unsupportable archway.

“Did you say Keiller?”

The stern adjudicator’s face dropped a modicum of its composure.

“Did she say Keiller?” the effervescent lady with jovial hair leant covertly towards her co-worker, whispering like a child revealing its deepest secrets.

“Of the Dundee Keillers?” she whispered again, this time to Isla, excitement simmering in every tone.

Isla nodded.

Another squeal emitted from that kaleidoscope of a woman, of a tone higher in pitch and more unbridled than the first.

“Oh my! A Keiller!” she exclaimed, brimming with a palpable and very infectious excitement.

She looked with anticipation at her colleague, who held her pen fixed throughout her friend’s tenuous exclamations, hopeful of completing her registration tasks.

“‘Tis an honour to meet with marmalade royalty”, she continued, making her way under the table with enviable speed and flexibility for one of her age and physical size.

She took Isla’s hand and shook it with an enthusiastic vigour.

“An honour”, she continued. “A real honour.”

Her smile was as bright and clear as a new moon and Isla smiled with the dutiful distinction of an adopted daughter.

Registration eventually, and rather embarrassingly completed, Isla stood by the entrance and watched as her little jar was swallowed up by many more on an undistinguished table of entrants. The seemingly unremarkable marmalade sat amongst the gingham wrappings and colourful labels of entrants who had also similar hopes for their own imaginative creations. They too had stored their happiness in pots now filed away for anonymous consumption by official strangers. She watched new applicants tentatively approach the table long after she, meekly offer their marmalade. Then she turned away and began to make her way back through the oak panelled hallways which criss-crossed the Caird Hall, masking the outside bright sunlight.

Waiting was a tenuous affair. Isla gazed out upon the bustling life of Dundee, rustling with a winter air which breezed across its surface and teased with the promise of dampness. She scanned their surrounds, barren trees striving to attain the blueness of a sky, stretching tall and proud, grazing the lowness of ethereal clouds, but their object perpetually denied. She watched James gently rock Billy, the child smiling with delight at the absolute affection. Their connection had been a slow burn which had fanned to flame, so unlike the sudden ignition of her previous affair which had burnt brighter but extinguished quicker. Isla lent back on the steps of the Hall. Her mind drifted to distant thoughts of her tousle-haired boy, but his image was blurred and unclear. She tried to force the clarity of those eyes which had drawn her in, but she changed their colour a thousand times. She had fallen for an idyll and found it lacking. But this new Scottish boy had been different from the start. There was no obvious infatuation. Nothing in his person had excited her. Everything about him represented a marked contrast to her first disastrous affair. Perhaps the outcome would be a contrast too. She had grown into him - his courage, his perseverance and his tenderness. He had awoken greater feeling within her with his unremarkable appearance than any antagonistic attitude ever could.

James had an inkling that Isla's thoughts, like her gaze, were fixed in his direction. There lingered within him a gaping hole where family should have been. For fifteen years the expectation of his mother's return had filled that void, but now that was gone. This emptiness bothered him and he had no notion of how to fill it. There was a growing consciousness that although she had not physically walked with him through the passing of all those years, he had never mourned her loss. The potential for reunion existed, and while it did, she lived a life like any other, just desperately removed from his. Death was a finality he had never considered but here it was and he was filled with the grief which should have been his at four years old. She had never aged, and now it seemed she never would. Nothing she could say or do would ever dismantle the image of perfection he had constructed for her. He found idle play with the baby a necessary distraction. The child swung in his arms with a newly discovered rush of excitement. The colours, the smells and senses, would never be remembered, but the feeling of happiness would always be retained.

The hour of competition finally arrived and, carried by an enthusiastic wave, the party of hopefuls found themselves once again in the surrounds of the Mirror Room. Jars of marmalade proliferated on every surface, reflecting back the centuries old light which pierced through staid panes.

Isla searched for her familiar jar amongst the cornucopia of colour, size and shape in the glorious room. It was a game of 'hide and seek' on a grander scale than the one she had played not a year before in Rose Cottage but her pursuit was now a more personal one. Resting on an eclectic table at the back of the hall, she found her treasure. Quietly standing, unassuming, the lid disturbed to facilitate the tasting process, the jar stood comfortably reflecting the historic magnificence of the four walls which contained it, somehow at home. Isla stood silently admiring it for a moment. She had poured her soul into that little pot, which sat innocuously on a hallowed surface. She had suffered for the little flecks of peel which peeked out from within the silky orange liquid and she felt proud at the resurgence of her faith, both in herself and in those who stood beside her. The subtle inflection of a smile upturned unseen in the corners of her mouth. It was a contentment which marked a very personal triumph. She touched the glass shell of her marmalade, glistening in the sunshine, admiring her own precious jar, lost to a world of private thoughts. Then she reluctantly continued on her tour around the room, a disinclined distance growing between her and the pot of marmalade. She strolled a little slower past subsequent jars and for just a moment, she thought she could smell the faint aroma of musk and cinnamon floating in the air.

The fortuitous moment finally arrived, announced from atop of a small podium erected especially for the occasion. A small crowd of expectant marmalade enthusiasts pressed closer to its colourful bunting as the final preparations were made for the celebrated announcement.

Isla shuffled from one foot to the next, her heartbeat accelerating with every moment. She could feel each reverberation as it resounded in the base of her throat, blood racing through her veins at an unsteady speed, numbing her fingers and aching her wrists.

James placed a conciliatory hand in hers.

"Ladies and gentlemen". The influential speaker coughed, tapping unconvincingly at the microphone, calling to arms an obedient crowd.

"Fellow marmalade enthusiasts…"

Isla looked at the dignitary, his composure, his trimmed moustache. She imagined his poise and formality when he arrived each morning at the breakfast table and that of his wife as she served him toast and marmalade.

The setting was the same, the hall no more magnificent than the one in which Maggie had stood awaiting her own silver spoon in 1932. She was a grieving young woman with a heavy heart when she won her prize and Isla knew that Maggie would have forgone all accolades for a chance to liberate herself from her personal loss. Almost forty years later and death had brought her eventual relief, but not before pilfering her dignity and unravelling her mind. Isla stood on the cusp of her own potential success and she lowered her head in expectation of destiny's decision.

"The Dundee Marmalade Silver Spoon of 1970 is awarded to…" the dignitary's words echoed around the old oak rafters, appearing even more clichéd than those uttered by Lord Tavistock forty years before.

Isla felt anxiety churning inside her, and feared that at any moment she would drop to the floor like a pebble launched from the cliff tops at the Leap. She would make no greater impact than that little stone and travel no greater distance than it, to meet her maker. She realised that she had pinned her future on this precise moment and the words which were destined to drop from a stranger's lips. He held her unsteady fate in his unremarkable hands, along with her life and those closest to her. All bonded irrevocably to the next few seconds of breath.

"Isla Keiller of Rose Cottage. Congratulations Ms Keiller."

Isla released a long repressed cry of relief as her long overdue moment of recompense arrived. It was the expelling of shock intertwined with a pure, unbounded happiness. Liberation from her deepest fears, the weight of a difficult destiny forgot. She shook with the unburdening of it all.

The room resounded with the deafening applause, rising gently through the crest of heads which bobbed about the stage.

Isla smiled. It was a contained smile, a knowing smile, one which was not yet sure of the truth in a glorious moment. She felt the spirit of every Mrs. Keiller who had gone before her, standing at her shoulder in solidarity at her triumph. It was not her prize, it was theirs. She sensed that somehow they had moved the heavens and delivered her success. Booming applause increased with her acceptance of her prize, resonating through the arches of an historic hall, cheering its rafters and breathing out life.

The surprise in her accomplishment was only secondary to that of returned optimism, which had been long in its absence and often missed. Isla had struck out upon her own path and had succeeded where she expected no success to lie. The small, innocuous silver spoon in her hands was a small reward, but it was not her real prize. That victory lay within and Isla understood that the return of her heart had been the true trophy of it all.

That evening, the intimate party returned to the enclave of Rose Cottage. Isla placed the Silver Spoon in the drawer beneath the sink where she knew Maggie had placed her own prize forty years previous. As she rested the new marmalade accolade in the dark hollows of the rusty drawer, a wooden panel at the back of the drawer compliantly dislodged, revealing a musty, discoloured envelope. Isla retrieved it and peering inside she discovered the inheritance her mother had so desperately sought. Alongside the banker's draft signed by John Keiller, was a simple note, in Maggie's hand, which read 'One final ingredient, all in good time.'

Step 21: Leave the Marmalade to Set

They arrived as all secrets do, under the cover of an early dawn and the perfect stillness of a soothed earth, transported by a new but willing hand, in happy fulfilment of a necessary duty. By the gate they passed Constance and Hamish, long retired but still a contented audience; and at the door a young woman awaited the delivery of this new batch of her Seville Oranges with warm tea and marmalade tablet.

In the kitchen, the arrival of another Marmalade season meant that its occupants were entirely distracted by the consuming activity of its production. The citrus smell of oranges on the stove and upon the floor, a morning's gift of pristine jars, waiting patiently for their reward. In the garden enjoying the fruits of spring's ripened berries was the young boy, Billy, with fresh eyes to see them, and a willing tongue to savour their delights. Next to him stood an attentive James, studying the boy and the sky, which was an unashamed blue.

After the fervour of the stewing, came the Marmalade creation, the batching and dispatching to new homes on the shelves of modern Scotland. After all frenetic activity had subsided; Isla found herself reflecting upon her transformation just two years after her first arrival at Rose Cottage. She sat quietly at the old kitchen table, on the cusp of a long awaited adulthood with 'Mrs Keiller's Recipes for Marmalade' once more unfurled before her. Carefully turning the pages until she reached a blank leaf, she stopped for a moment, her mind wandering down pathways of recipes and flavours. Taking a pencil in hand, she allowed the words to flow with the desire her ancestors had placed inside her.

Rose Cottage Marmalade:

1 cup of freshly picked Rose Petals

13 Seville oranges

A pound of sugar

Water

& An ounce of heart

Step 1:

Select the sturdiest Seville oranges for your marmalade

These glorious fruit should be soft and tender, including those with the bumps and bruises of their journey from the orange groves. A perfect appearance can sometimes mean too much shade or shelter, a fruit with little life experience. Without exposure to the midday sun, an orange will never be ripe enough to produce a fiery Marmalade. Without the blemishes of life, there can be no deep reward.

Step 2:

Scrub the fruit to release their natural goodness

Scrub the surface of the fruit with a delicate hand to bring it back to life. Gently clean every lump and indentation to repair and restore its previous splendour, reinstating that which nature had worn down. Sooth each minutiae, each bump, gradually removing every trace of the earth from which this fruit sprung.

Step 3:

Immerse the Oranges in Water

Simmer the oranges in a pan of hot water to warm their surfaces like the heat in which they sweltered when born from a scorched earth. Soak the fruit for two hour until they ooze moisture, shining from the crevices like an orange moon.

Step 4:

Disassemble the Fruit

Take the oranges from the water and remove their outer peel. The skin should easily be separated from its protective casing. Gently squeeze the juices from the fruit and gather in a suitable container. The liquid should be inconsistent and cloudy but wonderfully bright.

Step 5:

Separate the Pulp from the heart of the Orange

Cut the pulp into rough chunks as imperfect as the fruit's history. Tear the uneven pieces of pulp into smaller, more irregular parts. Your hands should now be tinged a passionate, orange shade.

Step 6:

Finely dissect the Segments of Peel

Finely slice the peel, chopping with a sharp knife through the pectin and into the bright orange skin. Shred into delicate flecks which will become the heart of the marmalade.

Step 7:

Extract the Pips of the Orange from its Whole

Cut the skinned oranges in half and scoop out any of the remaining pips from the heart. Add the pips to the rough pulp and the cloudy juice extracted from the oranges. Boil the mixture for a short time.

Step 8:

Place the Pips in a delicate Muslin Bag

Gather the heated mixture of pips, pulp and juice and place all within a muslin bag. Hold the bag firm over a large bowl and press the coarse contents against the tiny perforations of the bag with the rounded side of a steel spoon. The resulting juice will contain pectin, necessary to make the marmalade set.

Step 9:

Add the Juice, Pulp and Peel to a Large Pan

Place the juice into a fiery pan. Add to this mixture the delicate flecks of orange peel, which should float upon the surface of the marmalade mixture like beautiful islands of indulgence.

Step 10:

Diffuse the Rose Petals with Water

Immerse the rose petals in a bowl of warm, still water. Stew and stir to infuse the liquid with their perfumed scent. Add the rose water to the orange mixture simmering in the pot.

Step 11:

Introduce the Orange Pips into the Pan

Bled of their juices, wrap the pips and pulp tightly within their muslin bag to ensure they are contained, and add to the hopeful juices and rose scented water. This final addition will add zest to the marmalade and aid in the setting process. This marks the end of the preparation of the marmalade. The rest is down to destiny.

Step 12:

Gently Cook until the Peel is Tender

Gently heat the mixture for the encompassment of an afternoon, allowing it to steep and develop. As the mixture infuses, oozing flavours and textures, this is where the heart of the Marmalade is created and its unique taste is born. Only when the peel has softened, should the mixture be removed from the intensity of the flame.

Step 13:

Extricate the Pectin from the Muslin Bag

With a wooden spoon, remove the muslin bag and press against the side of the pot to wring out any remaining pectin. This will produce a firm but moist Marmalade to tantalise every taste-bud.

Step 14:

Discard the Remaining Pips

Discard the muslin bag and its pips. The pectin will have dissolved within the bitter juices of the orange to encourage setting and the production of a delicious marmalade.

Step 15:

Add Sugary Sweetness to the Orange Mixture

Stir into this magical mixture the sugar which will give the tart citric sharpness of the oranges its warm, syrupy taste of comfort.

Step 16:

Increase the Heat to Fuse the Ingredients

Boil rapidly this delicate balance of sharp and sweet, raising the temperature of the pan sharply to induce setting of the Marmalade. The contents of the pan will bubble with energy as the sugar dissolves into the orange liquid and its islands of peel.

Step 17:

Boil to Setting Point

Continue to increase the heat beneath this glorious mixture to integrate completely the contents of the pan. Simmer gently for an hour to create wonderful warmth within the belly of the marmalade.

Step 18:

Skim off the Excess from the Marmalade

Carefully skim the excess from the top of the mixture, revealing the intense orange marmalade buried beneath. To the marmalade maker, the joy of a new batch of marmalade, one which is unique to this moment and the fruit selected to create it.

Step 19:

Transfer to pristine Glass Pots

Place the glorious marmalade inside freshly boiled glass jars, the perfect container in which to display the dancing orange colour and the sparkling flecks of peel. Clean from the glass any droplets of stickiness, so that the jar is as perfect as the marmalade it contains.

Step 20:

Cover the Pleasing Pots with a Protective Lid

Cover the jars with a thin piece of parchment paper to seal in the warm delights of the orange marmalade. Allow the fiery liquid to settle in its containers, developing its character and its flavour.

Step 21:

Leave the Marmalade to Set

Place the jars in full exposure of nature's sunlight, allowing the warm rays to pierce the happy jars of marmalade. Once set, enjoy the delights of a warming marmalade which skips wonderfully on the tongue and soothes the heartache generated for a lifetime.

Isla Keiller

1971

Printed in Great Britain
by Amazon

54787360R00199